CONT[illegible]

ULYSSES THE SACKER OF CITIES

THE WANDERINGS OF ULYSSES

THE FLEECE OF GOLD

THESEUS

PERSEUS

THE AUTHOR, ANDREW LANG,
DEDICATES THIS BOOK,
Tales of Troy and Greece,
TO
H. RIDER HAGGARD

ULYSSES
THE SACKER OF CITIES

GREECE
THRACIANS
Troy
Lemnos
Delphi (Pytho)
Ithaca
Aulis
Eleusis
Megara
ATHENS
Mycenæ
Argos
Tiryns
Troezen
Seriphos
Lacedæmon
Pylos
Cnossos
CRETE

– I –

THE BOYHOOD AND PARENTS OF ULYSSES

LONG AGO, IN A LITTLE ISLAND CALLED Ithaca, on the west coast of Greece, there lived a King named Laertes. His kingdom was small and mountainous. People used to say that Ithaca 'lay like a shield upon the sea', which sounds as if it were a flat country. But in those times shields were very large, and rose at the middle into two peaks with a hollow between them, so that Ithaca, seen far off in the sea, with her two chief mountain peaks, and a cloven valley between them, looked exactly like a shield. The country was so rough that men kept no horses, for, at that time, people drove, standing up in little light chariots with two horses; they never rode, and there was no cavalry in battle: men fought from chariots. When Ulysses, the son of Laertes, King of Ithaca grew up, he never fought from a chariot, for he had none, but always on foot.

If there were no horses in Ithaca, there was plenty

of cattle. The father of Ulysses had flocks of sheep, and herds of swine, and wild goats, deer, and hares lived in the hills and in the plains. The sea was full of fish of many sorts, which men caught with nets, and with rod and line and hook.

Thus Ithaca was a good island to live in. The summer was long, and there was hardly any winter; only a few cold weeks, and then the swallows came back, and the plains were like a garden, all covered with wild flowers – violets, lilies, narcissus, and roses. With the blue sky and the blue sea, the island was beautiful. White temples stood on the shores; and the nymphs, a sort of fairies, had their little shrines built of stone, with wild rose-bushes hanging over them.

Other islands lay within sight, crowned with mountains, stretching away, one behind the other, into the sunset. Ulysses in the course of his life saw many rich countries, and great cities of men, but, wherever he was, his heart was always in the little isle of Ithaca, where he had learned how to row, and how to sail a boat, and how to shoot with bow and arrow, and to hunt boars and stags, and manage his hounds.

The mother of Ulysses was called Anticleia: she was the daughter of King Autolycus, who lived near Parnassus, a mountain on the mainland. This King Autolycus was the most cunning of men. He was a Master Thief, and could steal a man's pillow from under his head, but he does not seem to have been thought worse of for this. The Greeks had a God of Thieves, named Hermes, whom Autolycus worshipped, and people thought more good of his cunning tricks than harm of his dishonesty. Perhaps these tricks of his were only practised for amusement; however that may be, Ulysses became as artful as his grandfather; he was both the bravest and the most cunning of men, but Ulysses never stole things, except once, as we shall hear, from the enemy in time of war. He showed his cunning in stratagems of war, and in many strange escapes from giants and man-eaters.

Soon after Ulysses was born, his grandfather came to see his mother and father in Ithaca. He was sitting at supper when the nurse of Ulysses, whose name was Eurycleia, brought in the baby, and set him on the knees of Autolycus, saying, 'Find a name for your grandson, for he is a child of many prayers.'

'I am very angry with many men and women in the world,' said Autolycus, 'so let the child's name be *A Man of Wrath*,' which, in Greek, was Odysseus. So the child was called Odysseus by his own people, but the name was changed into Ulysses, and we shall call him Ulysses.

We do not know much about Ulysses when he

was a little boy, except that he used to run about the garden with his father, asking questions, and begging that he might have fruit trees 'for his very own'. He was a great pet, for his parents had no other son, so his father gave him thirteen pear trees, and forty fig trees, and promised him fifty rows of vines, all covered with grapes, which he could eat when he liked, without asking leave of the gardener. So he was not tempted to steal fruit, like his grandfather.

When Autolycus gave Ulysses his name, he said that he must come to stay with him when he was a big boy, and he would get splendid presents. Ulysses was told about this, so, when he was a tall lad, he crossed the sea and drove in his chariot to the old man's house on Mount Parnassus. Everybody welcomed him, and next day his uncles and cousins and he went out to hunt a fierce wild boar, early in the morning. Probably Ulysses took his own dog, named Argos, the best of hounds, of which we shall hear again, long afterwards, for the dog lived to be very old. Soon the hounds came on the scent of a wild boar, and after them the men went, with spears in their hands, and Ulysses ran foremost, for he was already the swiftest runner in Greece.

He came on a great boar lying in a tangled thicket of boughs and bracken, a dark place where the sun never shone, nor could the rain pierce through. Then the noise of the men's shouts and the barking of the dogs awakened the boar, and up he sprang, bristling all over his back, and with fire shining from his eyes. In rushed Ulysses first of all, with his spear raised to strike, but the boar was too quick for him, and ran in, and drove his sharp tusk sideways, ripping up the thigh of Ulysses. But the boar's tusk missed the bone, and Ulysses sent his sharp spear into the beast's right shoulder, and the spear went clean through, and the boar fell dead, with a loud cry. The uncles of Ulysses bound up his wound carefully, and sang a magical song over it, as the French soldiers wanted to do to Joan of Arc when the arrow pierced her shoulder at the siege of Orleans. Then the blood ceased to flow, and soon Ulysses was quite healed of his wound. They thought that he would be a good warrior, and gave him splendid presents, and when he went home again he told all that had happened to his father and mother, and his nurse, Eurycleia. But there was always a long white mark or scar above his left knee, and about that scar we shall hear again, many years afterwards.

– 2 –

HOW PEOPLE LIVED IN THE TIME OF ULYSSES

WHEN ULYSSES WAS A YOUNG MAN HE wished to marry a princess of his own rank. Now there were at that time many kings in Greece, and you must be told how they lived. Each king had his own little kingdom, with his chief town, walled with huge walls of enormous stone. Many of these walls are still standing, though the grass has grown over the ruins of most of them, and in later years, men believed that those walls must have been built by giants, the stones are so enormous. Each king had nobles under him, rich men, and all had their palaces, each with its courtyard, and its long hall, where the fire burned in the midst, and the King and Queen sat beside it on high thrones, between the four chief carved pillars that held up the roof. The thrones were made of cedar wood and ivory, inlaid with gold, and there were many other chairs and small tables for guests, and the walls and doors were covered with bronze plates, and gold and silver, and sheets of blue glass. Sometimes they were painted with pictures of bull hunts, and a few of these pictures may still be seen. At night torches were lit, and placed in the hands of golden figures of boys, but all the smoke of fire and torches escaped by a hole in the roof, and made the ceiling black. On the walls hung swords and spears and helmets and shields, which needed to be often cleaned from the stains of the smoke. The minstrel or poet sat beside the King and Queen, and after supper he struck his harp, and sang stories of old wars. At night the King and Queen slept in their own place, and the women in their own rooms; the princesses had their chambers upstairs, and the young princes had each his room built separate in the courtyard.

There were bath rooms with polished baths, where guests were taken when they arrived dirty from a journey. The guests lay at night on beds in the portico, for the climate was warm. There were plenty of servants, who were usually slaves taken in war, but they were very kindly treated, and were friendly with their masters. No coined money was used; people paid for things in cattle, or in weighed pieces of gold. Rich men had plenty of gold cups, and gold-hilted swords, and bracelets, and brooches. The kings were the leaders in war and judges in peace, and did sacrifices to the Gods, killing cattle and swine and sheep, on which they afterwards dined.

They dressed in a simple way, in a long smock of linen or silk, which fell almost to the feet, but was tucked up into a belt round the waist, and worn longer or shorter, as they happened to choose. Where it needed fastening at the throat, golden brooches were used, beautifully made, with safety pins. This garment was much like the plaid that the Highlanders used to wear, with its belt and brooches. Over it the Greeks wore great cloaks of woollen cloth when the weather was cold, but these they did not use in battle. They fastened their breastplates, in war, over their smocks, and had other armour covering the lower parts of the body, and leg armour called 'greaves'; while the great shield which guarded the whole body from throat to ankles was carried by a broad belt slung round the neck. The sword was worn in another belt, crossing the shield belt. They had light shoes in peace, and higher and heavier boots in war, or for walking across country.

The women wore the smock, with more brooches and jewels than the men, and had head coverings, with veils, and mantles over all, and necklaces of gold and amber, earrings, and bracelets of gold or of bronze. The colours of their dresses were various, chiefly white and purple; and, when in mourning, they wore very dark blue, not black. All the armour, and the sword-blades and spear-heads were made, not of steel or iron, but of bronze, a mixture of copper and tin. The shields were made of several thicknesses of leather, with a plating of bronze above; tools, such as axes and ploughshares, were either of iron or bronze; and so were the blades of knives and daggers.

To us the houses and way of living would have seemed very splendid, and also, in some ways, rather rough. The palace floors, at least in the house of Ulysses, were littered with bones and feet of the oxen slain for food, but this happened when Ulysses had been long from home. The floor of the hall in the house of Ulysses was not boarded with planks, or paved with stone: it was made of clay; for he was a poor king of small islands. The cooking was coarse: a pig or sheep was killed, roasted and eaten immediately. We never hear of boiling meat, and though people probably ate fish, we do not hear of their doing so, except when no meat could be procured. Still some people must have liked them; for in the pictures that were painted or cut in precious stones in these times we see the half-naked fisherman walking home, carrying large fish.

The people were wonderful workers of gold and bronze. Hundreds of their golden jewels have been found in their graves, but probably these were made and buried two or three centuries before the time of Ulysses. The dagger blades had pictures of fights with lions, and of flowers, inlaid on them, in gold of various colours, and in silver; nothing so beautiful is made now. There are figures of men hunting bulls on some of the gold cups, and these are wonderfully lifelike. The vases and pots of earthenware were painted in charming patterns: in short, it was a splendid world to live in.

The people believed in many Gods, male and female, under the chief God, Zeus. The Gods were thought to be taller than men, and immortal, and to live in much the same way as men did, eating, drinking, and sleeping in glorious palaces. Though they were supposed to reward good men, and to punish people who broke their oaths and were unkind to strangers, there were many stories told in which the Gods were fickle, cruel, selfish, and set very bad examples to men. How far these stories were believed is not sure; it is certain that 'all men felt a need of the Gods', and thought that they were pleased by good actions and displeased by evil. Yet, when a man felt that his behaviour had been bad, he often threw the blame on the Gods, and said that they had misled him, which really meant no more than that 'he could not help it'.

There was a curious custom by which the princes bought wives from the fathers of the princesses, giving cattle and gold, and bronze and iron, but sometimes a prince got a wife as the reward for some very brave action. A man would not give his daughter to a wooer whom she did not love, even if he offered the highest price, at least this must have been the general rule, for husbands and wives were very fond of each other, and of their children, and husbands always allowed their wives to rule the house, and give their advice on everything. It was thought a very wicked thing for a woman to like another man better than her husband, and there were few such wives, but among them was the most beautiful woman who ever lived.

– 3 –

THE WOOING OF HELEN OF TROY

THIS WAS THE WAY IN WHICH PEOPLE lived when Ulysses was young, and wished to be married. The worst thing in the way of life was that the greatest and most beautiful princesses might be taken prisoner, and carried off as slaves to the towns of the men who had killed their fathers and husbands. Now at that time one lady was far the fairest in the world: namely, Helen, daughter of King Tyndarus. Every young prince heard of her and desired to marry her; so her father invited them all to his palace, and entertained them, and found out what they would give. Among the rest Ulysses went, but his father had a little kingdom, a rough island, with others near it, and Ulysses had not a good chance. He was not tall; though very strong and active, he was a short man with broad shoulders, but his face was handsome, and, like all the princes, he wore long yellow hair, clustering like a hyacinth flower.

His manner was rather hesitating, and he seemed to speak very slowly at first, though afterwards his words came freely. He was good at everything a man can do; he could plough, and build houses, and make ships, and he was the best archer in Greece, except one, and could bend the great bow of a dead king, Euryrus, which no other man could string. But he had no horses, and had no great train of followers; and, in short, neither Helen nor her father thought of choosing Ulysses for her husband out of so many tall, handsome young princes, glittering with gold ornaments. Still, Helen was very kind to Ulysses, and there was great friendship between them, which was fortunate for her in the end.

Tyndarus first made all the princes take an oath that they would stand by the prince whom he chose, and would fight for him in all his quarrels. Then he named for her husband Menelaus, King of Lacedaemon. He was a very brave man, but not one of the strongest; he was not such a fighter as the gigantic Ajax, the tallest and strongest of men; or as Diomedes, the friend of Ulysses; or as his own brother, Agamemnon, the King of the rich city of Mycenae, who was chief over all other princes, and general of the whole army in war. The great lions carved in stone that seemed to guard his city are still standing above the gate through which Agamemnon used to drive his chariot.

The man who proved to be the best fighter of all, Achilles, was not among the lovers of Helen, for he was still a boy, and his mother, Thetis of the silver feet, a Goddess of the sea, had sent him to be brought up as a girl, among the daughters of Lycomedes of Scyros, in an island far away. Thetis did this because Achilles was her only child, and there was a prophecy that, if he went to the wars, he would win the greatest glory, but die very young, and never see his mother again. She thought that if war broke out he would not be found hiding in girl's dress, among girls, far away.

So at last, after thinking over the matter for long, Tyndarus gave fair Helen to Menelaus, the rich King of Lacedaemon; and her twin sister Clytemnestra, who was also very beautiful, was given to King Agamemnon, the chief over all the princes. They all lived very happily together at first, but not for long.

In the meantime King Tyndarus spoke to his brother Icarius, who had a daughter named Penelope. She also was very pretty, but not nearly so beautiful as her cousin, fair Helen, and we know that Penelope was not very fond of her cousin. Icarius, admiring the strength and wisdom of Ulysses, gave him his daughter Penelope to be his wife, and Ulysses loved her very dearly, no man and wife were ever dearer to each other. They went away together to rocky Ithaca, and perhaps Penelope was not sorry that a wide sea lay between her home and that of Helen; for Helen was not only the fairest woman that ever lived in the world, but she was so kind and gracious and charming that no man could see her without loving her. When she was only a child, the famous prince Theseus, whose story is to be told later, carried her away to his own city of Athens, meaning to marry her when she grew up, and, even at that time, there was a war for her sake, for her brothers followed Theseus with an army, and fought him, and brought her home.

She had fairy gifts: for instance, she had a great red jewel, called the 'Star', and when she wore it red drops seemed to fall from it and vanished before they touched and stained her white breast – so white that people called her the 'Daughter of the Swan'. She could speak in the very voice of any man or woman, so folk also named her Echo, and it was believed that she could neither grow old nor die, but would at last pass away to the Elysian plain and the world's end, where life is easiest for men. No snow comes thither, nor great storm, nor any rain; but always the river of Ocean that rings round the whole earth sends forth the west wind to blow cool on the people of King Rhadamanthus of the fair hair. These were some of the stories that men told of fair Helen, but Ulysses was never sorry that he had not the fortune to marry her, so fond he was of her cousin, his wife, Penelope, who was very wise and good.

When Ulysses brought his wife home they lived, as the custom was, in the palace of his father, King Laertes, but Ulysses, with his own hands, built a chamber for Penelope and himself. There grew a great olive tree in the inner court of the palace, and its stem was as large as one of the tall carved, pillars of the hall. Round about this tree Ulysses built the chamber, and finished it with close-set stones, and roofed it over, and made close-fastening doors. Then he cut off all the branches of the olive tree, and smoothed the trunk, and shaped it into the bedpost, and made the bedstead beautiful with inlaid work of gold and silver and ivory. There was no such bed in Greece, and no man could move it from its place, and this bed comes again into the story, at the very end.

Now time went by and Ulysses and Penelope had one son called Telemachus; and Eurycleia, who had been his father's nurse, took care of him. They were all very happy, and lived in peace in rocky Ithaca, and Ulysses looked after his lands, and flocks, and herds, and went hunting with his dog Argos, the swiftest of hounds.

– 4 –

THE STEALING OF HELEN

THIS HAPPY TIME DID NOT LAST LONG, and Telemachus was still a baby when war arose, so great and mighty and marvellous as had never been known in the world. Far across the sea that lies on the east of Greece, there dwelt the rich King Priam. His town was called Troy, or Ilios, and it stood on a hill near the seashore, where are the straits of Hellespont, between Europe and Asia; it was a great city surrounded by strong walls, and its ruins are still standing. The kings could make merchants who passed through the straits pay toll to them, and they had allies in Thrace, a part of Europe opposite Troy, and Priam was chief of all princes on his side of the sea, as Agamemnon was chief king in Greece. Priam had many beautiful things; he had a vine made of gold, with golden leaves and clusters, and he had the swiftest horses, and many strong and brave sons; the strongest and bravest was named Hector, and the youngest and most beautiful was named Paris.

There was a prophecy that Priam's wife would give birth to a burning torch, so, when Paris was born, Priam sent a servant to carry the baby into a wild wood on Mount Ida, and leave him to die or be eaten by wolves and wild cats. The servant left the child, but a shepherd found him, and brought him up as his own son. The boy became as beautiful, for a boy, as Helen was for a girl, and was the best runner, and hunter, and archer among the country people. He was loved by the beautiful Oenone, a nymph – that is, a kind of fairy – who dwelt in a cave among the woods of Ida. The Greeks and Trojans believed in these days that such fair nymphs haunted all beautiful woodland places, and the mountains, and wells, and had crystal palaces, like mermaids, beneath the waves of the sea. These fairies were not mischievous, but gentle and kind. Sometimes they married mortal men, and Oenone was the bride of Paris, and hoped to keep him for her own all the days of his life.

It was believed that she had the magical power of healing wounded men, however sorely they were hurt. Paris and Oenone lived most happily together in the forest; but one day, when the servants of Priam had driven off a beautiful bull that was in the herd of Paris, he left the hills to seek it, and came into the town of Troy. His mother, Hecuba, saw him, and looking at him closely, perceived that he wore a ring which she had tied round her baby's neck when he was taken away from her soon after his birth. Then Hecuba, beholding him so beautiful, and knowing him to be her son, wept for joy, and they all forgot the prophecy that he would be a burning torch of fire, and Priam gave him a house like those of his brothers, the Trojan princes.

The fame of beautiful Helen reached Troy, and Paris quite forgot unhappy Oenone, and must needs go to see Helen for himself. Perhaps he meant to try to win her for his wife, before her marriage. But sailing was little understood in these times, and the water was wide, and men were often driven for years out of their course, to Egypt and Africa and far away into the unknown seas, where fairies lived in enchanted islands, and cannibals dwelt in caves of the hills.

Paris came much too late to have a chance of marrying Helen; however, he was determined to see her, and he made his way to her palace beneath the mountain Taygetus, beside the clear swift river Eurotas. The servants came out of the hall when thcy heard the sound of wheels and horses' feet, and some of them took the horses to the stables, and tilted the chariots against the gateway, while others led Paris into the hall, which shone like the sun with gold and silver. Then Paris and his companions were led to the baths, where they were bathed, and clad in new clothes, mantles of white, and robes of purple, and next they were brought before King Menelaus, and he welcomed them kindly, and meat was set before them, and wine in cups of gold. While they were talking, Helen came forth from her fragrant chamber, like a Goddess, her maidens following her, and carrying for her an ivory distaff with violet-coloured wool, which she span as she sat, and heard Paris tell how far he had travelled to see her who was so famous for her beauty even in countries far away.

Then Paris knew that he had never seen, and never could see, a lady so lovely and gracious as Helen as she sat and span, while the red drops fell and vanished from the ruby called the Star; and Helen knew that among all the princes in the world there was none so beautiful as Paris. Now some say that Paris, by art magic, put on the appearance of Menelaus, and asked Helen to come sailing with him, and that she, thinking he was her husband, followed him, and he carried her across the wide waters of Troy, away from her lord and her one beautiful little daughter, the child Hermione. And others say that the Gods carried Helen herself off to Egypt, and that they made in her likeness a beautiful ghost, out of flowers and sunset clouds, whom Paris bore to Troy, and this they did to cause war between Greeks and Trojans. Another story is that Helen and her bower maiden and her jewels were seized by force, when Menelaus was out hunting. It is only certain that Paris and Helen did cross the seas together, and that Menelaus and little Hermione were left alone in the melancholy palace beside the Eurotas. Penelope, we know for certain, made no excuses for her beautiful cousin, but hated her as the cause of her own sorrows and of the deaths of thousands of men in war, for all the Greek princes were bound by their oath to fight for Menelaus against anyone who injured him and stole his wife away. But Helen was very unhappy in Troy, and blamed herself as bitterly as all the other women blamed her, and most of all Oenone, who had been the love of Paris. The men were much more kind to Helen, and were determined to fight to the death rather than lose the sight of her beauty among them.

The news of the dishonour done to Menelaus and to all the princes of Greece ran through the country like fire through a forest. East and west and south and north went the news: to kings in their castles on the hills, and beside the rivers and on cliffs above the sea. The cry came to ancient Nestor of the white beard at Pylos, Nestor who had reigned over two generations of men, who had fought against the wild folk of the hills, and remembered the strong Heracles, and Eurytus of the black bow that sang before the day of battle.

The cry came to black-bearded Agamemnon, in his strong town called 'golden Mycenae', because it was so rich; it came to the people in Thisbe, where the wild doves haunt; and it came to rocky Pytho, where is the sacred temple of Apollo and the maid who prophesies. It came to Ajax, the tallest and strongest of men, in his little isle of Salamis; and to Diomedes of the loud war-cry, the bravest of warriors, who held Argos and Tiryns of the black walls of huge stones, that are still standing. The summons came to the western islands and to Ulysses in Ithaca, and even far south to the great island of Crete of the hundred cities, where Idomeneus ruled in Knossos; Idomeneus, whose ruined palace may still be seen with the throne of the King, and pictures painted on the walls, and the King's own draughtboard of gold and silver, and hundreds of tablets of clay, on which are written the lists of royal treasures. Far north went the news to Pelasgian Argos, and Hellas, where the people of Peleus dwelt, the Myrmidons; but Peleus was too old to fight, and his boy, Achilles, dwelt far away, in the island of Scyros, dressed as a girl, among the daughters of King Lycomedes. To many another town and to a hundred islands went the bitter news of approaching war, for all princes knew that their honour and their oaths compelled them to gather their spearmen, and bowmen, and slingers from the fields and the fishing, and to make ready their ships, and meet King Agamemnon in the harbour of Aulis, and cross the wide sea to besiege Troy town.

Now the story is told that Ulysses was very unwilling to leave his island and his wife Penelope, and little Telemachus; while Penelope had no wish that he should pass into danger, and into the sight of Helen of the fair hands. So it is said that when two of the princes came to summon Ulysses, he pretended to be mad, and went ploughing the sea sand with oxen, and sowing the sand with salt. Then the prince Palamedes took the baby Telemachus from the arms of his nurse, Eurycleia, and laid him in the line of the furrow, where the ploughshare would strike him and kill him. But Ulysses turned the plough aside, and they cried that he was not mad, but sane, and he must keep his oath, and join the fleet at Aulis, a long voyage for him to sail, round the stormy southern Cape of Maleia.

Whether this talc be true or not, Ulysses did go, leading twelve black ships, with high beaks painted red at prow and stern. The ships had oars, and the warriors manned the oars, to row when there was no wind. There was a small raised deck at each end of the ships; on these decks men stood to fight with sword and spear when there was a battle at sea. Each ship had but one mast, with a broad lugger sail, and for anchors they had only heavy stones attached to cables. They generally landed at night, and slept on the shore of one of the many islands when they could, for they greatly feared to sail out of sight of land.

The fleet consisted of more than a thousand ships, each with fifty warriors, so the army was of more than fifty thousand men. Agamemnon had a hundred ships, Diomedes had eighty, Nestor had ninety, the Cretans with Idomeneus, had eighty, Menelaus had sixty; but Ajax and Ulysses, who lived in small islands, had only twelve ships apiece. Yet Ajax was so brave and strong, and Ulysses so brave and wise, that they were ranked among the greatest chiefs and advisers of Agamemnon, with Menelaus, Diomedes, Idomeneus, Nestor, Menestheus of Athens, and two or three others. These chiefs were called the Council, and gave advice to Agamemnon, who was commander-in-chief. He was a brave fighter, but so anxious and fearful of losing the lives of his soldiers that Ulysses and Diomedes were often obliged to speak to him very severely. Agamemnon was also very insolent and greedy, though, when anybody stood up to him, he was ready to apologise, for fear the injured chief should renounce his service and take away his soldiers.

Nestor was much respected because he remained brave, though he was too old to be very useful in battle. He generally tried to make peace when the princes quarrelled with Agamemnon. He loved to tell long stories about his great deeds when he was young, and he wished the chiefs to fight in old-fashioned ways.

For instance, in his time the Greeks had fought in clan regiments, and the princely men had never dismounted in battle, but had fought in squadrons of chariots, but now the owners of chariots fought on foot, each man for himself, while his squire kept the chariot near him to escape on if he had to retreat. Nestor wished to go back to the good old way of chariot charges against the crowds of foot soldiers of the enemy. In short, he was a fine example of the old-fashioned soldier.

Ajax, though so very tall, strong, and brave, was rather stupid. He seldom spoke, but he was always ready to fight, and the last to retreat. Menelaus was weak of body, but as brave as the best, or more brave, for he had a keen sense of honour, and would attempt what he had not the strength to do. Diomedes and Ulysses were great friends, and always fought side by side, when they could, and helped each other in the most dangerous adventures.

These were the chiefs who led the great Greek armada from the harbour of Aulis. A long time had passed, after the flight of Helen, before the large fleet could be collected, and more time went by in the attempt to cross the sea to Troy. There were tempests that scattered the ships, so they were driven back to Aulis to refit; and they fought, as they went out again, with the peoples of unfriendly islands, and besieged their towns. What they wanted most of all was to have Achilles with them, for he was the leader of fifty ships and 2,500 men, and he had magical armour made, men said, for his father, by Hephaestus, the God of armour-making and smithy work.

At last the fleet came to the Isle of Scyros, where they suspected that Achilles was concealed. King Lycomedes received the chiefs kindly, and they saw all his beautiful daughters dancing and playing at ball, but Achilles was still so young and slim and so beautiful that they did not know him among the others. There was a prophecy that they could not take Troy without him, and yet they could not find him out. Then Ulysses had a plan. He blackened his eyebrows and beard and put on the dress of a Phoenician merchant. The Phoenicians were a people who lived near the Jews, and were of the same race, and spoke much the same language, but, unlike the Jews, who at that time were farmers in Palestine, tilling the ground, and keeping flocks and herds, the Phoenicians were the greatest of traders and sailors, and stealers of slaves. They carried cargoes of beautiful cloths, and embroideries, and jewels of gold, and necklaces of amber, and sold these everywhere about the shores of Greece and the islands.

Ulysses then dressed himself like a Phoenician pedlar, with his pack on his back: he only took a stick in his hand, his long hair was turned up, and hidden under a red sailor's cap, and in this figure he came, stooping beneath his pack, into the courtyard of King Lycomedes. The girls heard that a pedlar had come, and out they all ran, Achilles with the rest, to watch the pedlar undo his pack. Each chose what she liked best: one took a wreath of gold; another a necklace of gold and amber; another earrings; a fourth a set of brooches, another a dress of embroidered scarlet cloth; another a veil; another a pair of bracelets; but at the bottom of the pack lay a great sword of bronze, the hilt studded with golden nails. Achilles seized the sword. 'This is for me!' he said, and drew the sword from the gilded sheath, and made it whistle round his head.

'You are Achilles, Peleus' son!' said Ulysses; 'and you are to be the chief warrior of the Achaeans,' for the Greeks then called themselves Achaeans. Achilles was only too glad to hear these words, for he was quite tired of living among maidens. Ulysses led him into the hall where the chiefs were sitting at their wine, and Achilles was blushing like any girl.

'Here is the Queen of the Amazons,' said Ulysses – for the Amazons were a race of warlike maidens – 'or rather here is Achilles, Peleus' son, with sword in hand.' Then they all took his hand, and welcomed him, and he was clothed in man's dress, with the sword by his side, and presently they sent him back with ten ships to his home. There his mother, Thetis, of the silver feet, the Goddess of the sea, wept over him, saying, 'My child, thou hast the choice of a long and happy and peaceful life here with me, or of a brief time of war and undying renown. Never shall I see thee again in Argos if thy choice is for war.' But Achilles chose to die young, and to be famous as long as the world stands. So his father gave him fifty ships, with Patroclus, who was older than he, to be his friend, and with an old man, Phoenix, to advise him; and his mother gave him the glorious armour that the God had made for his father, and the heavy ashen spear that none but he could wield, and he sailed to join the host of the Achaeans, who all praised and thanked Ulysses that had found for them such a prince. For Achilles was the fiercest fighter of them all, and the swiftest-footed man, and the most courteous prince, and the gentlest with women and children, but he was proud and high of heart, and when he was angered his anger was terrible.

The Trojans would have had no chance against the Greeks if only the men of the city of Troy had fought to keep Helen of the fair hands. But they had allies, who spoke different languages, and came to fight for them both from Europe and from Asia. On the Trojan as well as on the Greek side were people called Pelasgians, who seem to have lived on both shores of the sea. There were Thracians, too, who dwelt much further north than Achilles, in Europe and beside the strait of Hellespont, where the narrow sea runs like a river. There were warriors of Lycia, led by Sarpedon and Glaucus; there were Carians, who spoke in a strange tongue; there were Mysians and men from Alybe, which was called 'the birthplace of silver', and many other peoples sent their armies, so that the war was between Eastern Europe, on one side, and Western Asia Minor on the other. The people of Egypt took no part in the war: the Greeks and Islesmen used to come down in their ships and attack the Egyptians as the Danes used to invade England. You may see the warriors from the islands, with their horned helmets, in old Egyptian pictures.

The commander-in-chief, as we say now, of the Trojans was Hector, the son of Priam. He was thought a match for any one of the Greeks, and was brave and good. His brothers also were leaders, but Paris preferred to fight from a distance with bow and arrows. He and Pandarus, who dwelt on the slopes of Mount Ida, were the best archers in the Trojan army. The princes usually fought with heavy spears, which they threw at each other, and with swords, leaving archery to the common soldiers who had no armour of bronze. But Teucer, Meriones, and Ulysses were the best archers of the Achaeans. People called Dardanians were led by Aeneas, who was said to be the son of the most beautiful of the Goddesses. These, with Sarpedon and Glaucus, were the most famous of the men who fought for Troy.

Troy was a strong town on a hill: Mount Ida lay behind it, and in front was a plain sloping to the sea shore. Through this plain ran two beautiful clear rivers, and there were scattered here and there what you would have taken for steep knolls, but they were really mounds piled up over the ashes of warriors who had died long ago. On these mounds sentinels used to stand and look across the water to give warning if the Greek fleet drew near, for the Trojans had heard that it was on its way. At last the fleet came in view, and the sea was black with ships, the oarsmen pulling with all their might for the honour of being the first to land. The race was won by the ship of the princc Protesilaus, who was first of all to leap on shore, but as he leaped he was struck to the heart by an arrow from the bow of Paris. This must have seemed a good omen to the Trojans, and to the Greeks evil, but we do not hear that the landing was resisted in great force, any more than that of Norman William was, when he invaded England.

The Greeks drew up all their ships on shore, and the men camped in huts built in front of the ships. There was thus a long row of huts with the ships behind them, and in these huts the Greeks lived all through the ten years that the siege of Troy lasted. In those days they do not seem to have understood how to conduct a siege. You would have expected the Greeks to build towers and dig trenches all round Troy, and from the towers watch the roads, so that provisions might not be brought in from the country. This is called 'investing' a town, but the Greeks never invested Troy. Perhaps they had not men enough; at all events the place remained open, and cattle could always be driven in to feed the warriors and the women and children.

Moreover, the Greeks for long never seem to have tried to break down one of the gates, nor to scale the walls, which were very high, with ladders. On the other hand, the Trojans and allies never ventured to drive the Greeks into the sea; they commonly remained within the walls or skirmished just beneath them. The older men insisted on this way of fighting, in spite of Hector, who always wished to attack and storm the camp of the Greeks. Neither side had machines for throwing heavy stones, such as the Romans used later, and the most that the Greeks did was to follow Achilles and capture small neighbouring cities, and take the women for slaves, and drive the cattle. They got provisions and wine from the Phoenicians, who came in ships, and made much profit out of the war.

It was not till the tenth year that the war began in real earnest, and scarcely any of the chief leaders had fallen. Fever came upon the Greeks, and all day the camp was black with smoke, and all night shone with fire from the great piles of burning wood, on which the Greeks burned their dead, whose bones they then buried under hillocks of earth. Many of these hillocks are still standing on the plain of Troy. When the plague had raged for ten days, Achilles called an assembly of the whole army, to try to find out why the Gods were angry. They thought that the beautiful God Apollo (who took the Trojan side) was shooting invisible arrows at them from his silver bow, though fevers in armies are usually caused by dirt and drinking bad water. The great heat of the sun, too, may have helped to cause the disease; but we must tell the story as the Greeks told it themselves. So Achilles spoke in the assembly, and proposed to ask some prophet why Apollo was angry. The chief prophet was Calchas. He rose and said that he would declare the truth if Achilles would promise to protect him from the anger of any prince whom the truth might offend.

Achilles knew well whom Calchas meant. Ten days before, a priest of Apollo had come to the camp and offered ransom for his daughter Chryseis, a beautiful girl, whom Achilles had taken prisoner, with many others, when he captured a small town. Chryseis had been given as a slave to Agamemnon, who always got the best of the plunder because he was chief king, whether he had taken part in the fighting or not. As a rule he did not. To Achilles had been given another girl, Briseis, of whom he was very fond. Now when Achilles had promised to protect Calchas, the prophet spoke out, and boldly said, what all men knew already, that Apollo caused the plague because Agamemnon would not return Chryseis, and had insulted her father, the priest of the God.

On hearing this, Agamemnon was very angry. He said that he would send Chryseis home, but that he would take Briseis away from Achilles. Then Achilles was drawing his great sword from the sheath to kill Agamemnon, but even in his anger he knew that this was wrong, so he merely called Agamemnon a greedy coward, 'with face of dog and heart of deer', and he swore that he and his men would fight no more against the Trojans. Old Nestor tried to make peace, and swords were not drawn, but Briseis was taken away from Achilles, and Ulysses put Chryseis on board of his ship and sailed away with her to her father's town, and gave her up to her father. Then her father prayed to Apollo that the plague might cease, and it did cease – when the Greeks had cleansed their camp, and purified themselves and cast their filth into the sea.

We know how fierce and brave Achilles was, and we may wonder that he did not challenge Agamemnon to fight a duel. But the Greeks never fought duels, and Agamemnon was believed to be chief king by right divine. Achilles went alone to the sea shore when his dear Briseis was led away, and he wept, and called to his mother, the silver-footed lady of the waters. Then she arose from the grey sea, like a mist, and sat down beside her son, and stroked his hair with her hand, and he told her all his sorrows. So she said that she would go up to the dwelling of the Gods, and pray Zeus, the chief of them all, to make the Trojans win a great battle, so that Agamemnon should feel his need of Achilles, and make amends for his insolence, and do him honour.

Thetis kept her promise, and Zeus gave his word that the Trojans should defeat the Greeks. That night Zeus sent a deceitful dream to Agamemnon. The dream took the shape of old Nestor, and said that Zeus would give him victory that day. While he was still asleep, Agamemnon was full of hope that he would instantly take Troy, but, when he woke, he seems not to have been nearly so confident, for in place of putting on his armour, and bidding the Greeks arm themselves, he merely dressed in his robe and mantle, took his sceptre, and went and told the chiefs about his dream. They did not feel much encouraged, so he said that he would try the temper of the army. He would call them together, and propose to return to Greece; but, if the soldiers took him at his word, the other chiefs were to stop them. This was a foolish plan, for the soldiers were wearying for beautiful Greece, and their homes, and wives and children. Therefore, when Agamemnon did as he had said, the whole army rose, like the sea under the west wind, and, with a shout, they rushed to the ships, while the dust blew in clouds from under their feet. Then they began to launch their ships, and it seems that the princes were carried away in the rush, and were as eager as the rest to go home.

But Ulysses only stood in sorrow and anger beside his ship, and never put hand to it, for he felt how disgraceful it was to run away. At last he threw down his mantle, which his herald Eurybates of Ithaca, a round-shouldered, brown, curly-haired man, picked up, and he ran to find Agamemnon, and took his sceptre, a gold-studded staff, like a marshal's baton, and he gently told the chiefs whom he met that they were doing a shameful thing; but he drove the common soldiers back to the place of meeting with the sceptre. They all returned, puzzled and chattering, but one lame, bandy-legged, bald, round-shouldered, impudent fellow, named Thersites, jumped up and made an insolent speech, insulting the princes, and advising the army to run away. Then Ulysses took him and beat him till the blood came, and he sat down, wiping away his tears, and looking so foolish that the whole army laughed at him, and cheered Ulysses when he and Nestor bade them arm and fight. Agamemnon still believed a good deal in his dream, and prayed that he might take Troy that very day, and kill Hector. Thus Ulysses alone saved the army from a cowardly retreat; but for him the ships would have been launched in an hour. But the Greeks armed and advanced in full force, all except Achilles and his friend Patroclus with their two or three thousand men. The Trojans also took heart, knowing that Achilles would not fight, and the armies approached each other. Paris himself, with two spears and a bow, and without armour, walked into the space between the hosts, and challenged any Greek prince to single combat. Menelaus, whose wife Paris had carried away, was as glad as a hungry lion when he finds a stag or a goat, and leaped in armour from his chariot, but Paris turned and slunk away, like a man when he meets a great serpent on a narrow path in the hills. Then Hector rebuked Paris for his cowardice, and Paris was ashamed and offered to end the war by fighting Menelaus. If he himself fell, the Trojans must give up Helen and all her jewels; if Menelaus fell, the Greeks were to return without fair Helen. The Greeks accepted this plan, and both sides disarmed themselves to look on at the fight in comfort, and they meant to take the most solemn oaths to keep peace till the combat was lost and won, and the quarrel settled. Hector sent into Troy for two lambs, which were to be sacrificed when the oaths were taken.

In the meantime Helen of the fair hands was at

home working at a great purple tapestry on which she embroidered the battles of the Greeks and Trojans. It was just like the tapestry at Bayeux on which Norman ladies embroidered the battles in the Norman Conquest of England. Helen was very fond of embroidering, like poor Mary, Queen of Scots, when a prisoner in Loch Leven Castle. Probably the work kept both Helen and Mary from thinking of their past lives and their sorrows.

When Helen heard that her husband was to fight Paris, she wept, and threw a shining veil over her head, and with her two bower maidens went to the roof of the gate tower, where King Priam was sitting with the old Trojan chiefs. They saw her and said that it was small blame to fight for so beautiful a lady, and Priam called her 'dear child', and said, 'I do not blame you, I blame the Gods who brought about this war.' But Helen said that she wished she had died before she left her little daughter and her husband, and her home: 'Alas! shameless me!' Then she told Priam the names of the chief Greek warriors, and of Ulysses, who was shorter by a head than Agamemnon but broader in chest and shoulders. She wondered that she could not see her own two brothers, Castor and Polydeuces, and thought that they kept aloof in shame for her sin; but the green grass covered their graves, for they had both died in battle, far away in Lacedaemon, their own country.

Then the lambs were sacrificed, and the oaths were taken, and Paris put on his brother's armour: helmet, breastplate, shield and leg-armour. Lots were drawn to decide whether Paris or Menelaus should throw his spear first, and, as Paris won, he threw his spear, but the point was blunted against the shield of Menelaus. But when Menelaus threw his spear it went clean through the shield of Paris, and through the side of his breastplate, but only grazed his robe. Menelaus drew his sword, and rushed in, and smote at the crest of the helmet of Paris, but his bronze blade broke into four pieces. Menelaus caught Paris by the horsehair crest of his helmet, and dragged him towards the Greeks, but the chin-strap broke, and Menelaus, turning round, threw the helmet into the ranks of the Greeks. But when Menelaus looked again for Paris, with a spear in his hand, he could see him nowhere! The Greeks believed that the beautiful Goddess Aphrodite, whom the Romans called Venus, hid him in a thick cloud of darkness and carried him to his own house, where Helen of the fair hands found him and said to him, 'Would that thou hadst perished, conquered by that great warrior who was my lord! Go forth again and challenge him to fight thee face to face.' But

Paris had no more desire to fight, and the Goddess threatened Helen, and compelled her to remain with him in Troy, coward as he had proved himself. Yet on other days Paris fought well; it seems that he was afraid of Menelaus because, in his heart, he was ashamed of himself.

Meanwhile Menelaus was seeking for Paris everywhere, and the Trojans, who hated him, would have shown his hiding-place. But they knew not where he was, and the Greeks claimed the victory, and thought that, as Paris had the worst of the fight, Helen would be restored to them, and they would all sail home.

– 5 –

TROJAN VICTORIES

THE WAR MIGHT NOW HAVE ENDED, BUT an evil and foolish thought came to Pandarus, a prince of Ida, who fought for the Trojans. He chose to shoot an arrow at Menelaus, contrary to the sworn vows of peace, and the arrow pierced the breastplate of Menelaus through the place where the clasped plates meet, and drew his blood. Then Agamemnon, who loved his brother dearly, began to lament, saying that, if he died, the army would all go home and Trojans would dance on the grave of Menelaus. 'Do not alarm all our army,' said Menelaus, 'the arrow has done me little harm;' and so it proved, for the surgeon easily drew the arrow out of the wound.

Then Agamemnon hastened here and there, bidding the Greeks arm and attack the Trojans, who would certainly be defeated, for they had broken the oaths of peace. But with his usual insolence he chose to accuse Ulysses and Diomedes of cowardice, though Diomedes was as brave as any man, and Ulysses had just prevented the whole army from launching their ships and going home. Ulysses answered him with spirit, but Diomedes said nothing at the moment; later he spoke his mind. He leaped from his chariot, and all the chiefs leaped down and advanced in line, the chariots following them, while the spearmen and bowmen followed the chariots. The Trojan army advanced, all shouting in their different languages, but the Greeks came on silently. Then the two front lines clashed, shield against shield, and the noise was like the roaring of many flooded torrents among the hills. When a man fell he who had slain him tried to strip off his armour, and his friends fought over his body to save the dead from this dishonour.

Ulysses fought above a wounded friend, and drove his spear through head and helmet of a Trojan prince, and everywhere men were falling beneath spears and arrows and heavy stones which the warriors threw. Here Menelaus speared the man who built the ships with which Paris had sailed to Greece; and the dust rose like a cloud, and a mist went up from the fighting men, while Diomedes stormed across the plain like a river in flood, leaving dead bodies behind him as the river leaves boughs of trees and grass to mark its course. Pandarus wounded Diomedes with an arrow, but Diomedes slew him, and the Trojans were being driven in flight, when Sarpedon and

Hector turned and hurled themselves on the Greeks; and even Diomedes shuddered when Hector came on, and charged at Ulysses, who was slaying Trojans as he went, and the battle swayed this way and that, and the arrows fell like rain.

But Hector was sent into the city to bid the women pray to the Goddess Athene for help, and he went to the house of Paris, whom Helen was imploring to go and fight like a man, saying: 'Would that the winds had wafted me away, and the tides drowned me, shameless that I am, before these things came to pass!'

Then Hector went to see his dear wife, Andromache, whose father had been slain by Achilles early in the siege, and he found her and her nurse carrying her little boy, Hector's son, and like a star upon her bosom lay his beautiful and shining golden head. Now, while Helen urged Paris to go into the fight, Andromache prayed Hector to stay with her in the town, and fight no more lest he should be slain and leave her a widow, and the boy an orphan, with none to protect him. The army, she said, should come back within the walls, where they had so long been safe, not fight in the open plain. But Hector answered that he would never shrink from battle, 'yet I know this in my heart, the day shall come for holy Troy to be laid low, and Priam and the people of Priam. But this and my own death do not trouble me so much as the thought of you, when you shall be carried as a slave to Greece, to spin at another woman's bidding, and bear water from a Grecian well. May the heaped up earth of my tomb cover me ere I hear thy cries and the tale of thy captivity.'

Then Hector stretched out his hands to his little boy, but the child was afraid when he saw the great glittering helmet of his father and the nodding horsehair crest. So Hector laid his helmet on the ground and dandled the child in his arms, and tried to comfort his wife, and said goodbye for the last time, for he never came back to Troy alive. He went on his way back to the battle, and Paris went with him, in glorious armour, and soon they were slaying the princes of the Greeks.

The battle raged till nightfall, and in the night the Greeks and Trojans burned their dead; and the Greeks made a trench and wall round their camp, which they needed for safety now that the Trojans came from their town and fought in the open plain.

Next day the Trojans were so successful that they did not retreat behind their walls at night, but lit great fires on the plain: a thousand fires, with fifty men taking supper round each of them, and drinking their wine to the music of flutes. But the

Greeks were much discouraged, and Agamemnon called the whole army together, and proposed that they should launch their ships in the night and sail away home. Then Diomedes stood up, and said: 'You called me a coward lately. You are the coward! Sail away if you are afraid to remain here, but all the rest of us will fight till we take Troy town.'

Then all shouted in praise of Diomedes, and Nestor advised them to send five hundred young men, under his own son, Thrasymedes, to watch the Trojans, and guard the new wall and the ditch, in case the Trojans attacked them in the darkness. Next Nestor counselled Agamemnon to send Ulysses and Ajax to Achilles, and promise to give back Briseis, and rich presents of gold, and beg pardon for his insolence. If Achilles would be friends again with Agamemnon, and fight as he used to fight, the Trojans would soon be driven back into the town.

Agamemnon was very ready to beg pardon, for he feared that the whole army would be defeated, and cut off from their ships, and killed or kept as slaves. So Ulysses and Ajax and the old tutor of Achilles, Phoenix, went to Achilles and argued with him, praying him to accept the rich presents, and help the Greeks. But Achilles answered that he did not believe a word that Agamemnon said; Agamemnon had always hated him, and always would hate him.

No; he would not cease to be angry, he would sail away next day with all his men, and he advised the rest to come with him. 'Why be so fierce?' said tall Ajax, who seldom spoke. 'Why make so much trouble about one girl? We offer you seven girls, and plenty of other gifts.'

Then Achilles said that he would not sail away next day, but he would not fight till the Trojans tried to burn his own ships, and there he thought that Hector would find work enough to do. This was the most that Achilles would promise, and all the Greeks were silent when Ulysses delivered his message. But Diomedes arose and said that, with or without Achilles, fight they must; and all men, heavy at heart, went to sleep in their huts or in the open air at their doors.

Agamemnon was much too anxious to sleep. He saw the glow of the thousand fires of the Trojans in the dark, and heard their merry flutes, and he groaned and pulled out his long hair by handfuls. When he was tired of crying and groaning and tearing his hair, he thought that he would go for advice to old Nestor. He threw a lion skin, the coverlet of his bed, over his shoulder, took his spear, went out and met Menelaus – for he, too, could not sleep – and Menelaus proposed to send a spy among the Trojans, if any man were brave enough to go, for the Trojan camp was all alight with fires, and the adventure was dangerous. Therefore the two wakened Nestor and the other chiefs, who came just as they were, wrapped in the fur coverlets of their beds, without any armour. First they visited the five hundred young men set to watch the wall, and then they crossed the ditch and sat down outside and considered what might be done. 'Will nobody go as a spy among the Trojans?' said Nestor; he meant would none of the young men go. Diomedes said that he would take the risk if any other man would share it with him, and, if he might choose a companion, he would take Ulysses.

'Come, then, let us be going,' said Ulysses, 'for the night is late, and the dawn is near.' As these two chiefs had no armour on, they borrowed shields and leather caps from the young men of the guard, for leather would not shine as bronze helmets shine in the firelight. The cap lent to Ulysses was strengthened outside with rows of boars' tusks. Many of these tusks, shaped for this purpose, have been found, with swords and armour, in a tomb in Mycenae, the town of Agamemnon. This cap which was lent to Ulysses had once been stolen by his grandfather, Autolycus, who was a Master Thief, and he gave it as a present to a friend, and so, through several hands, it had come to young Meriones of Crete, one of the five hundred guards, who now lent it to Ulysses. So the two princes set forth in the dark, so dark it was that though they heard a heron cry, they could not see it as it flew away.

While Ulysses and Diomedes stole through the night silently, like two wolves among the bodies of dead men, the Trojan leaders met and considered what they ought to do. They did not know whether the Greeks had set sentinels and outposts, as usual, to give warning if the enemy were approaching; or whether they were too weary to keep a good watch; or whether perhaps they were getting ready their ships to sail homewards in the dawn. So Hector offered a reward to any man who would creep through the night and spy on the Greeks; he said he would give the spy the two best horses in the Greek camp.

Now among the Trojans there was a young man named Dolon, the son of a rich father, and he was the only boy in a family of five sisters. He was ugly, but a very swift runner, and he cared for horses more than for anything else in the world. Dolon arose and said, 'If you will swear to give me the horses and chariot of Achilles, son of Peleus, I will steal to the hut of Agamemnon and listen and find out whether the Greeks mean to fight or flee.' Hector swore to give these horses, which were the best in the world, to Dolon, so he took his bow and threw a grey wolf's hide over his shoulders, and ran towards the ships of the Greeks.

Now Ulysses saw Dolon as he came, and said to Diomedes, 'Let us suffer him to pass us, and then do you keep driving him with your spear towards the ships, and away from Troy.' So Ulysses and Diomedes lay down among the dead men who had fallen in the battle, and Dolon ran on past them towards the Greeks. Then they rose and chased him as two greyhounds course a hare, and, when Dolon was near the sentinels, Diomedes cried 'Stand, or I will slay you with my spear!' and he threw his spear just over Dolon's shoulder. So Dolon stood still, green with fear, and with his teeth chattering. When the two came up, he cried, and said that his father was a rich man, who would pay much gold, and bronze, and iron for his ransom.

Ulysses said, 'Take heart, and put death out of your mind, and tell us what you are doing here.' Dolon said that Hector had promised him the horses of Achilles if he would go and spy on the Greeks. 'You set your hopes high,' said Ulysses, 'for the horses of Achilles are not earthly steeds, but divine; a gift of the Gods, and Achilles alone can drive them. But, tell me, do the Trojans keep good watch, and where is Hector with his horses?' for Ulysses thought that it would be a great adventure to drive away the horses of Hector.

'Hector is with the chiefs, holding council at the tomb of Ilus,' said Dolon; 'but no regular guard is set. The people of Troy, indeed, are round their watchfires, for they have to think of the safety of their wives and children; but the allies from far lands keep no watch, for their wives and children are safe at home.' Then he told where all the different peoples who fought for Priam had their stations; but, said he, 'if you want to steal horses, the best are those of Rhesus, King of the Thracians, who has only joined us tonight. He and his men are asleep at the farthest end of the line, and his horses are the best and greatest that ever I saw: tall, white as snow, and swift as the wind, and his chariot is adorned with gold and silver, and golden is his armour. Now take me prisoner to the ships, or bind me and leave me here while you go and try whether I have told you truth or lies.'

'No,' said Diomedes, 'if I spare your life you may come spying again,' and he drew his sword and smote off the head of Dolon. They hid his cap and bow and spear where they could find them easily, and marked the spot, and went through the night to the dark camp of King Rhesus, who had no watchfire and no guards. Then Diomedes silently stabbed each sleeping man to the heart, and Ulysses seized the dead by the feet and threw them aside lest they should frighten the horses, which had never been in battle, and would shy if they were led over the bodies of dead men. Last of all Diomedes killed King Rhesus, and Ulysses led forth his horses, beating them with his bow, for he had forgotten to take the whip from the chariot. Then Ulysses and Diomedes leaped on the backs of the horses, as they had not time to bring away the chariot, and they galloped to the ships, stopping to pick up the spear, and bow, and cap of Dolon. They rode to the princes, who welcomed them, and all laughed for glee when they saw the white horses and heard that King Rhesus was dead, for they guessed that all his army would now go home to Thrace. This they must have done, for we never hear of them in the battles that followed, so Ulysses and Diomedes deprived the Trojans of thousands of men. The other princes went to bed in good spirits, but Ulysses and Diomedes took a swim in the sea, and then went into hot baths, and so to breakfast, for rosy-fingered Dawn was coming up the sky.

- 6 -

BATTLE AT THE SHIPS

WITH DAWN AGAMEMNON AWOKE, AND fear had gone out of his heart. He put on his armour, and arrayed the chiefs on foot in front of their chariots, and behind them came the spearmen, with the bowmen and slingers on the wings of the army. Then a great black cloud spread over the sky, and red was the rain that fell from it. The Trojans gathered on a height in the plain, and Hector, shining in armour, went here and there, in front and rear, like a star that now gleams forth and now is hidden in a cloud.

The armies rushed on each other and hewed each other down, as reapers cut their way through a field of tall corn. Neither side gave ground, though the helmets of the bravest Trojans might be seen deep in the ranks of the Greeks; and the swords of the bravest Greeks rose and fell in the ranks of the Trojans, and all the while the arrows showered like rain. But at noonday, when the weary woodman rests from cutting trees, and takes his dinner in the quiet hills, the Greeks of the first line made a charge, Agamemnon running in front of them, and he speared two Trojans, and took their breastplates, which he laid in his chariot, and then he speared one brother of Hector and struck another down with his sword, and killed two more who vainly asked to be made prisoners of war. Footmen slew footmen, and chariot men slew chariot men, and they broke into the Trojan line as fire falls on a forest in a windy day, leaping and roaring and racing through the trees. Many an empty chariot did the horses hurry madly through the field, for the charioteers were lying dead, with the greedy vultures hovering above them, flapping their wide wings. Still Agamemnon followed and slew the hindmost Trojans, but the rest fled till they came to the gates, and the oak tree that grew outside the gates, and there they stopped.

But Hector held his hands from fighting, for in the meantime he was making his men face the enemy and form up in line and take breath, and was encouraging them, for they had retreated from the wall of the Greeks across the whole plain, past the hill that was the tomb of Ilus, a king of old, and past the place of the wild fig tree. Much ado had Hector to rally the Trojans, but he knew that when men do turn again they are hard to beat. So it proved, for when the Trojans had rallied and formed in line,

Agamemnon slew a Thracian chief who had come to fight for Troy before King Rhesus came. But the eldest brother of the slain man smote Agamemnon through the arm with his spear, and, though Agamemnon slew him in turn, his wound bled much and he was in great pain, so he leaped into his chariot and was driven back to the ships.

Then Hector gave the word to charge, as a huntsman cries on his hounds against a lion, and he rushed forward at the head of the Trojan line, slaying as he went. Nine chiefs of the Greeks he slew, and fell upon the spearmen and scattered them, as the spray of the waves is scattered by the wandering wind.

Now the ranks of the Greeks were broken, and they would have been driven among their ships and killed without mercy, had not Ulysses and Diomedes stood firm in the centre, and slain four Trojan leaders. The Greeks began to come back and face their enemies in line of battle again, though Hector, who had been fighting on the Trojan right, rushed against them. But Diomedes took good aim with his spear at the helmet of Hector, and struck it fairly. The spear-point did not go through the helmet, but Hector was stunned and fell; and, when he came to himself, he leaped into his chariot, and his squire drove him against the Pylians and Cretans, under Nestor and Idomeneus, who were on the left wing of the Greek army. Then Diomedes fought on till Paris, who stood beside the pillar on the hillock that was the tomb of old King Ilus, sent an arrow clean through his foot. Ulysses went and stood in front of Diomedes, who sat down, and Ulysses drew the arrow from his foot, and Diomedes stepped into his chariot and was driven back to the ships.

Ulysses was now the only Greek chief that still fought in the centre. The Greeks all fled, and he was alone in the crowd of Trojans, who rushed on him as hounds and hunters press round a wild boar that stands at bay in a wood. 'They are cowards that flee from the fight,' said Ulysses to himself; 'but I will stand here, one man against a multitude.' He covered the front of his body with his great shield, that hung by a belt round his neck, and he smote four Trojans and wounded a fifth. But the brother of the wounded man drove a spear through the shield and breastplate of Ulysses, and tore clean through his side. Then Ulysses turned on this Trojan, and he fled, and Ulysses sent a spear through his shoulder and out at his breast, and he died. Ulysses dragged from his own side the spear that had wounded him, and called thrice with a great voice to the other Greeks, and Menelaus and Ajax rushed to rescue him, for many Trojans were round him, like jackals round a wounded stag that a man has struck with an arrow. But Ajax ran and covered the wounded Ulysses with his huge shield till he could climb into the chariot of Menelaus, who drove him back to the ships.

Meanwhile, Hector was slaying the Greeks on the left of their battle, and Paris struck the Greek surgeon, Machaon, with an arrow; and Idomeneus bade Nestor put Machaon in his chariot and drive him to Nestor's hut, where his wound might be tended. Meanwhile, Hector sped to the centre of the line, where Ajax was slaying the Trojans; but Eurypylus, a Greek chief, was wounded by an arrow from the bow of Paris, and his friends guarded him with their shields and spears.

Thus the best of the Greeks were wounded and out of the battle, save Ajax, and the spearmen were in flight. Meanwhile Achilles was standing by the stern of his ship watching the defeat of the Greeks, but when he saw Machaon being carried past, sorely wounded, in the chariot of Nestor, he bade his friend Patroclus, whom he loved better than all the rest, to go and ask how Machaon did. He was sitting drinking wine with Nestor when Patroclus came, and Nestor told Patroclus how many of the chiefs were wounded, and though Patroclus was in a hurry Nestor began a very long story about his own great deeds of war, done when he was a young man. At last he bade Patroclus tell Achilles that, if he would not fight himself, he should at least send out his men under Patroclus, who should wear the splendid armour of Achilles. Then the Trojans would think that Achilles himself had returned to the battle, and they would be afraid, for none of them dared to meet Achilles hand to hand.

So Patroclus ran off to Achilles; but, on his way, he met the wounded Eurypylus, and he took him to his hut and cut the arrow out of his thigh with a knife, and washed the wound with warm water, and rubbed over it a bitter root to take the pain away. Thus he waited for some time with Eurypylus, but the advice of Nestor was in the end to cause the death of Patroclus. The battle now raged more fiercely, while Agamemnon and Diomedes and Ulysses could only limp about leaning on their spears; and again Agamemnon wished to moor the ships near shore, and embark in the night and run away. But Ulysses was very angry with him, and said: 'You should lead some other inglorious army, not us, who will fight on till every soul of us perish, rather than flee like cowards! Be silent, lest the soldiers hear you speaking of flight, such words as no man should utter. I wholly scorn your counsel, for the Greeks will lose heart if, in the midst of battle, you bid them launch the ships.'

Agamemnon was ashamed, and, by Diomedes's advice, the wounded kings went down to the verge of the war to encourage the others, though they were themselves unable to fight. They rallied the Greeks, and Ajax led them and struck Hector full in the breast with a great rock, so that his friends carried him out of the battle to the river side, where they poured water over him, but he lay fainting on the ground, the black blood gushing up from his mouth. While Hector lay there, and all men thought that he would die, Ajax and Idomeneus were driving back the Trojans, and it seemed that, even without Achilles and his men, the Greeks were able to hold their own against the Trojans. But the battle was never lost while Hector lived. People in those days believed in 'omens': they thought that the appearance of birds on the right or left hand meant good or bad luck. Once during the battle a Trojan showed Hector an unlucky bird, and wanted him to retreat into the town. But Hector said, 'One omen is the best: to fight for our own country.' While Hector lay between death and life the Greeks were winning, for the Trojans had no other great chief to lead them. But Hector awoke from his faint, and leaped to his feet and ran here and there, encouraging the men of Troy. Then most of the Greeks fled when they saw him; but Ajax and Idomeneus, and the rest of the bravest, formed in a square between the Trojans and the ships, and down on them came Hector and Aeneas and Paris, throwing their spears, and slaying on every hand. The Greeks turned and ran, and the Trojans would have stopped to strip the armour from the slain men, but Hector cried: 'Haste to the ships and leave the spoils of war. I will slay any man who lags behind!'

On this, all the Trojans drove their chariots down into the ditch that guarded the ships of the Greeks, as when a great wave sweeps at sea over the side of a vessel; and the Greeks were on the ship decks, thrusting with very long spears, used in sea fights, and the Trojans were boarding the ships, and striking with swords and axes. Hector had a lighted torch and tried to set fire to the ship of Ajax; but Ajax kept him back with the long spear, and slew a Trojan, whose lighted torch fell from his hand. And Ajax kept shouting: 'Come on, and drive away Hector; it is not to a dance that he is calling his men, but to battle.'

The dead fell in heaps, and the living ran over them to mount the heaps of slain and climb the ships. Hector rushed forward like a sea wave against a great steep rock, but like the rock stood the Greeks; still the Trojans charged past the beaks of the foremost ships, while Ajax, thrusting with a spear more than twenty feet long, leaped from deck to deck like a man that drives four horses abreast, and leaps from the back of one to the back of another. Hector seized with his hand the stern of the ship of Protesilaus, the prince whom Paris shot when he leaped ashore on the day when the Greeks first landed; and Hector kept calling: 'Bring fire!' and even Ajax, in this strange sea fight on land, left the decks and went below, thrusting with his spear through the port-holes. Twelve men lay dead who had brought fire against the ship which Ajax guarded.

– 7 –

THE SLAYING AND AVENGING OF PATROCLUS

AT THIS MOMENT, WHEN TORCHES WERE blazing round the ships, and all seemed lost, Patroclus came out of the hut of Eurypylus, whose wound he had been tending, and he saw that the Greeks were in great danger, and ran weeping to Achilles. 'Why do you weep,' said Achilles, 'like a little girl that runs by her mother's side, and plucks at her gown and looks at her with tears in her eyes, till her mother takes her up in her arms? Is there bad news from home that your father is dead, or mine; or are you sorry that the Greeks are getting what they deserve for their folly?' Then Patroclus told Achilles how Ulysses and many other princes were wounded and could not fight, and begged to be allowed to put on Achilles' armour and lead his men, who were all fresh and unwearied, into the battle, for a charge of two thousand fresh warriors might turn the fortune of the day.

Then Achilles was sorry that he had sworn not to fight himself till Hector brought fire to his own ships. He would lend Patroclus his armour, and his horses, and his men; but Patroclus must only drive the Trojans from the ships, and not pursue them. At, this moment Ajax was weary, so many spears smote his armour, and he could hardly hold up his great shield, and Hector cut off his spear-head with the sword; the bronze head fell ringing on the ground, and Ajax brandished only the pointless shaft. So he shrank back and fire blazed all over his ship; and Achilles saw it, and smote his thigh, and bade Patroclus make haste. Patroclus armed himself in the shining armour of Achilles, which all Trojans feared, and leaped into the chariot where Automedon, the squire, had harnessed Xanthus and Balius, two horses that were the children, men said, of the West Wind, and a led horse was harnessed beside them in the side traces. Meanwhile the two thousand men of Achilles, who were called Myrmidons, had met in armour, five companies of four hundred apiece, under five chiefs of noble names. Forth they came, as eager as a pack of wolves that have eaten a great red deer and run to slake their thirst with the dark water of a well in the hills.

So all in close array, helmet touching helmet and shield touching shield, like a moving wall of shining bronze, the men of Achilles charged, and Patroclus in the chariot led the way. Down they came at full speed on the flank of the Trojans, who saw the leader, and knew the bright armour and the horses of the terrible Achilles, and thought that he had returned to the war. Then each Trojan looked round to see by what way he could escape, and when men do that in battle they soon run by the way they have chosen. Patroclus rushed to the ship of Protesilaus, and slew the leader of the Trojans there, and drove them out, and quenched the fire; while they of Troy drew back from the ships, and Ajax and the other unwounded Greek princes leaped among them, smiting with sword and spear. Well did Hector know that the break in the battle had come again; but even so he stood, and did what he might, while the Trojans were driven back in disorder across the ditch, where the poles of many chariots were broken and the horses fled loose across the plain.

The horses of Achilles cleared the ditch, and Patroclus drove them between the Trojans and the wall of their own town, slaying many men, and, chief of all, Sarpedon, King of the Lycians; and round the body of Sarpedon the Trojans rallied under Hector, and the fight swayed this way and that, and there was such a noise of spears and swords smiting shields and helmets as when many woodcutters fell trees in a glen of the hills. At last the Trojans gave way, and the Greeks stripped the armour from the body of brave Sarpedon; but men say that Sleep and Death, like two winged angels, bore his body away to his own country. Now Patroclus forgot how Achilles had told him not to pursue the Trojans across the plain, but to return when he had driven them from the ships. On he raced, slaying as he went, even till he reached the foot of the wall of Troy. Thrice he tried to climb it, but thrice he fell back.

Hector was in his chariot in the gateway, and he bade his squire lash his horses into the war, and struck at no other man, great or small, but drove straight against Patroclus, who stood and threw a heavy stone at Hector; which missed him, but killed his charioteer. Then Patroclus leaped on the charioteer to strip his armour, but Hector stood over the body, grasping it by the head, while Patroclus dragged at the feet, and spears and arrows flew in clouds around the fallen man. At last, towards sunset, the Greeks drew him out of the war, and Patroclus thrice charged into the thick of the Trojans. But the helmet of Achilles was loosened in the fight, and fell from the head of Patroclus, and he was wounded from behind, and Hector, in front, drove his spear clean through his body. With his last breath Patroclus prophesied: 'Death stands near thee, Hector, at the hands of noble Achilles.' But Automedon was driving back the swift horses, carrying to Achilles the news that his dearest friend was slain.

After Ulysses was wounded, early in this great battle, he was not able to fight for several days, and, as the story is about Ulysses, we must tell quite shortly how Achilles returned to the war to take vengeance for Patroclus, and how he slew Hector. When Patroclus fell, Hector seized the armour which the Gods had given to Peleus, and Peleus to his son Achilles, while Achilles had lent it to Patroclus that he might terrify the Trojans. Retiring out of reach of spears, Hector took off his own armour and put on that of Achilles, and Greeks and Trojans fought for the dead body of Patroclus. Then Zeus, the chief of the Gods, looked down and said that Hector should never come home out of the battle to his wife, Andromache. But Hector returned into the fight around the dead Patroclus, and here all the best men fought, and even Automedon, who had been driving the chariot of Patroclus. Now when the Trojans seemed to have the better of the fight, the Greeks sent Antilochus, a son of old Nestor, to tell Achilles that his friend was slain, and Antilochus ran, and Ajax and his brother protected the Greeks who were trying to carry the body of Patroclus back to the ships.

Swiftly Antilochus came running to Achilles, saying: 'Fallen is Patroclus, and they are fighting round his naked body, for Hector has his armour.' Then Achilles said never a word, but fell on the floor of his hut, and threw black ashes on his yellow hair, till Antilochus seized his hands, fearing that he would cut his own throat with his dagger, for very sorrow. His mother, Thetis, arose from the sea to comfort him, but he said that he desired to die if he could not slay Hector, who had slain his friend. Then Thetis told him that he could not fight without armour, and now he had none; but she would go to the God of armour-making and bring from him such a shield and helmet and breastplate as had never been seen by men.

Meanwhile the fight raged round the dead body of Patroclus, which was defiled with blood and dust, near the ships, and was being dragged this way and that, and torn and wounded. Achilles could not bear this sight, yet his mother had warned him not to enter without armour the battle where stones and arrows and spears were flying like hail; and he was so tall and broad that he could put on the arms of no other man. So he went down to the ditch as he was, unarmed, and as he stood high above it, against the red sunset, fire seemed to flow from his golden hair like the beacon blaze that soars into the dark sky when an island town is attacked at night, and men light beacons that their neighbours may see them and come to their help from other isles. There Achilles stood in a splendour of fire, and he shouted aloud, as clear as a clarion rings when men fall on to attack a besieged city wall. Thrice Achilles shouted mightily, and thrice the horses of the Trojans shuddered for fear and turned back from the onslaught, and thrice the men of Troy were confounded and shaken with terror. Then the Greeks drew the body of Patroclus out of the dust and the arrows, and laid him on a bier, and Achilles followed, weeping, for he had sent his friend with chariot and horses to the war; but home again he welcomed him never more. Then the sun set and it was night.

Now one of the Trojans wished Hector to retire within the walls of Troy, for certainly Achilles would tomorrow be foremost in the war. But Hector said, 'Have ye not had your fill of being shut up behind walls? Let Achilles fight; I will meet him in the open field.' The Trojans cheered, and they camped in the plain; while in the hut of Achilles women washed the dead body of Patroclus, and Achilles swore that he would slay Hector.

In the dawn came Thetis, bearing to Achilles the new splendid armour that the God had made for him. Then Achilles put on that armour, and roused his men; but Ulysses, who knew all the rules of honour, would not let him fight till peace had been made, with a sacrifice and other ceremonies, between him and Agamemnon, and till Agamemnon had given him all the presents which Achilles had before refused. Achilles did not want them; he wanted only to fight, but Ulysses made him obey, and do what was usual. Then the gifts were brought, and Agamemnon stood up, and said that he was sorry for his insolence, and the men took breakfast, but Achilles would neither eat nor drink. He mounted his chariot, but the horse Xanthus bowed his head till his long mane touched the ground, and, being a fairy horse, the child of the West Wind, he spoke (or so men said), and these were his words: 'We shall bear thee swiftly and speedily, but thou shalt be slain in fight, and thy dying day is near at hand.' 'Well I know it,' said Achilles, 'but I will not cease from fighting till I have given the Trojans their fill of war.'

So all that day he chased and slew the Trojans. He drove them into the river, and, though the river came down in a red flood, he crossed, and slew them on the plain. The plain caught fire, the bushes and long dry grass blazed round him, but he fought his way through the fire, and drove the Trojans to their walls. The gates were thrown open, and the Trojans rushed through like frightened fawns, and then they climbed to the battlements, and looked down in safety, while the whole Greek army advanced in line under their shields.

But Hector stood still, alone, in front of the gate, and old Priam, who saw Achilles rushing on, shining like a star in his new armour, called with tears to Hector, 'Come within the gate! This man has slain many of my sons, and if he slays thee, whom have I to help me in my old age?' His mother also called to Hector, but he stood firm, waiting for Achilles. Now the story says that he was afraid, and ran thrice in full armour round Troy, with Achilles in pursuit. But this cannot be true, for no mortal men could run thrice, in heavy armour, with great shields that clanked against their ankles, round the town of Troy: moreover Hector was the bravest of men, and all the Trojan women were looking down at him from the walls.

We cannot believe that he ran away, and the story goes on to tell that he asked Achilles to make an agreement with him. The conqueror in the fight should give back the body of the fallen to be buried by his friends, but should keep his armour. But Achilles said that he could make no agreement with Hector, and threw his spear, which flew over Hector's shoulder. Then Hector threw his spear, but it could not pierce the shield which the God had made for Achilles. Hector had no other spear, and Achilles had one, so Hector cried, 'Let me not die without honour!' and drew his sword, and rushed at Achilles, who sprang to meet him, but before Hector could come within a sword-stroke Achilles had sent his spear clean through the neck of Hector. He fell in the dust and Achilles said, 'Dogs and birds shall tear your flesh unburied.' With his dying breath Hector prayed him to take gold from Priam, and give back his body to be burned in Troy. But Achilles said, 'Hound! would that I could bring myself to carve and eat thy raw flesh, but dogs shall devour it, even if thy father offered me thy weight in gold.' With his last words Hector prophesied and said, 'Remember me in the day when Paris shall slay thee in the Scaean gate.' Then his brave soul went to the Land of the Dead, which the Greeks called Hades. To that land Ulysses sailed while he was still a living man, as the story tells later.

Then Achilles did a dreadful deed; he slit the feet of dead Hector from heel to ankle, and thrust thongs through, and bound him by the thongs to his chariot and trailed the body in the dust. All the women of Troy who were on the walls raised a shriek, and Hector's wife, Andromache, heard the sound. She had been in an inner room of her house, weaving a purple web, and embroidering flowers on it, and she was calling her bower maidens to make ready a bath for Hector when he should come back tired from battle. But when she heard the cry from the wall she trembled, and the shuttle with which she was weaving fell from her hands. 'Surely I heard the cry of my husband's mother,' she said, and she bade two of her maidens come with her to see why the people lamented.

She ran swiftly, and reached the battlements, and thence she saw her dear husband's body being whirled through the dust towards the ships, behind the chariot of Achilles. Then night came over her eyes and she fainted. But when she returned to herself she cried out that now none would defend her little boy, and other children would push him away from feasts, saying, 'Out with you; no father of thine is at our table,' and his father, Hector, would lie naked at the ships, unclad, unburned, unlamented. To be unburned and unburied was thought the greatest of misfortunes, because the dead man unburned could not go into the House of Hades, God of the Dead, but must always wander, alone and comfortless, in the dark borderland between the dead and the living.

– 8 –

THE CRUELTY OF ACHILLES, AND THE RANSOMING OF HECTOR

WHEN ACHILLES WAS ASLEEP THAT night the ghost of Patroclus came, saying, 'Why dost thou not burn and bury me? for the other shadows of dead men suffer me not to come near them, and lonely I wander along the dark dwelling of Hades.' Then Achilles awoke, and he sent men to cut down trees, and make a huge pile of faggots and logs. On this they laid Patroclus, covered with white linen, and then they slew many cattle, and Achilles cut the throats of twelve Trojan prisoners of war, meaning to burn them with Patroclus to do him honour. This was a deed of shame, for Achilles was mad with sorrow and anger for the death of his friend. Then they drenched with wine the great pile of wood, which was thirty yards long and broad, and set fire to it, and the fire blazed all through the night and died down in the morning. They put the white bones of Patroclus in a golden casket, and laid it in the hut of Achilles, who said that, when he died, they must burn his body, and mix the ashes with the ashes of his friend, and build over it a chamber of stone, and cover the chamber with a great hill of earth, and set a pillar of stone above it. This is one of the hills on the plain of Troy, but the pillar has fallen from the tomb, long ago.

Then, as the custom was, Achilles held games – chariot races, foot races, boxing, wrestling, and archery – in honour of Patroclus. Ulysses won the prize for the foot race, and for the wrestling, so now his wound must have been healed.

But Achilles still kept trailing Hector's dead body each day round the hill that had been raised for the tomb of Patroclus, till the Gods in heaven were angry, and bade Thetis tell her son that he must give back the dead body to Priam, and take ransom for it, and they sent a messenger to Priam to bid him redeem the body of his son. It was terrible for Priam to have to go and humble himself before Achilles, whose hands had been red with the blood of his sons, but he did not disobey the Gods. He opened his chests, and took out twenty-four beautiful embroidered changes of raiment; and he weighed out ten heavy bars, or talents, of gold, and chose a beautiful golden cup, and he called nine of his sons, Paris, and Helenus, and

Deiphobus, and the rest, saying, 'Go, ye bad sons, my shame; would that Hector lived and all of you were dead!' for sorrow made him angry; 'go, and get ready for me a wain, and lay on it these treasures.' So they harnessed mules to the wain, and placed in it the treasures, and, after praying, Priam drove through the night to the hut of Achilles. In he went, when no man looked for him, and kneeled to Achilles, and kissed his terrible death-dealing hands. 'Have pity on me, and fear the Gods, and give me back my dead son,' he said, 'and remember thine own father. Have pity on me, who have endured to do what no man born has ever done before, to kiss the hands that slew my sons.'

Then Achilles remembered his own father, far away, who now was old and weak: and he wept, and Priam wept with him, and then Achilles raised Priam from his knees and spoke kindly to him, admiring how beautiful he still was in his old age, and Priam himself wondered at the beauty of Achilles. And Achilles thought how Priam had long been rich and happy, like his own father, Peleus, and now old age and weakness and sorrow were laid upon both of them, for Achilles knew that his own day of death was at hand, even at the doors. So Achilles bade the women make ready the body of Hector for burial, and they clothed him in a white mantle that Priam had brought, and laid him in the wain; and supper was made ready, and Priam and Achilles ate and drank together, and the women spread a bed for Priam, who would not stay long, but stole away back to Troy while Achilles was asleep.

All the women came out to meet him, and to lament for Hector. They carried the body into the house of Andromache and laid it on a bed, and the women gathered around, and each in turn sang her song over the great dead warrior. His mother bewailed him, and his wife, and Helen of the fair hands, clad in dark mourning raiment, lifted up her white arms, and said: 'Hector, of all my brethren in Troy thou wert the dearest, since Paris brought me hither. Would that ere that day I had died! For this is now the twentieth year since I came, and in all these twenty years never heard I a word from thee that was bitter and unkind; others might upbraid me, thy sisters or thy mother, for thy father was good to me as if he had been my own; but then thou wouldst restrain them that spoke evil by the courtesy of thy heart and thy gentle words. Ah! woe for thee, and woe for me, whom all men shudder at, for there is now none in wide Troyland to be my friend like thee, my brother and my friend!'

So Helen lamented, but now was done all that men might do; a great pile of wood was raised, and Hector was burned, and his ashes were placed in a golden urn, in a dark chamber of stone, within a hollow hill.

9

HOW ULYSSES STOLE THE LUCK OF TROY

AFTER HECTOR WAS BURIED, THE SIEGE went on slowly, as it had done during the first nine years of the war. The Greeks did not know at that time how to besiege a city, as we saw, by way of digging trenches and building towers, and battering the walls with machines that threw heavy stones. The Trojans had lost courage, and dared not go into the open plain, and they were waiting for the coming up of new armies of allies – the Amazons, who were girl warriors from far away, and an Eastern people called the Khita, whose king was Memnon, the son of the bright Dawn.

Now everyone knew that, in the temple of the Goddess Pallas Athene, in Troy, was a sacred image, which fell from heaven, called the Palladium, and this very ancient image was the Luck of Troy. While it remained safe in the temple people believed that Troy could never be taken, but as it was in a guarded temple in the middle of the town, and was watched by priestesses day and night, it seemed impossible that the Greeks should ever enter the city secretly and steal the Luck away.

As Ulysses was the grandson of Autolycus, the Master Thief, he often wished that the old man was with the Greeks, for if there was a thing to steal Autolycus could steal it. But by this time Autolycus was dead, and so Ulysses could only puzzle over the way to steal the Luck of Troy, and wonder how his grandfather would have set about it. He prayed for help secretly to Hermes, the God of Thieves, when he sacrificed goats to him, and at last he had a plan.

There was a story that Anius, the King of the Isle of Delos, had three daughters, named Oeno, Spermo and Elais, and that Oeno could turn water into wine, while Spermo could turn stones into bread, and Elais could change mud into olive oil. Those fairy gifts, people said, were given to the maidens by the Wine God, Dionysus, and by the Goddess of Corn, Demeter. Now corn, and wine, and oil were sorely needed by the Greeks, who were tired of paying much gold and bronze to the Phoenician merchants for their supplies. Ulysses therefore went to Agamemnon one day, and asked leave to take his ship and voyage to Delos, to bring, if he could, the three maidens to the camp, if indeed they could do these miracles. As no fighting was going on, Agamemnon gave Ulysses leave to depart, so he went on board his ship, with a crew of fifty men of Ithaca, and away they sailed, promising to return in a month.

Two or three days after that, a dirty old beggar man began to be seen in the Greek camp. He had crawled in late one evening, dressed in a dirty smock and a very dirty old cloak, full of holes, and stained with smoke. Over everything he wore the skin of a stag, with half the hair worn off, and he carried a staff, and a filthy tattered wallet, to put food in, which swung from his neck by a cord. He came crouching and smiling up to the door of the hut of Diomedes, and sat down just within the doorway, where beggars still sit in the East. Diomedes saw him, and sent him a loaf and two handfuls of flesh, which the beggar laid on his wallet, between his feet, and he made his supper greedily, gnawing a bone like a dog.

After supper Diomedes asked him who he was and whence he came, and he told a long story about how he had been a Cretan pirate, and had been taken prisoner by the Egyptians when he was robbing there, and how he had worked for many years in their stone quarries, where the sun had burned him brown, and had escaped by hiding among the great stones, carried down the Nile in a raft, for building a temple on the seashore. The raft arrived at night, and the beggar said that he stole out from it in the dark and found a Phoenician ship in the harbour, and the Phoenicians took him on board, meaning to sell him somewhere as a slave. But a tempest came on and wrecked the ship off the Isle of Tenedos, which is near Troy, and the beggar alone escaped to the island on a plank of the ship. From Tenedos he had come to Troy in a fisher's boat, hoping to make himself useful in the camp, and earn enough to keep body and soul together till he could find a ship sailing to Crete.

He made his story rather amusing, describing the strange ways of the Egyptians; how they worshipped cats and bulls, and did everything in just the opposite of the Greek way of doing things. So Diomedes let him have a rug and blankets to sleep on in the portico of the hut, and next day the old wretch went begging about the camp and talking with the soldiers. Now he was a most impudent and annoying old vagabond, and was always in quarrels. If there was a disagreeable story about the father or grandfather of any of the princes, he knew it and told it, so that he got a blow from the baton of Agamemnon, and Ajax gave him a kick, and Idomeneus drubbed him with the butt of his spear for a tale about his grandmother, and everybody hated him and called him a nuisance. He was forever jeering at Ulysses, who was far away, and telling tales about Autolycus, and at last he stole a gold cup, a very large cup, with two handles, and a dove sitting on each handle, from the hut of Nestor. The old chief was fond of this cup, which he had brought from home, and, when it was found in the beggar's dirty wallet, everybody cried that he must be driven out of the camp and well whipped. So Nestor's son, young Thrasymedes, with other young men, laughing and shouting, pushed and dragged the beggar close up to the Scaean gate of Troy, where Thrasymedes called with a loud voice, 'O Trojans, we are sick of this shameless beggar. First we shall whip him well, and if he comes back we shall put out his eyes and cut off his hands and feet, and give him to the dogs to eat. He may go to you, if he likes; if not, he must wander till he dies of hunger.'

The young men of Troy heard this and laughed, and a crowd gathered on the wall to see the beggar punished. So Thrasymedes whipped him with his bowstring till he was tired, and they did not leave off beating the beggar till he ceased howling and fell, all bleeding, and lay still. Then Thrasymedes gave him a parting kick, and went away with his friends. The beggar lay quiet for some time, then he began to stir, and sat up, wiping the tears from his eyes, and shouting curses and bad words after the Greeks, praying that they might be speared in the back, and eaten by dogs.

At last he tried to stand up, but fell down again, and began to crawl on hands and knees towards the Scaean gate. There he sat down, within the two side walls of the gate, where he cried and lamented. Now Helen of the fair hands came down from the gate tower, being sorry to see any man treated so much worse than a beast, and she spoke to the beggar and asked him why he had been used in this cruel way?

At first he only moaned, and rubbed his sore sides, but at last he said that he was an unhappy man, who had been shipwrecked, and was begging his way home, and that the Greeks suspected him of being a spy sent out by the Trojans. But he had been in Lacedaemon, her own country, he said, and could tell her about her father, if she were, as he supposed, the beautiful Helen, and about her brothers, Castor and Polydeuces, and her little daughter, Hermione.

'But perhaps,' he said, 'you are no mortal woman, but some Goddess who favours the Trojans, and if indeed you are a Goddess then I liken you to Aphrodite, for beauty, and stature, and shapeliness.' Then Helen wept; for many a year had passed since she had heard any word of her father, and daughter, and her brothers, who were dead, though she knew it not. So she stretched out her white hand, and raised the beggar, who was kneeling at her feet, and bade him follow her to her own house, within the palace garden of King Priam.

Helen walked forward, with a bower maiden at either side, and the beggar crawling after her. When she had entered her house, Paris was not there, so she ordered the bath to be filled with warm water, and new clothes to be brought, and she herself washed the old beggar and anointed him with oil. This appears very strange to us, for though Saint Elizabeth of Hungary used to wash and clothe beggars, we are surprised that Helen should do so, who was not a saint. But long afterwards she herself told the son of Ulysses, Telemachus, that she had washed his father when he came into Troy disguised as a beggar who had been sorely beaten.

You must have guessed that the beggar was Ulysses, who had not gone to Delos in his ship, but stolen back in a boat, and appeared disguised among the Greeks. He did all this to make sure that nobody could recognise him, and he behaved so as to deserve a whipping that he might not be suspected as a Greek spy by the Trojans, but rather be pitied by them. Certainly he deserved his name of 'the much-enduring Ulysses'.

Meanwhile he sat in his bath and Helen washed his feet. But when she had done, and had anointed his wounds with olive oil, and when she had clothed him in a white tunic and a purple mantle, then she opened her lips to cry out with amazement, for she knew Ulysses; but he laid his finger on her lips, saying 'Hush!' Then she remembered how great danger he was in, for the Trojans, if they found him, would put him to some cruel death, and she sat down, trembling and weeping, while he watched her.

'Oh thou strange one,' she said, 'how enduring is thy heart and how cunning beyond measure! How hast thou borne to be thus beaten and disgraced, and to come within the walls of Troy? Well it is for thee that Paris, my lord, is far from home, having gone to guide Penthesilea, the Queen of the warrior maids whom men call Amazons, who is on her way to help the Trojans.'

Then Ulysses smiled, and Helen saw that she had said a word which she ought not to have spoken, and had revealed the secret hope of the Trojans. Then she wept, and said, 'Oh cruel and cunning! You have made me betray the people with whom I live, though woe is me that ever I left my own people, and my husband dear, and my child! And now if you escape alive out of Troy, you will tell the Greeks, and they will lie in ambush by night for the Amazons on the way to Troy and will slay them all. If you and I were not friends long ago, I would tell the Trojans that you are here, and they would give your body to the dogs to eat, and fix your head on the palisade above the wall. Woe is me that ever I was born.'

Ulysses answered, 'Lady, as you have said, we two are friends from of old, and your friend I will be till the last, when the Greeks break into Troy, and slay the men, and carry the women captives. If I live till that hour no man shall harm you, but safely and in honour you shall come to your palace in Lacedaemon of the rifted hills. Moreover, I swear to you a great oath, by Zeus above, and by Them that under earth punish the souls of men who swear falsely, that I shall tell no man the thing which you have spoken.'

So when he had sworn and done that oath, Helen was comforted and dried her tears. Then she told him how unhappy she was, and how she had lost her last comfort when Hector died. 'Always am I wretched,' she said, 'save when sweet sleep falls on me. Now the wife of Thon, King of Egypt, gave me this gift when we were in Egypt, on our way to Troy, namely, a drug that brings sleep even to the most unhappy, and it is pressed from the poppy heads of the garland of the God of Sleep.' Then she showed him strange phials of gold, full of this drug: phials wrought by the Egyptians, and covered with magic spells and shapes of beasts and flowers. 'One of these I will give you,' she said, 'that even from Troy town you may not go without a gift in memory of the hands of Helen.' So Ulysses took the phial of gold, and was glad in his heart, and Helen set before him meat and wine. When he had eaten and drunk, and his strength had come back to him, he said: 'Now I must dress me again in my old rags, and take my wallet, and my staff, and go forth, and beg through Troy town. For here I must abide for some days as a beggar man, lest if I now escape from your house in the night the Trojans may think that you have told me the secrets of their counsel, which I am carrying to the Greeks, and may be angry with you.' So he clothed himself again as a beggar, and took his staff, and hid the phial of gold with the Egyptian drug in his rags, and in his wallet also he put the new clothes that Helen had given him, and a sword, and he took farewell, saying, 'Be of good heart, for the end of your sorrows is at hand. But if you see me among the beggars in the street, or by the well, take no heed of me, only I will salute you as a beggar who has been kindly treated by a Queen.'

So they parted, and Ulysses went out, and when it was day he was with the beggars in the streets, but by night he commonly slept near the fire of a smithy forge, as is the way of beggars. So for some days he begged, saying that he was gathering food to eat while he walked to some town far away that was at peace, where he might find work to do. He was not impudent now, and did not go to rich men's houses or tell evil tales, or laugh, but he was much in the temples, praying to the Gods, and above all in the temple of Pallas Athene. The Trojans thought that he was a pious man for a beggar.

Now there was a custom in these times that men and women who were sick or in distress should sleep at night on the floors of the temples. They did this hoping that the God would send them a dream to show them how their diseases might be cured, or how they might find what they had lost, or might escape from their distresses.

Ulysses slept in more than one temple, and once in that of Pallas Athene, and the priests and priestesses were kind to him, and gave him food in the morning when the gates of the temple were opened.

In the temple of Pallas Athene, where the Luck of Troy lay always on her altar, the custom was that priestesses kept watch, each for two hours, all through the night, and soldiers kept guard within call. So one night Ulysses slept there, on the floor, with other distressed people, seeking for dreams from the Gods. He lay still all through the night till the turn of the last priestess came to watch. The priestess used to walk up and down with bare feet among the dreaming people, having a torch in her hand, and muttering hymns to the Goddess. Then Ulysses, when her back was turned, slipped the gold phial out of his rags, and let it lie on the polished floor beside him. When the priestess came back again, the light from her torch fell on the glittering phial, and she stooped and picked it up, and looked at it curiously. There came from it a sweet fragrance, and she opened it, and tasted the drug. It seemed to her the sweetest thing that ever she had tasted, and she took more and more, and then closed the phial and laid it down, and went along murmuring her hymn.

But soon a great drowsiness came over her, and she sat down on the step of the altar, and fell sound asleep, and the torch sunk in her hand, and went out, and all was dark. Then Ulysses put the phial in his wallet, and crept very cautiously to the altar, in the dark, and stole the Luck of Troy. It was only a small black mass of what is now called meteoric iron, which sometimes comes down with meteorites from the sky, but it was shaped like a shield, and the people thought it an image of the warlike shielded Goddess, fallen from heaven. Such sacred shields, made of glass and ivory, are found deep in the earth in the ruined cities of Ulysses' time. Swiftly Ulysses hid the Luck in his rags and left in its place on the altar a copy of the Luck, which he had made of blackened clay. Then he stole back to the place where he had lain, and remained there till dawn appeared, and the sleepers who sought for dreams awoke, and the temple gates were opened, and Ulysses walked out with the rest of them.

He stole down a lane, where as yet no people were stirring, and crept along, leaning on his staff, till he came to the eastern gate, at the back of the city, which the Greeks never attacked, for they had never drawn their army in a circle round the town. There Ulysses explained to the sentinels that he had gathered food enough to last for a long journey to some other town, and opened his bag, which seemed full of bread and broken meat. The soldiers said he was a lucky beggar, and let him out. He walked slowly along the waggon road by which wood was brought into Troy from the forests on Mount Ida, and when he found that nobody was within sight he slipped into the forest, and stole into a dark thicket, hiding beneath the tangled boughs. Here he lay and slept till evening, and then took the new clothes which Helen had given him out of his wallet, and put them on, and threw the belt of the sword over his shoulder, and hid the Luck of Troy in his bosom. He washed himself clean in a mountain brook, and now all who saw him must have known that he was no beggar, but Ulysses of Ithaca, Laertes' son.

So he walked cautiously down the side of the brook which ran between high banks deep in trees, and followed it till it reached the river Xanthus, on the left of the Greek lines. Here he found Greek sentinels set to guard the camp, who cried aloud in joy and surprise, for his ship had not yet returned from Delos, and they could not guess how Ulysses had come back alone across the sea. So two of the sentinels guided Ulysses to the hut of Agamemnon, where he and Achilles and all the chiefs were sitting at a feast. They all leaped up, but when Ulysses took the Luck of Troy from within his mantle, they cried that this was the bravest deed that had been done in the war, and they sacrificed ten oxen to Zeus.

'So you were the old beggar,' said young Thrasymedes.

'Yes,' said Ulysses, 'and when next you beat a beggar, Thrasymedes, do not strike so hard and so long.'

That night all the Greeks were full of hope, for now they had the Luck of Troy, but the Trojans were in despair, and guessed that the beggar was the thief, and that Ulysses had been the beggar. The priestess, Theano, could tell them nothing; they found her, with the extinguished torch drooping in her hand, asleep, as she sat on the step of the altar, and she never woke again.

– 10 –

THE BATTLES WITH THE AMAZONS AND MEMNON – THE DEATH OF ACHILLES

ULYSSES THOUGHT MUCH AND OFTEN OF Helen, without whose kindness he could not have saved the Greeks by stealing the Luck of Troy. He saw that, though she remained as beautiful as when the princes all sought her hand, she was most unhappy, knowing herself to be the cause of so much misery, and fearing what the future might bring. Ulysses told nobody about the secret which she had let fall, the coming of the Amazons.

The Amazons were a race of warlike maids, who lived far away on the banks of the river Thermodon. They had fought against Troy in former times, and one of the great hill-graves on the plain of Troy covered the ashes of an Amazon, swift-footed Myrine. People believed that they were the daughters of the God of War, and they were reckoned equal in battle to the bravest men. Their young Queen, Penthesilea, had two reasons for coming to fight at Troy: one was her ambition to win renown, and the other her sleepless sorrow for having accidentally killed her sister, Hippolyte, when hunting. The spear which she threw at a stag struck Hippolyte and slew her, and Penthesilea cared no longer for her own life, and desired to fall gloriously in battle. So Penthesilea and her bodyguard of twelve Amazons set forth from the wide streams of Thermodon, and rode into Troy. The story says that they did not drive in chariots, like all the Greek and Trojan chiefs, but rode horses, which must have been the manner of their country.

Penthesilea was the tallest and most beautiful of the Amazons, and shone among her twelve maidens like the moon among the stars, or the bright Dawn among the Hours which follow her chariot wheels. The Trojans rejoiced when they beheld her, for she looked both terrible and beautiful, with a frown on her brow, and fair shining eyes, and a blush on her cheeks. To the Trojans she came like Iris, the Rainbow, after a storm, and they gathered round her cheering, and throwing flowers and kissing her stirrup, as the people of Orleans welcomed Joan of Arc when she came to deliver them. Even Priam was glad, as is a man long blind, when he has been healed, and again looks upon the light of the sun.

Priam held a great feast, and gave to Penthesilea many beautiful gifts: cups of gold, and embroideries, and a sword with a hilt of silver, and she vowed that she would slay Achilles. But when Andromache, the wife of Hector, heard her she said within herself, 'Ah, unhappy girl, what is this boast of thine! Thou hast not the strength to fight the unconquerable son of Peleus, for if Hector could not slay him, what chance hast thou? But the piled-up earth covers Hector!'

In the morning Penthesilea sprang up from sleep and put on her glorious armour, with spear in hand, and sword at side, and bow and quiver hung behind her back, and her great shield covering her side from neck to stirrup, and mounted her horse, and galloped to the plain. Beside her charged the twelve maidens of her bodyguard, and all the company of Hector's brothers and kinsfolk. These headed the Trojan lines, and they rushed towards the ships of the Greeks.

Then the Greeks asked each other, 'Who is this that leads the Trojans as Hector led them, surely some God rides in the van of the charioteers!' Ulysses could have told them who the new leader of the Trojans was, but it seems that he had not the heart to fight against women, for his name is not mentioned in this day's battle. So the two lines clashed, and the plain of Troy ran red with blood, for Penthesilea slew

Molios, and Persinöos, and Eilissos, and Antiphates, and Lernos high of heart, and Hippalmos of the loud war-cry, and Haemonides, and strong Elasippus, while her maidens Derinoe and Clonie slew each a chief of the Greeks. But Clonie fell beneath the spear of Podarkes, whose hand Penthesilea cut off with the sword, while Idomeneus speared the Amazon Bremousa, and Meriones of Crete slew Evadre, and Diomedes killed Alcibie and Derimacheia in close fight with the sword, so the company of the Twelve were thinned, the bodyguard of Penthesilea.

The Trojans and Greeks kept slaying each other, but Penthesilea avenged her maidens, driving the ranks of Greece as a lioness drives the cattle on the hills, for they could not stand before her. Then she shouted, 'Dogs! today shall you pay for the sorrows of Priam! Where is Diomedes, where is Achilles, where is Ajax, that, men say, are your bravest? Will none of them stand before my spear?' Then she charged again, at the head of the Household of Priam, brothers and kinsmen of Hector, and where they came the Greeks fell like yellow leaves before the wind of autumn. The white horse that Penthesilea rode, a gift from the wife of the North Wind, flashed like lightning through a dark cloud among the companies of the Greeks, and the chariots that followed the charge of the Amazon rocked as they swept over the bodies of the slain. Then the old Trojans, watching from the walls, cried: 'This is no mortal maiden but a Goddess, and today she will burn the ships of the Greeks, and they will all perish in Troyland, and see Greece never more again.'

Now it so was that Ajax and Achilles had not heard the din and the cry of war, for both had gone to weep over the great new grave of Patroclus. Penthesilea and the Trojans had driven back the Greeks within their ditch, and they were hiding here and there among the ships, and torches were blazing in men's hands to burn the ships, as in the day of the valour of Hector: when Ajax heard the din of battle, and called to Achilles to make speed towards the ships.

So they ran swiftly to their huts, and armed themselves, and Ajax fell smiting and slaying upon the Trojans, but Achilles slew five of the bodyguard of Penthesilea. She, beholding her maidens fallen, rode straight against Ajax and Achilles, like a dove defying two falcons, and cast her spear, but it fell back blunted from the glorious shield that the God had made for the son of Peleus. Then she threw another spear at Ajax, crying, 'I am the daughter of the God of War,' but his armour kept out the spear, and he and Achilles laughed aloud. Ajax paid no more heed to the Amazon, but rushed against the Trojan men; while Achilles raised the heavy spear that none but he could throw, and drove it down through breastplate and breast of Penthesilea, yet still her hand grasped her sword-hilt. But, ere she could draw her sword, Achilles speared her horse, and horse and rider fell, and died in their fall.

There lay fair Penthesilea in the dust, like a tall poplar tree that the wind has overthrown, and her helmet fell, and the Greeks who gathered round marvelled to see her lie so beautiful in death, like Artemis, the Goddess of the Woods, when she sleeps alone, weary with hunting on the hills. Then the heart of Achilles was pierced with pity and sorrow, thinking how she might have been his wife in his own country, had he spared her, but he was never to see pleasant Phthia, his native land, again. So Achilles stood and wept over Penthesilea dead.

Now the Greeks, in pity and sorrow, held their hands, and did not pursue the Trojans who had fled, nor did they strip the armour from Penthesilea and her twelve maidens, but laid the bodies on biers, and sent them back in peace to Priam. Then the Trojans burned Penthesilea in the midst of her dead maidens, on a great pile of dry wood, and placed their ashes in a golden casket, and buried them all in the great hill-grave of Laomedon, an ancient King of Troy, while the Greeks with lamentation buried them whom the Amazon had slain.

The old men of Troy and the chiefs now held a council, and Priam said that they must not yet despair, for, if they had lost many of their bravest warriors, many of the Greeks had also fallen. Their best plan was to fight only with arrows from the walls and towers, till King Memnon came to their rescue with a great army of Aethiopes. Now Memnon was the son of the bright Dawn, a beautiful Goddess who had loved and married a mortal man, Tithonus. She had asked Zeus, the chief of the Gods, to make her lover immortal, and her prayer was granted. Tithonus could not die, but he began to grow grey, and then white-haired, with a long white beard, and very weak, till nothing of him seemed to be left but his voice, always feebly chattering like the grasshoppers on a summer day.

Memnon was the most beautiful of men, except Paris and Achilles, and his home was in a country that borders on the land of sunrising. There he was reared by the lily maidens called Hesperides, till he came to his full strength, and commanded the whole army of the Aethiopes. For their arrival Priam wished to wait, but Polydamas advised that the Trojans should give back Helen to the Greeks, with jewels twice as valuable as those which she had brought from the house of Menelaus. Then Paris was very angry, and said that Polydamas was a coward, for it was little to Paris that Troy should be taken and burned in a month if for a month he could keep Helen of the fair hands.

At length Memnon came, leading a great army of men who had nothing white about them but the teeth, so fiercely the sun burned on them in their own country. The Trojans had all the more hopes of Memnon because, on his long journey from the land of sunrising, and the river Oceanus that girdles the round world, he had been obliged to cross the country of the Solymi. Now the Solymi were the fiercest of men and rose up against Memnon, but he and his army fought them for a whole day, and defeated them, and drove them to the hills. When Memnon came, Priam gave him a great cup of gold, full of wine to the brim, and Memnon drank the wine at one draught. But he did not make great boasts of what he could do, like poor Penthesilea, 'for,' said he, 'whether I am a good man at arms will be known in battle, where the strength of men is tried. So now let us turn to sleep, for to wake and drink wine all through the night is an ill beginning of war.'

Then Priam praised his wisdom, and all men betook them to bed, but the bright Dawn rose unwillingly next day, to throw light on the battle where her son was to risk his life. Then Memnon led out the dark clouds of his men into the plain, and the Greeks foreboded evil when they saw so great a new army of fresh and unwearied warriors, but Achilles, leading them in his shining armour, gave them courage. Memnon fell upon the left wing of the Greeks, and on the men of Nestor, and first he slew Ereuthus, and then attacked Nestor's young son, Antilochus, who, now that Patroclus had fallen, was the dearest friend of Achilles. On him Memnon leaped, like a lion on a kid, but Antilochus lifted a huge stone from the plain, a pillar that had been set on the tomb of some great warrior long ago, and the stone smote full on the helmet of Memnon, who reeled beneath the stroke. But Memnon seized his heavy spear, and drove it through shield and corselet of Antilochus, even into his heart, and he fell and died beneath his father's eyes. Then Nestor in great sorrow and anger strode across the body of Antilochus and called to his other son, Thrasymedes, 'Come and drive afar this man that has slain thy brother, for if fear be in thy heart thou art no son of mine, nor of the race of Periclymenus, who stood up in battle even against the strong man Heracles!'

But Memnon was too strong for Thrasymedes, and drove him off, while old Nestor himself charged sword in hand, though Memnon bade him begone, for he was not minded to strike so aged a man, and

Nestor drew back, for he was weak with age. Then Memnon and his army charged the Greeks, slaying and stripping the dead. But Nestor had mounted his chariot and driven to Achilles, weeping, and imploring him to come swiftly and save the body of Antilochus, and he sped to meet Memnon, who lifted a great stone, the landmark of a field, and drove it against the shield of the son of Peleus. But Achilles was not shaken by the blow; he ran forward, and wounded Memnon over the rim of his shield. Yet wounded as he was Memnon fought on and struck his spear through the arm of Achilles, for the Greeks fought with no sleeves of bronze to protect their arms.

Then Achilles drew his great sword, and flew on Memnon, and with sword-strokes they lashed at each other on shield and helmet, and the long horsehair crests of the helmets were shorn off, and flew down the wind, and their shields rang terribly beneath the sword-strokes. They thrust at each other's throats between shield and visor of the helmet, they smote at knee, and thrust at breast, and the armour rang about their bodies, and the dust from beneath their feet rose up in a cloud around them, like mist round the falls of a great river in flood. So they fought, neither of them yielding a step, till Achilles made so rapid a thrust that Memnon could not parry it, and the bronze sword passed clean through his body beneath the breastbone, and he fell, and his armour clashed as he fell.

Then Achilles, wounded as he was and weak from loss of blood, did not stay to strip the golden armour of Memnon, but shouted his war-cry, and pressed on, for he hoped to enter the gate of Troy with the fleeing Trojans, and all the Greeks followed after him. So they pursued, slaying as they went, and the Scaean gate was choked with the crowd of men, pursuing and pursued. In that hour would the Greeks have entered Troy, and burned the city, and taken the women captive, but Paris stood on the tower above the gate, and in his mind was anger for the death of his brother Hector. He tried the string of his bow, and found it frayed, for all day he had showered his arrows on the Greeks; so he chose a new bowstring, and fitted it, and strung the bow, and chose an arrow from his quiver, and aimed at the ankle of Achilles, where it was bare beneath the greave, or leg-guard of metal, that the God had fashioned for him. Through the ankle flew the arrow, and Achilles wheeled round, weak as he was, and stumbled, and fell, and the armour that the God had wrought was defiled with dust and blood.

Then Achilles rose again, and cried: 'What coward has smitten me with a secret arrow from afar? Let him stand forth and meet me with sword and spear!' So speaking he seized the shaft with his strong hands and tore it out of the wound, and much blood gushed, and darkness came over his eyes. Yet he staggered forward, striking blindly, and smote Orythaon, a dear friend of Hector, through the helmet, and others he smote, but now his force failed him and he leaned on his spear, and cried his war-cry, and said, 'Cowards of Troy, ye shall not all escape my spear, dying as I am.' But as he spoke he fell, and all his armour rang around him, yet the Trojans stood apart and watched; and as hunters watch a dying lion not daring to go nigh him, so the Trojans stood in fear till Achilles drew his latest breath. Then from the wall the Trojan women raised a great cry of joy over him who had slain the noble Hector: and thus was fulfilled the prophecy of Hector, that Achilles should fall in the Scaean gateway, by the hand of Paris.

Then the best of the Trojans rushed forth from the gate to seize the body of Achilles, and his glorious armour, but the Greeks were as eager to carry the body to the ships that it might have due burial. Round the dead Achilles men fought long and sore, and both sides were mixed, Greeks and Trojans, so that men dared not shoot arrows from the walls of Troy lest they should kill their own friends. Paris, and Aeneas, and Glaucus, who had been the friend of Sarpedon, led the Trojans, and Ajax and Ulysses led the Greeks, for we are not told that Agamemnon was fighting in this great battle of the war. Now as angry wild bees flock round a man who is taking their honeycombs, so the Trojans gathered round Ajax, striving to stab him, but he set his great shield in front, and smote and slew all that came within reach of his spear. Ulysses, too, struck down many, and though a spear was thrown and pierced his leg near the knee he stood firm, protecting the body of Achilles. At last Ulysses caught the body of Achilles by the hands, and heaved it upon his back, and so limped towards the ships, but Ajax and the men of Ajax followed, turning round if ever the Trojans ventured to come near, and charging into the midst of them. Thus very slowly they bore the dead Achilles across the plain, through the bodies of the fallen and the blood, till they met Nestor in his chariot and placed Achilles therein, and swiftly Nestor drove to the ships.

There the women, weeping, washed Achilles' comely body, and laid him on a bier with a great white mantle over him, and all the women lamented and sang dirges; and the first was Briseis, who loved Achilles better than her own country, and her father, and her brothers whom he had slain in war. The

Greek princes, too, stood round the body, weeping and cutting off their long locks of yellow hair, a token of grief and an offering to the dead.

Men say that forth from the sea came Thetis of the silver feet, the mother of Achilles, with her ladies, the deathless maidens of the waters. They rose up from their glassy chambers below the sea, moving on, many and beautiful, like the waves on a summer day, and their sweet song echoed along the shores, and fear came upon the Greeks. Then they would have fled, but Nestor cried: 'Hold, flee not, young lords of the Achaeans! Lo, she that comes from the sea is his mother, with the deathless maidens of the waters, to look on the face of her dead son.' Then the sea nymphs stood around the dead Achilles and clothed him in the garments of the Gods, fragrant raiment, and all the Nine Muses, one to the other replying with sweet voices, began their lament.

Next the Greeks made a great pile of dry wood, and laid Achilles on it, and set fire to it, till the flames had consumed his body except the white ashes. These they placed in a great golden cup and mingled with them the ashes of Patroclus, and above all they built a tomb like a hill, high on a headland above the sea, that men for all time may see it as they go sailing by, and may remember Achilles. Next they held in his honour foot races and chariot races, and other games, and Thetis gave splendid prizes. Last of all, when the games were ended, Thetis placed before the chiefs the glorious armour that the God had made for her son on the night after the slaying of Patroclus by Hector. 'Let these arms be the prize of the best of the Greeks,' she said, 'and of him that saved the body of Achilles out of the hands of the Trojans.'

Then stood up on one side Ajax and on the other Ulysses, for these two had rescued the body, and neither thought himself a worse warrior than the other. Both were the bravest of the brave, and if Ajax was the taller and stronger, and upheld the fight at the ships on the day of the valour of Hector; Ulysses had alone withstood the Trojans, and refused to retreat even when wounded, and his courage and cunning had won for the Greeks the Luck of Troy. Therefore old Nestor arose and said: 'This is a luckless day, when the best of the Greeks are rivals for such a prize. He who is not the winner will be heavy at heart, and will not stand firm by us in battle, as of old, and hence will come great loss to the Greeks. Who can be a just judge in this question, for some men will love Ajax better, and some will prefer Ulysses, and thus will arise disputes among ourselves. Lo! have we not here among us many Trojan prisoners, waiting till their friends pay their ransom in cattle and gold and bronze and iron? These hate all the Greeks alike, and will favour neither Ajax nor Ulysses. Let *them* be the judges, and decide who is the best of the Greeks, and the man who has done most harm to the Trojans.'

Agamemnon said that Nestor had spoken wisely. The Trojans were then made to sit as judges in the midst of the Assembly, and Ajax and Ulysses spoke, and told the stories of their own great deeds, of which we have heard already, but Ajax spoke roughly and discourteously, calling Ulysses a coward and a weakling. 'Perhaps the Trojans know,' said Ulysses quietly, 'whether they think that I deserve what Ajax has said about me, that I am a coward; and perhaps Ajax may remember that he did not find me so weak when we wrestled for a prize at the funeral of Patroclus.'

Then the Trojans all with one voice said that Ulysses was the best man among the Greeks, and the most feared by them, both for his courage and his skill in stratagems of war. On this, the blood of Ajax flew into his face, and he stood silent and unmoving, and could not speak a word, till his friends came round him and led him away to his hut, and there he sat down and would not eat or drink, and the night fell.

Long he sat, musing in his mind, and then rose

and put on all his armour, and seized a sword that Hector had given him one day when they two fought in a gentle passage of arms, and took courteous farewell of each other, and Ajax had given Hector a broad sword-belt, wrought with gold. This sword, Hector's gift, Ajax took, and went towards the hut of Ulysses, meaning to carve him limb from limb, for madness had come upon him in his great grief. Rushing through the night to slay Ulysses he fell upon the flock of sheep that the Greeks kept for their meat. And up and down among them he went, smiting blindly till the dawn came, and, lo! his senses returned to him, and he saw that he had not smitten Ulysses, but stood in a pool of blood among the sheep that he had slain. He could not endure the disgrace of his madness, and he fixed the sword, Hector's gift, with its hilt firmly in the ground, and went back a little way, and ran and fell upon the sword, which pierced his heart, and so died the great Ajax, choosing death before a dishonoured life.

– 11 –

ULYSSES SAILS TO SEEK THE SON OF ACHILLES – THE VALOUR OF EURYPYLUS

WHEN THE GREEKS FOUND AJAX LYING dead, slain by his own hand, they made great lament, and above all the brother of Ajax, and his wife Tecmessa bewailed him, and the shores of the sea rang with their sorrow. But of all no man was more grieved than Ulysses, and he stood up and said: 'Would that the sons of the Trojans had never awarded to me the arms of Achilles, for far rather would I have given them to Ajax than that this loss should have befallen the whole army of the Greeks. Let no man blame me, or be angry with me, for I have not sought for wealth, to enrich myself, but for honour only, and to win a name that will be remembered among men in times to come.' Then they made a great fire of wood, and burned the body of Ajax, lamenting him as they had sorrowed for Achilles.

Now it seemed that though the Greeks had won the Luck of Troy and had defeated the Amazons and the army of Memnon, they were no nearer taking Troy than ever. They had slain Hector, indeed, and many other Trojans, but they had lost the great Achilles, and Ajax, and Patroclus, and Antilochus, with the princes whom Penthesilea and Memnon slew, and the bands of the dead chiefs were weary of fighting, and eager to go home. The chiefs met in council, and Menelaus arose and said that his heart was wasted with sorrow for the death of so many brave men who had sailed to Troy for his sake. 'Would that death had come upon me before I gathered this host,' he said, 'but come, let the rest of us launch our swift ships, and return each to our own country.'

He spoke thus to try the Greeks, and see of what courage they were, for his desire was still to burn Troy town and to slay Paris with his own hand. Then up rose Diomedes, and swore that never would the Greeks turn cowards. No! He bade them sharpen their swords, and make ready for battle. The prophet Calchas, too, arose and reminded the Greeks how he had always foretold that they would take Troy in the tenth year of the siege, and how the tenth year had come, and victory was almost in their hands. Next Ulysses stood up and said that, though Achilles was dead, and there was no prince to lead his men, yet a son had been born to Achilles, while he was in the isle of Scyros, and that son he would bring to fill his father's place.

'Surely he will come, and for a token I will carry to him those unhappy arms of the great Achilles. Unworthy am I to wear them, and they bring back to my mind our sorrow for Ajax. But his son will wear them, in the front of the spearmen of Greece and in the thickest ranks of Troy shall the helmet of Achilles shine, as it was wont to do, for always he fought among the foremost.' Thus Ulysses spoke, and he and Diomedes, with fifty oarsmen, went on board a swift ship, and sitting all in order on the benches they smote the grey sea into foam, and Ulysses held the helm and steered them towards the isle of Scyros.

Now the Trojans had rest from war for a while, and Priam, with a heavy heart, bade men take his chief treasure, the great golden vine, with leaves and clusters of gold, and carry it to the mother of Eurypylus, the king of the people who dwell where the wide marshlands of the river Caycus clang with the cries of the cranes and herons and wild swans. For the mother of Eurypylus had sworn that never would she let her son go to the war unless Priam sent her the vine of gold, a gift of the Gods to an ancient King of Troy.

With a heavy heart, then, Priam sent the golden vine, but Eurypylus was glad when he saw it, and bade all his men arm, and harness the horses to the chariots, and glad were the Trojans when the long line of the new army wound along the road and into the town. Then Paris welcomed Eurypylus who was his nephew, son of his sister Astyoche, a daughter of Priam; but the grandfather of Eurypylus was the famous Heracles, the strongest man who ever lived on earth. So Paris brought Eurypylus to his house, where Helen sat working at her embroideries with her four bower maidens, and Eurypylus marvelled when he saw her, she was so beautiful. But the Khita, the people of Eurypylus, feasted in the open air among the Trojans, by the light of great fires burning, and to the music of pipes and flutes. The Greeks saw the fires, and heard the merry music, and they watched all night lest the Trojans should attack the ships before the dawn. But in the dawn Eurypylus rose from sleep and put on his armour, and hung from his neck by the belt the great shield on which were fashioned, in gold of many colours and in silver, the Twelve Adventures of Heracles, his grandfather; strange deeds that he did, fighting with monsters and giants and with the Hound of Hades, who guards the dwellings of the dead. Then Eurypylus led on his whole army, and with the brothers of Hector he charged against the Greeks, who were led by Agamemnon.

In that battle Eurypylus first smote Nireus, who was the most beautiful of the Greeks now that Achilles had fallen. There lay Nireus, like an apple tree, all covered with blossoms red and white, that the wind has overthrown in a rich man's orchard. Then Eurypylus would have stripped off his armour, but Machaon rushed in, Machaon who had been wounded and taken to the tent of Nestor, on the day of the Valour of Hector, when he brought fire against the ships. Machaon drove his spear through the left shoulder of Eurypylus, but Eurypylus struck at his shoulder with his sword, and the blood flowed; nevertheless, Machaon stooped, and grasped a great stone, and sent it against the helmet of Eurypylus. He was shaken, but he did not fall, he drove his spear through breastplate and breast of Machaon, who fell and died. With his last breath he said, 'Thou, too, shalt fall,' but Eurypylus made answer, 'So let it be! Men cannot live for ever, and such is the fortune of war.'

Thus the battle rang, and shone, and shifted, till few of the Greeks kept steadfast, except those with Menelaus and Agamemnon, for Diomedes and Ulysses were far away upon the sea, bringing from Scyros the son of Achilles. But Teucer slew

Polydamas, who had warned Hector to come within the walls of Troy; and Menelaus wounded Deiphobus, the bravest of the sons of Priam who were still in arms, for many had fallen; and Agamemnon slew certain spearmen of the Trojans. Round Eurypylus fought Paris, and Aeneas, who wounded Teucer with a great stone, breaking in his helmet, but he drove back in his chariot to the ships. Menelaus and Agamemnon stood alone and fought in the crowd of Trojans, like two wild boars that a circle of hunters surrounds with spears, so fiercely they stood at bay. There they would both have fallen, but Idomeneus, and Meriones of Crete, and Thrasymedes, Nestor's son, ran to their rescue, and fiercer grew the fighting. Eurypylus desired to slay Agamemnon and Menelaus, and end the war, but, as the spears of the Scots encompassed King James at Flodden Field till he ran forward, and fell within a lance's length of the English general, so the men of Crete and Pylos guarded the two princes with their spears.

There Paris was wounded in the thigh with a spear, and he retreated a little way, and showered his arrows among the Greeks; and Idomeneus lifted and hurled a great stone at Eurypylus which struck his spear out of his hand, and he went back to find it, and Menelaus and Agamemnon had a breathing space in the battle. But soon Eurypylus returned, crying on his men, and they drove back foot by foot the ring of spears round Agamemnon, and Aeneas and Paris slew men of Crete and of Mycenae till the Greeks were pushed to the ditch round the camp; and then great stones and spears and arrows rained down on the Trojans and the people of Eurypylus from the battlements and towers of the Grecian wall. Now night fell, and Eurypylus knew that he could not win the wall in the dark, so he withdrew his men, and they built great fires, and camped upon the plain.

The case of the Greeks was now like that of the Trojans after the death of Hector. They buried Machaon and the other chiefs who had fallen, and they remained within their ditch and their wall, for they dared not come out into the open plain. They knew not whether Ulysses and Diomedes had come safely to Scyros, or whether their ship had been wrecked or driven into unknown seas. So they sent a herald to Eurypylus, asking for a truce, that they might gather their dead and burn them, and the Trojans and Khita also buried their dead.

Meanwhile the swift ship of Ulysses had swept through the sea to Scyros, and to the palace of King Lycomedes. There they found Neoptolemus, the son of Achilles, in the court before the doors. He was as tall as his father, and very like him in face and shape, and he was practising the throwing of the spear at a mark. Right glad were Ulysses and Diomedes to behold him, and Ulysses told Neoptolemus who they were, and why they came, and implored him to take pity on the Greeks and help them.

'My friend is Diomedes, Prince of Argos,' said Ulysses, 'and I am Ulysses of Ithaca. Come with us, and we Greeks will give you countless gifts, and I myself will present you with the armour of your father, such as it is not lawful for any other mortal man to wear, seeing that it is golden, and wrought by the hands of a God. Moreover, when we have taken Troy, and gone home, Menelaus will give you his daughter, the beautiful Hermione, to be your wife, with gold in great plenty.'

Then Neoptolemus answered: 'It is enough that the Greeks need my sword. Tomorrow we shall sail for Troy.' He led them into the palace to dine, and there they found his mother, beautiful Deidamia, in mourning raiment, and she wept when she heard that they had come to take her son away. But Neoptolemus comforted her, promising to return safely with the spoils of Troy, 'or, even if I fall,' he said, 'it will be after doing deeds worthy of my father's name.' So next day they sailed, leaving Deidamia mournful, like a swallow whose nest a serpent has found, and has killed her young ones; even so she wailed, and went up and down in the house. But the ship ran swiftly on her way, cleaving the dark waves till Ulysses showed Neoptolemus the far off snowy crest of Mount Ida; and Tenedos, the island near Troy; and they passed the plain where the tomb of Achilles stands, but Ulysses did not tell the son that it was his father's tomb.

Now all this time the Greeks, shut up within their wall and fighting from their towers, were looking back across the sea, eager to spy the ship of Ulysses, like men wrecked on a desert island, who keep watch every day for a sail afar off, hoping that the seamen will touch at their isle and have pity upon them, and carry them home, so the Greeks kept watch for the ship bearing Neoptolemus.

Diomedes, too, had been watching the shore, and when they came in sight of the ships of the Greeks, he saw that they were being besieged by the Trojans, and that all the Greek army was penned up within the wall, and was fighting from the towers. Then he cried aloud to Ulysses and Neoptolemus, 'Make haste, friends, let us arm before we land, for some great evil has fallen upon the Greeks. The Trojans are attacking our wall, and soon they will burn our ships, and for us there will be no return.'

Then all the men on the ship of Ulysses armed

themselves, and Neoptolemus, in the splendid armour of his father, was the first to leap ashore. The Greeks could not come from the wall to welcome him, for they were fighting hard and hand-to-hand with Eurypylus and his men. But they glanced back over their shoulders and it seemed to them that they saw Achilles himself, spear and sword in hand, rushing to help them. They raised a great battle-cry, and, when Neoptolemus reached the battlements, he and Ulysses, and Diomedes leaped down to the plain, the Greeks following them, and they all charged at once on the men of Eurypylus, with levelled spears, and drove them from the wall.

Then the Trojans trembled, for they knew the shields of Diomedes and Ulysses, and they thought that the tall chief in the armour of Achilles was Achilles himself, come back from the Land of the Dead to take vengeance for Antilochus. The Trojans fled, and gathered round Eurypylus, as in a thunderstorm little children, afraid of the lightning and the noise, run and cluster round their father, and hide their faces on his knees.

But Neoptolemus was spearing the Trojans, as a man who carries at night a beacon of fire in his boat on the sea spears the fishes that flock around, drawn by the blaze of the flame. Cruelly he avenged his father's death on many a Trojan, and the men whom

Achilles had led followed Achilles' son, slaying to right and left, and smiting the Trojans, as they ran, between the shoulders with the spear. Thus they fought and followed while daylight lasted, but when night fell, they led Neoptolemus to his father's hut, where the women washed him in the bath, and then he was taken to feast with Agamemnon and Menelaus and the princes. They all welcomed him, and gave him glorious gifts, swords with silver hilts, and cups of gold and silver, and they were glad, for they had driven the Trojans from their wall, and hoped that tomorrow they would slay Eurypylus, and take Troy town.

But their hope was not to be fulfilled, for though next day Eurypylus met Neoptolemus in the battle, and was slain by him, when the Greeks chased the Trojans into their city so great a storm of lightning and thunder and rain fell upon them that they retreated again to their camp. They believed that Zeus, the chief of the Gods, was angry with them, and the days went by, and Troy still stood unconquered.

– 12 –

THE SLAYING OF PARIS

WHEN THE GREEKS WERE DISHEARTENED, as they often were, they consulted Calchas the prophet. He usually found that they must do something, or send for somebody, and in doing so they diverted their minds from their many misfortunes. Now, as the Trojans were fighting more bravely than before, under Deiphobus, a brother of Hector, the Greeks went to Calchas for advice, and he told them that they must send Ulysses and Diomedes to bring Philoctetes the bowman from the isle of Lemnos. This was an unhappy deserted island, in which the married women, some years before, had murdered all their husbands, out of jealousy, in a single night. The Greeks had landed in Lemnos, on their way to Troy, and there Philoctetes had shot an arrow at a great water dragon which lived in a well within a cave in the lonely hills. But when he entered the cave the dragon bit him, and, though he killed it at last, its poisonous teeth wounded his foot. The wound never healed, but dripped with venom, and Philoctetes, in terrible pain, kept all the camp awake at night by his cries.

The Greeks were sorry for him, but he was not a pleasant companion, shrieking as he did, and exuding poison wherever he came. So they left him on the lonely island, and did not know whether he was alive or dead. Calchas ought to have told the Greeks not to desert Philoctetes at the time, if he was so important that Troy, as the prophet now said, could not be taken without him. But now, as he must give some advice, Calchas said that Philoctetes must be brought back, so Ulysses and Diomedes went to bring him. They sailed to Lemnos, a melancholy place they found it, with no smoke rising from the ruinous houses along the shore. As they were landing they learned that Philoctetes was not dead, for his dismal old cries of pain, *otototototoi, ai, ai; pheu, pheu; otototototoi*, came echoing from a cave on the beach. To this cave the princes went, and found a terrible-looking man, with long, dirty, dry hair and beard; he was worn to a skeleton, with hollow eyes, and lay moaning in a mass of the feathers of sea birds. His great bow and his arrows lay ready to his hand: with these he used to shoot the sea birds, which were all that he had to eat, and their feathers littered all the floor of his cave, and they were none the better for the poison that dripped from his wounded foot.

When this horrible creature saw Ulysses and Diomedes coming near, he seized his bow and fitted a poisonous arrow to the string, for he hated the Greeks, because they had left him in the desert isle. But the princes held up their hands in sign of peace, and cried out that they had come to do him kindness, so he laid down his bow, and they came in and sat on the rocks, and promised that his wound should be healed, for the Greeks were very much ashamed of having deserted him. It was difficult to resist Ulysses when he wished to persuade anyone, and at last Philoctetes consented to sail with them to Troy. The oarsmen carried him down to the ship on a litter, and there his dreadful wound was washed with warm water, and oil was poured into it, and it was bound up with soft linen, so that his pain grew less fierce, and they gave him a good supper and wine enough, which he had not tasted for many years.

Next morning they sailed, and had a fair west wind, so that they soon landed among the Greeks and carried Philoctetes on shore. Here Podalirius, the brother of Machaon, being a physician, did all that could be done to heal the wound, and the pain left Philoctetes. He was taken to the hut of Agamemnon, who welcomed him, and said that the Greeks repented of their cruelty. They gave him seven female slaves to take care of him, and twenty swift horses, and twelve great vessels of bronze, and told him that he was always to live with the greatest chiefs and feed at their table. So he was bathed, and his hair was cut and combed and anointed with oil, and soon he was eager and ready to fight, and to use his great bow and poisoned arrows on the Trojans. The use of poisoned arrow-tips was thought unfair, but Philoctetes had no scruples.

Now in the next battle Paris was shooting down the Greeks with his arrows, when Philoctetes saw him, and cried: 'Dog, you are proud of your archery and of the arrow that slew the great Achilles. But, behold, I am a better bowman than you, by far, and the bow in my hands was borne by the strong man Heracles!' So he cried and drew the bowstring to his breast and the poisoned arrowhead to the bow, and the bowstring rang, and the arrow flew, and did but graze the hand of Paris. Then the bitter pain of the poison came upon him, and the Trojans carried him into their city, where the physicians tended him all night. But he never slept, and lay tossing in agony till dawn, when he said: 'There is but one hope. Take me to Oenone, the nymph of Mount Ida!'

Then his friends laid Paris on a litter, and bore him up the steep path to Mount Ida. Often had he climbed it swiftly, when he was young, and went to see the nymph who loved him; but for many a day he had not trod the path where he was now carried in great pain and fear, for the poison turned his blood to fire. Little hope he had, for he knew how cruelly he had deserted Oenone, and he saw that all the birds which were disturbed in the wood flew away to the left hand, an omen of evil.

At last the bearers reached the cave where the nymph Oenone lived, and they smelled the sweet fragrance of the cedar fire that burned on the floor of the cave, and they heard the nymph singing a melancholy song. Then Paris called to her in the voice which she had once loved to hear, and she grew very pale, and rose up, saying to herself, 'The day has come for which I have prayed. He is sore hurt, and has come to bid me heal his wound.' So she came and stood in the doorway of the dark cave, white against the darkness, and the bearers laid Paris on the litter at the feet of Oenone, and he stretched forth his hands to touch her knees, as was the manner of suppliants. But she drew back and gathered her robe about her, that he might not touch it with his hands.

Then he said: 'Lady, despise me not, and hate me not, for my pain is more than I can bear. Truly it was by no will of mine that I left you lonely here, for the Fates that no man may escape led me to Helen. Would that I had died in your arms before I saw her face! But now I beseech you in the name of the Gods, and for the memory of our love, that you will have pity on me and heal my hurt, and not refuse your grace and let me die here at your feet.'

Then Oenone answered scornfully: 'Why have you come here to me? Surely for years you have not come this way, where the path was once worn with your feet. But long ago you left me lonely and lamenting, for the love of Helen of the fair hands. Surely she is much more beautiful than the love of your youth, and far more able to help you, for men say that she can never know old age and death. Go home to Helen and let her take away your pain.'

Thus Oenone spoke, and went within the cave, where she threw herself down among the ashes of the hearth and sobbed for anger and sorrow. In a little while she rose and went to the door of the cave, thinking that Paris had not been borne away back to Troy, but she found him not; for his bearers had carried him by another path, till he died beneath the boughs of the oak trees. Then his bearers carried him swiftly down to Troy, where his mother bewailed him, and Helen sang over him as she had sung over Hector, remembering many things, and fearing to think of what her own end might be. But the Trojans hastily built a great pile of dry wood, and thereon laid the body of Paris and set fire to it, and the flame went up through the darkness, for now night had fallen.

But Oenone was roaming in the dark woods, crying and calling after Paris, like a lioness whose cubs the hunters have carried away. The moon rose to give her light, and the flame of the funeral fire shone against the sky, and then Oenone knew that Paris had died – beautiful Paris – and that the Trojans were burning his body on the plain at the foot of Mount Ida. Then she cried that now Paris was all her own, and that Helen had no more hold on him: 'And though when he was living he left me, in death we shall not be divided,' she said, and she sped down the hill, and through the thickets where the wood nymphs were wailing for Paris, and she reached the plain, and, covering her head with her veil like a bride, she rushed through the throng of Trojans. She leaped upon the burning pile of wood, she clasped the body of Paris in her arms, and the flame of fire consumed the bridegroom and the bride, and their ashes mingled. No man could divide them any more, and the ashes were placed in a golden cup, within a chamber of stone, and the earth was mounded above them. On that grave the wood nymphs planted two rose trees, and their branches met and plaited together.

This was the end of Paris and Oenone.

- 13 -

HOW ULYSSES INVENTED THE DEVICE OF THE HORSE OF TREE

AFTER PARIS DIED, HELEN WAS NOT GIVEN back to Menelaus. We are often told that only fear of the anger of Paris had prevented the Trojans from surrendering Helen and making peace. Now Paris could not terrify them, yet for all that the men of the town would not part with Helen, whether because she was so beautiful, or because they thought it dishonourable to yield her to the Greeks, who might put her to a cruel death. So Helen was taken by Deiphobus, the brother of Paris, to live in his own house, and Deiphobus was at this time the best warrior and the chief captain of the men of Troy.

Meanwhile, the Greeks made an assault against the Trojan walls and fought long and hardily; but, being safe behind the battlements, and shooting through loopholes, the Trojans drove them back with loss of many of their men. It was in vain that Philoctetes shot his poisoned arrows, they fell back from the stone walls, or stuck in the palisades of wood above the walls, and the Greeks who tried to climb over were speared, or crushed with heavy stones. When night fell, they retreated to the ships and held a council, and, as usual, they asked the advice of the prophet Calchas. It was the business of Calchas to go about looking at birds, and taking omens from what he saw them doing, a way of prophesying which the Romans also used, and some savages do the same to this day. Calchas said that yesterday he had seen a hawk pursuing a dove, which hid herself in a hole in a rocky cliff. For a long while the hawk tried to find the hole, and follow the dove into it, but he could not reach her. So he flew away for a short distance and hid himself; then the dove fluttered out into the sunlight, and the hawk swooped on her and killed her.

The Greeks, said Calchas, ought to learn a lesson from the hawk, and take Troy by cunning, as by force they could do nothing. Then Ulysses stood up and described a trick which it is not easy to understand. The Greeks, he said, ought to make an enormous hollow horse of wood, and place the bravest men in the horse. Then all the rest of the

Greeks should embark in their ships and sail to the Isle of Tenedos, and lie hidden behind the island. The Trojans would then come out of the city, like the dove out of her hole in the rock, and would wander about the Greek camp, and wonder why the great horse of tree had been made, and why it had been left behind. Lest they should set fire to the horse, when they would soon have found out the warriors hidden in it, a cunning Greek, whom the Trojans did not know by sight, should be left in the camp or near it. He would tell the Trojans that the Greeks had given up all hope and gone home, and he was to say that they feared the Goddess Pallas was angry with them, because they had stolen her image that fell from heaven, and was called the Luck of Troy. To soothe Pallas and prevent her from sending great storms against the ships, the Greeks (so the man was to say) had built this wooden horse as an offering to the Goddess. The Trojans, believing this story, would drag the horse into Troy, and, in the night, the princes would come out, set fire to the city, and open the gates to the army, which would return from Tenedos as soon as darkness came on.

The prophet was much pleased with the plan of Ulysses, and, as two birds happened to fly away on the right hand, he declared that the stratagem would certainly be lucky. Neoptolemus, on the other hand, voted for taking Troy, without any trick, by sheer hard fighting. Ulysses replied that if Achilles could not do that, it could not be done at all, and that Epeius, a famous carpenter, had better set about making the horse at once.

Next day half the army, with axes in their hands, were sent to cut down trees on Mount Ida, and thousands of planks were cut from the trees by Epeius and his workmen, and in three days he had finished the horse. Ulysses then asked the best of the Greeks to come forward and go inside the machine; while one, whom the Trojans did not know by sight, should volunteer to stay behind in the camp and deceive the Trojans. Then a young man called Sinon stood up and said that he would risk himself and take the chance that the Trojans might disbelieve him, and burn him alive. Certainly, none of the Greeks did anything more courageous, yet Sinon had not been considered brave. Had he fought in the front ranks, the Trojans would have known him; but there were many brave fighters who would not have dared to do what Sinon undertook.

Then old Nestor was the first that volunteered to go into the horse; but Neoptolemus said that, brave as he was, he was too old, and that he must depart with the army to Tenedos. Neoptolemus himself would go into the horse, for he would rather die than turn his back on Troy. So Neoptolemus armed himself and climbed into the horse, as did Menelaus, Ulysses, Diomedes, Thrasymedes (Nestor's son), Idomeneus, Philoctetes, Meriones, and all the best men except Agamemnon, while Epeius himself entered last of all. Agamemnon was not allowed by the other Greeks to share their adventure, as he was to command the army when they returned from Tenedos. They meanwhile launched their ships and sailed away.

But first Menelaus had led Ulysses apart, and told him that if they took Troy (and now they must either take it or die at the hands of the Trojans), he would owe to Ulysses the glory. When they came back to Greece, he wished to give Ulysses one of his own cities, that they might always be near each other. Ulysses smiled and shook his head; he could not leave Ithaca, his own rough island kingdom. 'But if we both live through the night that is coming,' he said, 'I may ask you for one gift, and giving it will make you none the poorer.' Then Menelaus swore by the splendour of Zeus that Ulysses could ask him for no gift that he would not gladly give; so they embraced, and both armed themselves and went up into the horse. With them were all the chiefs except Nestor, whom they would not allow to come, and Agamemnon, who, as chief general, had to command the army. They swathed themselves and their arms in soft silks, that they might not ring and clash, when the Trojans, if they were so foolish, dragged the horse up into their town, and there they sat in the dark waiting. Meanwhile, the army burned their huts and launched their ships, and with oars and sails made their way to the back of the isle of Tenedos.

– 14 –

THE END OF TROY AND THE SAVING OF HELEN

FROM THE WALLS THE TROJANS SAW THE black smoke go up thick into the sky, and the whole fleet of the Greeks sailing out to sea. Never were men so glad, and they armed themselves for fear of an ambush, and went cautiously, sending forth scouts in front of them, down to the seashore. Here they found the huts burned down and the camp deserted, and some of the scouts also caught Sinon, who had hid himself in a place where he was likely to be found. They rushed on him with fierce cries, and bound his hands with a rope, and kicked and dragged him along to the place where Priam and the princes were wondering at the great horse of tree. Sinon looked round upon them, while some were saying that he ought to be tortured with fire to make him tell all the truth about the horse. The chiefs in the horse must have trembled for fear lest torture should wring the truth out of Sinon, for then the Trojans would simply burn the machine and them within it.

But Sinon said: 'Miserable man that I am, whom the Greeks hate and the Trojans are eager to slay!' When the Trojans heard that the Greeks hated him, they were curious, and asked who he was, and how he came to be there. 'I will tell you all, oh King!' he answered Priam. 'I was a friend and squire of an unhappy chief, Palamedes, whom the wicked Ulysses hated and slew secretly one day, when he found him alone, fishing in the sea. I was angry, and in my folly I did not hide my anger, and my words came to the ears of Ulysses. From that hour he sought occasion to slay me. Then Calchas –' here he stopped, saying: 'But why tell a long tale? If you hate all Greeks alike, then slay me; this is what Agamemnon and Ulysses desire; Menelaus would thank you for my head.'

The Trojans were now more curious than before. They bade him go on, and he said that the Greeks had consulted an Oracle, which advised them to sacrifice one of their army to appease the anger of the Gods and gain a fair wind homewards. 'But who was to be sacrificed? They asked Calchas, who for fifteen days refused to speak. At last, being bribed by Ulysses, he pointed to me, Sinon, and said that I must be the victim. I was bound and kept in prison, while they built their great horse as a present for Pallas Athene the Goddess. They made it so large that you Trojans might never be able to drag it into your city; while, if you destroyed it, the Goddess might turn her anger against you. And now they have gone home to bring back the image that fell from heaven, which they had sent to Greece, and to restore it to the Temple of Pallas Athene, when they have taken your town, for the Goddess is angry with them for that theft of Ulysses.'

The Trojans were foolish enough to believe the story of Sinon, and they pitied him and unbound his hands. Then they tied ropes to the wooden horse, and laid rollers in front of it, like men launching a ship, and they all took turns to drag the horse up to the Scaean gate. Children and women put their hands to the ropes and hauled, and with shouts and dances, and hymns they toiled, till about nightfall the horse stood in the courtyard of the inmost castle.

Then all the people of Troy began to dance, and drink, and sing. Such sentinels as were set at the gates got as drunk as all the rest, who danced about the city till after midnight, and then they went to their homes and slept heavily.

Meanwhile the Greek ships were returning from behind Tenedos as fast as the oarsmen could row them.

One Trojan did not drink or sleep; this was Deiphobus, at whose house Helen was now living. He bade her come with them, for he knew that she was able to speak in the very voice of all men and women whom she had ever seen, and he armed a few of his friends and went with them to the citadel. Then he stood beside the horse, holding Helen's hand, and whispered to her that she must call each of the chiefs in the voice of his wife. She was obliged to obey, and she called Menelaus in her own voice, and Diomedes in the voice of his wife, and Ulysses in the very voice of Penelope. Then Menelaus and Diomedes were eager to answer, but Ulysses grasped their hands and whispered the word 'Echo!' Then they remembered that this was a name of Helen, because she could speak in all voices, and they were silent; but Anticlus was still eager to answer, till Ulysses held his strong hand over his mouth. There was only silence, and Deiphobus led Helen back to his house. When they had gone away Epeius opened the side of the horse, and all the chiefs let themselves down softly to the ground. Some rushed to the gate, to open it, and they killed the sleeping sentinels and let in the Greeks. Others sped with torches to burn the houses of the Trojan princes, and terrible was the slaughter of men, unarmed and half-awake, and loud were the cries of the women. But Ulysses had slipped away at the first, none knew where. Neoptolemus ran to the palace of Priam, who was sitting at the altar in his courtyard, praying vainly to the Gods, for Neoptolemus slew the old man cruelly, and his white hair was dabbled in his blood. All through the city was fighting and slaying; but Menelaus went to the house of Deiphobus, knowing that Helen was there.

In the doorway he found Deiphobus lying dead in all his armour, a spear standing in his breast. There were footprints marked in blood, leading through the portico and into the hall. There Menelaus went, and found Ulysses leaning, wounded, against one of the central pillars of the great chamber, the firelight shining on his armour.

'Why hast thou slain Deiphobus and robbed me of my revenge?' said Menelaus. 'You swore to give me a gift,' said Ulysses, 'and will you keep your oath?' 'Ask what you will,' said Menelaus; 'it is yours and my oath cannot be broken.' 'I ask the life of Helen of the fair hands,' said Ulysses; 'this is my own life-price that I pay back to her, for she saved my life when I took the Luck of Troy, and I swore that hers should be saved.'

Then Helen stole, glimmering in white robes, from a recess in the dark hall, and fell at the feet of Menelaus; her golden hair lay in the dust of the hearth, and her hands moved to touch his knees.

His drawn sword fell from the hands of Menelaus, and pity and love came into his heart, and he raised her from the dust and her white arms were round his neck, and they both wept. That night Menelaus fought no more, but they tended the wound of Ulysses, for the sword of Deiphobus had bitten through his helmet.

When dawn came Troy lay in ashes, and the women were being driven with spear shafts to the ships, and the men were left unburied, a prey to dogs and all manner of birds. Thus the grey city fell, that had lorded it for many centuries. All the gold and silver and rich embroideries, and ivory and amber, the horses and chariots, were divided among the army; all but a treasure of silver and gold, hidden in a chest within a hollow of the wall, and this treasure was found, not very many years ago, by men digging deep on the hill where Troy once stood. The women, too, were given to the princes, and Neoptolemus took Andromache to his home in Argos, to draw water from the well and to be the slave of a master, and Agamemnon carried beautiful Cassandra, the daughter of Priam, to his palace in Mycenae, where they were both slain in one night. Only Helen was led with honour to the ship of Menelaus.

THE WANDERING OF ULYSSES

– I –

THE SLAYING OF AGAMEMNON AND THE SORROWS OF ULYSSES

THE GREEKS LEFT TROY A MASS OF smouldering ashes; the marks of fire are still to be seen in the ruins on the hill which is now called Hissarlik. The Greeks had many troubles on their way home, and years passed before some of the chiefs reached their own cities. As for Agamemnon, while he was at Troy his wife, Clytemnestra, the sister of Helen, had fallen in love with a young man named Aegisthus, who wished to be king, so he married Clytemnestra, just as if Agamemnon had been dead. Meanwhile Agamemnon was sailing home with his share of the wealth of Troy, and many a storm drove him out of his course. At last he reached the harbour, about seven miles from his city of Mycenae, and he kissed the earth when he landed, thinking that all his troubles were over, and that he would find his son and daughter, Orestes and Electra, grown up, and his wife happy because of his return.

But Aegisthus had set, a year before, a watchman on a high tower, to come with the news as soon as Agamemnon landed, and the watchman ran to Mycenae with the good news. Aegisthus placed twenty armed men in a hidden place in the great hall, and then he shouted for his chariots and horses, and drove down to meet Agamemnon, and welcome him, and carry him to his own palace. Then he gave a great feast, and when men had drunk much wine, the armed men, who had been hiding behind curtains, rushed out, with sword and spear, and fell on Agamemnon and his company. Though taken by surprise they drew their swords, and fought so well for their lives that none were left alive, not one, neither of the company of Agamemnon nor of the company of Aegisthus; they were all slain in the hall except Aegisthus, who had hidden himself when the fray began. The bodies lay round the great mixing bowl of wine, and about the tables, and the floor ran with blood. Before Agamemnon died he saw Clytemnestra herself stab Cassandra, the daughter of Priam, whom he had brought from Troy.

In the town of Agamemnon, Mycenae, deep down in the earth, have been found five graves, with bones of men and women, and these bones were all covered with beautiful ornaments of gold, hundreds of them, and swords and daggers inlaid with gold, and golden cups, and a sceptre of gold and crystal, and two gold breastplates. There were also golden masks that had been made to cover the faces of the dead kings, and who knows but that one of these masks may show us the features of the famous Agamemnon?

Ulysses, of course, knew nothing about these murders at the time, for he was being borne by the winds into undiscovered seas. But later he heard all the story from the ghost of a dead prophet, in the Land of the Dead, and he determined to be very cautious if ever he reached his own island, for who knew what the young men might do, that had grown up since he sailed to Troy?

Of the other Greeks Nestor soon and safely arrived at his town of Pylos, but Menelaus and Helen were borne by the winds to Egypt and other strange countries, and the ship of the brother of Ajax was wrecked on a rock, and there he was drowned, and Calchas the prophet died on land, on his way across Greece.

When Ulysses left Troy the wind carried him to the coast of Thrace, where the people were allies of the Trojans. It was a king of the Thracians that Diomedes killed when he and Ulysses stole into the camp of the Trojans in the night, and drove away the white horses of the king, as swift as the winds. Ismarus was the name of the Thracian town where Ulysses landed, and his men took it and plundered it, yet Ulysses allowed no one to harm the priest of Apollo, Maron, but protected him and his wife and child, in their house within the holy grove of the God. Maron was grateful, and gave Ulysses twelve talents, or little wedges, of gold, and a great bowl of silver, and twelve large clay jars, as big as barrels, full of the best and strongest wine. It was so strong that men put into the mixing bowl but one measure of wine to twenty measures of water. These presents Ulysses stored up in his ship, and lucky for him it was that he was kind to Maron.

Meanwhile his men, instead of leaving the town with their plunder, sat eating and drinking till dawn. By that time the people of the town had warned their neighbours in the country farms, who all came down in full armour, and attacked the men of Ulysses. In this fight he lost seventy-two men, six from each of his twelve ships, and it was only by hard fighting that the others were able to get on board their ships and sail away.

A great storm arose and beat upon the ships, and it seems that Ulysses and his men were driven into Fairyland, where they remained for ten years. We have heard that King Arthur and Thomas the

Rhymer were carried into Fairyland, but what adventures they met with there we do not know. About Ulysses we have the stories which are now to be told. For ten days his ships ran due south, and, on the tenth, they reached the land of the Lotus Eaters, who eat food of flowers. They went on shore and drew water, and three men were sent to try to find the people of that country, who were a quiet, friendly people, and gave the fruit of the lotus to the strange sailors. Now whoever tastes of that fruit has no mind ever to go home, but to sit between the setting sun and the rising moon, dreaming happy dreams, and forgetting the world. The three men ate the lotus, and sat down to dream, but Ulysses went after them, and drove them to the ships, and bound their hands and feet, and threw them on board, and sailed away. Then he with his ships reached the coast of the land of the Cyclopes, which means the round-eyed men, men with only one eye apiece, set in the middle of their foreheads. They lived not in houses, but in caves among the hills, and they had no king and no laws, and did not plough or sow, but wheat and vines grew wild, and they kept great flocks of sheep.

There was a beautiful wild desert island lying across the opening of a bay; the isle was full of wild goats, and made a bar against the waves, so that ships could lie behind it safely, run up on the beach, for there was no tide in that sea. There Ulysses ran up his ships, and the men passed the time in hunting wild goats, and feasting on fresh meat and the wine of Maron, the priest of Apollo. Next day Ulysses left all the ships and men there, except his own ship, and his own crew, and went to see what kind of people lived on the mainland, for as yet none had been seen. He found a large cave close to the sea, with laurels growing on the rocky roof, and a wall of rough stones built round a court in front. Ulysses left all his men but twelve with the ship; filled a goat skin with the strong wine of Maron, put some corn flour in a sack, and went up to the cave. Nobody was there, but there were all the things that are usually in a dairy, baskets full of cheese, pails and bowls full of milk and whey, and kids and lambs were playing in their folds.

All seemed very quiet and pleasant. The men wanted to take as much cheese as they could carry back to the ship, but Ulysses wished to see the owner of the cave. His men, making themselves at home, lit a fire, and toasted and ate the cheeses, far within the cave. Then a shadow thrown by the setting sun fell across the opening of the cave, and a monstrous man entered, and threw down a dry trunk of a tree that he carried for firewood. Next he drove, in the ewes of his flock, leaving the rams in the yard, and he picked up a huge flat stone, and set it so as to make a shut door to the cave, for twenty-four yoke of horses could not have dragged away that stone. Lastly the man milked his ewes, and put the milk in pails to drink at supper. All this while Ulysses and his men sat quiet and in great fear, for they were shut up in a cave with a one-eyed giant, whose cheese they had been eating.

Then the giant, when he had lit the fire, happened to see the men, and asked them who they were. Ulysses said that they were Greeks, who had taken Troy, and were wandering lost on the seas, and he asked the man to be kind to them in the name of their chief God, Zeus.

'We Cyclopes,' said the giant, 'do not care for Zeus or the Gods, for we think that we are better men than they. Where is your ship?' Ulysses answered that it had been wrecked on the coast, to which the man made no answer, but snatched up two of the twelve, knocked out their brains on the floor, tore the bodies limb from limb, roasted them at his fire, ate them, and, after drinking many pailfuls of milk, lay down and fell asleep. Now Ulysses had a mind to drive his sword-point into the giant's liver, and he felt for the place with his hand. But he remembered that, even if he killed the giant, he could not move the huge stone that was the door of the cave, so he and his men would die of hunger, when they had eaten all the cheeses.

In the morning the giant ate two more men for breakfast, drove out his ewes, and set the great stone in the doorway again, as lightly as a man would put a quiverlid on a quiver of arrows. Then away he went, driving his flock to graze on the green hills.

Ulysses did not give way to despair. The giant had left his stick in the cave: it was as large as the mast of a great ship. From this Ulysses cut a portion six feet long, and his men cut and rubbed as if they were making a spear shaft: Ulysses then sharpened it to a point, and hardened the point in the fire. It was a thick rounded bar of wood, and the men cast lots to choose four, who should twist the bar in the giant's eye when he fell asleep at night. Back he came at sunset, and drove his flocks into the cave, rams and all. Then he put up his stone door, milked his ewes, and killed two men and cooked them.

Ulysses meanwhile had filled one of the wooden ivy bowls full of the strong wine of Maron, without putting a drop of water into it. This bowl he offered to the giant, who had never heard of wine. He drank one bowl after another, and when he was merry he said that he would make Ulysses a present. 'What is your name?' he asked. 'My name is *Nobody*,' said Ulysses. 'Then I shall eat the others first and

Nobody last,' said the giant. 'That shall be your gift.' Then he fell asleep.

Ulysses took his bar of wood, and made the point red-hot in the fire. Next his four men rammed it into the giant's one eye, and held it down, while Ulysses twirled it round, and the eye hissed like red-hot iron when men dip it into cold water, which is the strength of iron. The Cyclops roared and leaped to his feet, and shouted for help to the other giants who lived in the neighbouring caves. 'Who is troubling you, Polyphemus?' they answered. 'Why do you wake us out of our sleep?' The giant answered, 'Nobody is killing me by his cunning, not at all in fair fight.' 'Then if nobody is harming you nobody can help you,' shouted a giant. 'If you are ill pray to your father, Poseidon, who is the God of the sea.' So the giants all went back to bed, and Ulysses laughed low to see how his cunning had deceived them. Then the giant went and took down his door and sat in the doorway, stretching out his arms, so as to catch his prisoners as they went out.

But Ulysses had a plan. He fastened sets of three rams together with twisted withies, and bound a man to each ram in the middle, so that the blind giant's hands would only feel the two outside rams. The biggest and strongest ram Ulysses seized, and held on by his hands and feet to its fleece, under its belly, and then all the sheep went out through the doorway, and the giant felt them, but did not know that they were carrying out the men. 'Dear ram!' he said to the biggest, which carried Ulysses, 'you do not come out first, as usual, but last, as if you were slow with sorrow for your master, whose eye Nobody has blinded!'

Then all the rams went out into the open country, and Ulysses unfastened his men, and drove the sheep down to his ship and so on board. His crew wept when they heard of the death of six of their friends, but Ulysses made them row out to sea. When he was just so far away from the cave as to be within hearing distance he shouted at the Cyclops and mocked him. Then that giant broke off the rocky peak of a great hill and threw it in the direction of the sound. The rock fell in front of the ship, and raised a wave that drove it back to shore, but Ulysses punted it off with a long pole, and his men rowed out again, far out. Ulysses again shouted to the giant, 'If anyone asks who blinded you, say that it was Ulysses, Laertes' son, of Ithaca, the stormer of cities.'

Then the giant prayed to the Sea God, his father, that Ulysses might never come home, or if he did, that he might come late and lonely, with loss of all his men, and find sorrow in his house. Then the giant heaved and threw another rock, but it fell at the stern of the ship, and the wave drove the ship further out to sea, to the shore of the island. There Ulysses and his men landed, and killed some of the giant's sheep, and took supper, and drank wine.

But the Sea God heard the prayer of his son the blind giant.

Ulysses and his men sailed on, in what direction and for how long we do not know, till they saw far off an island that shone in the sea. When they came nearer they found that it had a steep cliff of bronze, with a palace on the top. Here lived Aeolus, the King of the Winds, with his six sons and six daughters. He received Ulysses kindly on his island, and entertained him for a whole month. Then he gave him a leather bag, in which he had bound the ways of all the noisy winds. This bag was fastened with a silver cord, and Aeolus left no wind out except the West Wind, which would blow Ulysses straight home to Ithaca. Where he was we cannot guess, except that he was to the west of his own island.

So they sailed for nine days and nights towards the east, and Ulysses always held the helm and steered, but on the tenth day he fell asleep. Then his men said to each other, 'What treasure is it that he keeps in the leather bag, a present from King Aeolus? No doubt the bag is full of gold and silver, while we have only empty hands.' So they opened the bag when they were so near Ithaca that they could see people lighting fires on the shore. Then out rushed all the winds, and carried the ship into unknown seas, and when Ulysses woke he was so miserable that he had a mind to drown himself. But he was of an enduring heart, and he lay still, and the ship came back to the isle of Aeolus, who cried, 'Away with you! You are the most luckless of living men: you must be hated by the Gods.'

Thus Aeolus drove them away, and they sailed for seven days and nights, till they saw land, and came to a harbour with a narrow entrance, and with tall steep rocks on either side. The other eleven ships sailed into the haven, but Ulysses did not venture in; he fastened his ship to a rock at the outer end of the harbour. The place must have been very far north, for, as it was summer, the sun had hardly set till dawn began again, as it does in Norway and Iceland, where there are many such narrow harbours within walls of rock. These places are called *fiords*. Ulysses sent three men to spy out the country, and at a well outside the town they met a damsel drawing water; she was the child of the king of the people, the Laestrygonians. The damsel led them to her father's house; he was a giant and seized one of the men of Ulysses, meaning to kill and eat him. The two other men fled to the ships, but the Laestrygonians ran along the tops of the cliffs and threw down great rocks, sinking the vessels and killing the sailors. When Ulysses saw this he drew his sword and cut the cable that fastened his ship to the rock outside the harbour, and his crew rowed for dear life and so escaped, weeping for the death of their friends. Thus the prayer of the blind Cyclops was being fulfilled, for now out of twelve ships Ulysses had but one left.

– 2 –

THE ENCHANTRESS CIRCE, THE LAND OF THE DEAD AND THE SIRENS

On they sailed till they came to an island, and there they landed. What the place was they did not know, but it was called Aeaea, and here lived Circe, the enchantress, sister of the wizard king Aeëtes, who was the Lord of the Fleece of Gold, that Jason won from him by help of the king's daughter, Medea. For two days Ulysses and his men lay on land beside their ship, which they anchored in a bay of the island. On the third morning Ulysses took his sword and spear, and climbed to the top of a high hill, whence he saw the smoke rising out of the wood where Circe had her palace. He thought of going to the house, but it seemed better to return to his men and send some of them to spy out the place. Since the adventure of the Cyclops Ulysses did not care to risk himself among unknown people, and for all that he knew there might be man-eating giants on the island. So he went back, and, as he came to the bank of the river, he found a great red deer drinking under the shadow of the green boughs. He speared the stag, and, tying his feet together, slung the body from his neck, and so, leaning on his spear, he came to his fellows. Glad they were to see fresh venison, which they cooked, and so dined with plenty of wine.

Next morning Ulysses divided his men into two companies, Eurylochus led one company and he himself the other. Then they put two marked pieces of wood, one for Eurylochus, one for Ulysses, in a helmet, to decide who should go to the house in the wood. They shook the helmet, and the lot of Eurylochus leaped out, and, weeping for fear, he led his twenty-two men away into the forest. Ulysses and the other twenty-two waited, and, when Eurylochus came back alone, he was weeping, and unable to speak for sorrow. At last he told his story: they had come to the beautiful house of Circe, within the wood, and tame wolves and lions were walking about in front of the house. They wagged their tails, and jumped up, like friendly dogs, round the men of Ulysses, who stood in the gateway and heard Circe singing in a sweet voice, as she went up and down before the loom at which she was weaving. Then one of the men of Ulysses called to her, and she came out, a beautiful lady in white robes covered with jewels of gold. She opened the doors and bade them come in, but Eurylochus hid himself and watched, and saw Circe and her maidens mix honey and wine for the men, and bid them sit down on chairs at tables, but, when they had drunk of her cup, she touched them with her wand. Then they were all changed into swine, and Circe drove them out and shut them up in the sties.

When Ulysses heard that he slung his sword-belt round his shoulders, seized his bow, and bade Eurylochus come back with him to the house of Circe; but Eurylochus was afraid. Alone went Ulysses through the woods, and in a dell he met a most beautiful young man, who took his hand and said, 'Unhappy one! how shalt thou free thy friends from so great an enchantress?' Then the young man plucked a plant from the ground; the flower was as white as milk, but the root was black: it is a plant that men may not dig up, but to the Gods all things are easy, and the young man was the cunning God Hermes, whom Autolycus, the grandfather of Ulysses, used to worship. 'Take this herb of grace,' he said, 'and when Circe has made thee drink of the cup of her enchantments the herb will so work that they shall have no power over thee. Then draw thy sword, and rush at her, and make her swear that she will not harm thee with her magic'

Then Hermes departed, and Ulysses went to the house of Circe, and she asked him to enter, and seated him on a chair, and gave him the enchanted cup to drink, and then smote him with her wand and bade him go to the sties of the swine. But Ulysses drew his sword, and Circe, with a great cry, fell at his feet, saying, 'Who art thou on whom the cup has no power? Truly thou art Ulysses of Ithaca, for the God Hermes has told me that he should come to my island on his way from Troy. Come now, fear not; let us be friends!'

Then the maidens of Circe came to them, fairy damsels of the wells and woods and rivers. They threw covers of purple silk over the chairs, and on the silver tables they placed golden baskets, and mixed wine in a silver bowl, and heated water, and bathed Ulysses in a polished bath, and clothed him in new raiment, and led him to the table and bade him eat and drink. But he sat silent, neither eating nor drinking, in sorrow for his company, till Circe called them out from the sties and disenchanted them. Glad they were to see Ulysses, and they embraced him, and wept for joy.

So they went back to their friends at the ship, and told them how Circe would have them all to live with her; but Eurylochus tried to frighten them, saying that she would change them into wolves and lions. Ulysses drew his sword to cut off the head of Eurylochus for his cowardice, but the others prayed that he might be left alone to guard the ship. So Ulysses left him; but Eurylochus had not the courage to be alone, and slunk behind them to the house of Circe. There she welcomed them all, and gave them a feast, and there they dwelt for a whole year, and then they wearied for their wives and children, and longed to return to Ithaca. They did not guess by what a strange path they must sail.

When Ulysses was alone with Circe at night he told her that his men were homesick, and would fain go to Ithaca. Then Circe said, 'There is no way but this: you must sail to the last shore of the stream of the river Oceanus, that girdles round the world. There is the Land of the Dead, and the House of Hades and Persephone, the King and Queen of the ghosts. There you must call up the ghost of the blind prophet, Tiresias of Thebes, for he alone has knowledge of your way, and the other spirits sweep round shadow-like.'

Then Ulysses thought that his heart would break, for how should he, a living man, go down to the awful dwellings of the dead? But Circe told him the strange things that he must do, and she gave him a black ram and a black ewe, and next day Ulysses called his men together. All followed him to the ship, except one, Elpenor. He had been sleeping, for the sake of the cool air, on the flat roof of the house, and, when suddenly wakened, he missed his foothold on the tall ladder, and fell to the ground and broke his neck. They left him unburned and unburied, and, weeping, they followed Ulysses, as follow they must, to see the homes of the ghosts and the House of Hades. Very sorrowfully they all went on board, taking with them the black ram and the black ewe, and they set the sails, and the wind bore them at its will.

Now in midday they sailed out of the sunlight into darkness, for they had come to the land of the Cimmerian men, which the sun never sees, but all is dark cloud and mist. There they ran the ship ashore, and took out the two black sheep, and walked along the dark banks of the river Oceanus to a place of which Circe had told Ulysses. There the two rivers of the dead meet, where a rock divides the two dark roaring streams. There they dug a trench and poured out mead, and wine, and water, and prayed to the ghosts, and then they cut the throat of the black ewe, and the grey ghosts gathered to smell thc blood. Pale spectres came, spirits of brides who died long ago, and youths unwed, and old unhappy men; and many phantoms were there of men who fell in battle, with shadowy spears in their hands, and battered armour. Then Ulysses sacrificed the black ram to the ghost of the prophet Tiresias, and sat down with his sword in his hand, that no spirit before Tiresias might taste the blood in the trench.

First the spirit of Elpenor came, and begged Ulysses to burn his body, for till his body was burned he was not allowed to mingle with the other souls of dead men. So Ulysses promised to burn and bury him when he went back to Circe's island. Then came the shadow of the mother of Ulysses, who had died when he was at Troy, but, for all his grief, he would not allow the shadow to come near the blood till Tiresias had tasted it. At length came the spirit of the blind prophet, and he prayed Ulysses to sheathe his sword and let him drink the blood of the black sheep.

When he had tasted it he said that the Sea God was angry because of the blinding of his son, the Cyclops, and would make his voyaging vain. But if the men of Ulysses were wise, and did not slay and eat the sacred cattle of the Sun God, in the isle called Thrinacia, they might all win home. If they were unwise, and if Ulysses did come home, lonely and late he would arrive, on the ship of strangers, and he would find proud men wasting his goods and seeking to wed his wife, Penelope. Even if Ulysses alone could kill these men his troubles would not be ended. He must wander over the land, as he had wandered over the waters, carrying an oar on his shoulder, till he came to men who had never heard of the sea or of boats. When one of these men, not knowing what an oar was, came and told him that he carried a fan for winnowing corn, then Ulysses must fix the oar in the ground, and offer a sacrifice to the Sea God, and go home, where he would at last live in peace. Ulysses said, 'So be it!' and asked how he could have speech with the ghosts. Tiresias told him how this might be done, and then his mother told him how she died of sorrow for him, and Ulysses tried to embrace and kiss her, but his arms only clasped the empty air.

Then came up the beautiful spirits of many dead, unhappy ladies of old times, and then came the souls of Agamemnon, and of Achilles, and of Ajax. Achilles was glad when he heard how bravely his young son had fought at Troy, but he said it was better to be the servant of a poor farmer on earth than to rule over all the ghosts of the dead in the still grey land where the sun never shone, and no flowers grew but the mournful asphodel. Many other spirits of Greeks slain at Troy came and asked for news about their friends, but Ajax stood apart and silent, still in anger because the arms of Achilles had been given to Ulysses. In vain Ulysses told him that the Greeks had mourned as much for him as for

Achilles; he passed silently away into the House of Hades. At last the legions of the innumerable dead, all that have died since the world began, flocked, and filled the air with their low wailing cries, and fear fell on Ulysses, and he went back along that sad last shore of the world's end to his ship, and sailed again out of the darkness into the sunlight, and to the isle of Circe. There they burned the body of Elpenor, and piled a mound over it, and on the mound set the oar of the dead man, and so went to the palace of Circe.

Ulysses told Circe all his adventures, and then she warned him of dangers yet to come, and showed him how he might escape them. He listened, and remembered all that she spoke, and these two said goodbye for ever. Circe wandered away alone into the woods, and Ulysses and his men set sail and crossed the unknown seas. Presently the wind fell, and the sea was calm, and they saw a beautiful island from which came the sound of sweet singing. Ulysses knew who the singers were, for Circe had told him that they were the Sirens, a kind of beautiful Mermaids, deadly to men. Among the flowers they sit and sing, but the flowers hide the bones of men who have listened and landed on the island, and died of that strange music, which carries the soul away.

Ulysses now took a great cake of bees' wax and

cut it up into small pieces, which he bade his men soften and place in their ears, that they might not hear that singing. But, as he desired to hear it and yet live, he bade the sailors bind him tightly to the mast with ropes, and they must not unbind him, however much he might implore them to set him free. When all this was done the men sat down on the benches, all orderly, and smote the grey sea with their oars, and the ship rushed along through the clear still water, and came opposite the island. Then the sweet singing of the Sirens was borne over the sea,

'Hither, come hither, renowned Ulysses,
Great glory of the Achaean name.
Here stay thy ship, that thou mayest listen to
our song.
Never has any man driven his ship past
our island
Till he has heard our voices, sweet as
the honeycomb;
Gladly he has heard, and wiser has he gone
on his way.
Hither, come hither, for we know all things,
All that the Greeks wrought and endured
in Troyland,
All that shall hereafter be upon the
fruitful earth.'

Thus they sang, offering Ulysses all knowledge and wisdom, which they knew that he loved more than anything in the world. To other men, no doubt, they would have offered other pleasures. Ulysses desired to listen, and he nodded to his men to loosen his bonds. But Perimedes and Eurylochus arose, and laid on him yet stronger bonds, and the ship was driven past that island, till the song of the Sirens faded away, and then the men set Ulysses free and took the wax out of their ears.

– 3 –

THE WHIRLPOOL, THE SEA MONSTER AND THE CATTLE OF THE SUN

THEY HAD NOT SAILED FAR WHEN THEY heard the sea roaring, and saw a great wave, over which hung a thick shining cloud of spray. They had drifted to a place where the sea narrowed between two high black rocks; under the rock on the left was a boiling whirlpool in which no ship could live; the opposite rock showed nothing dangerous, but Ulysses had been warned by Circe that here too lay great peril. We may ask, Why did Ulysses pass through the narrows between these two rocks? why did he not steer on the outer side of one or the other? The reason seems to have been that, on the outer side of these cliffs, were the tall reefs which men called the Rocks Wandering. Between them the sea water leaped in high columns of white foam, and the rocks themselves rushed together, grinding and clashing, while fire flew out of the crevices and crests as from a volcano.

Circe had told Ulysses about the Rocks Wandering, which do not even allow flocks of doves to pass through them; even one of the doves is always caught and crushed, and no ship of men escapes that tries to pass that way, and the bodies of the sailors and the planks of the ships are confusedly tossed by the waves of the sea and the storms of ruinous fire. Of all ships that ever sailed the sea, only *Argo*, the ship of Jason, has escaped the Rocks Wandering, as you may read in the story of the Fleece of Gold. For these reasons Ulysses was forced to steer between the rock of the whirlpool and the rock which seemed harmless. In the narrows between these two cliffs the sea ran like a rushing river, and the men, in fear, ceased to hold the oars, and down the stream the oars splashed in confusion. But Ulysses, whom Circe had told of this new danger, bade them grasp the oars again and row hard. He told the man at the helm to steer under the great rocky cliff, on the right, and to keep clear of the whirlpool and the cloud of spray on the left. Well he knew the danger of the rock on the left, for within it was a deep cave, where a monster named Scylla lived, yelping with a shrill voice out of her six hideous heads. Each head hung down from a long, thin, scaly neck, and in each mouth were three rows of greedy teeth, and twelve long feelers, with claws at the ends of them, dropped down, ready to catch at men. There in her cave Scylla sits, fishing with her feelers for dolphins and other great fish, and for men, if any men sail by that way.* Against this deadly thing none may fight, for she cannot be slain with the spear.

All this Ulysses knew, for Circe had warned him. But he also knew that on the other side of the strait, where the sea spray forever flew high above the rock, was a whirlpool, called Charybdis, which would swallow up his ship if it came within the current, while Scylla could only catch some of his men. For this reason he bade the helmsman to steer close to the rock of Scylla, and he did not tell the sailors that she lurked there with her body hidden in her deep cave. He himself put on his armour, and took two spears, and went and stood in the raised half-deck at the front of the ship, thinking that, at least, he would have a stroke at Scylla. Then they rowed down the swift sea stream, while the wave of the whirlpool now rose up, till the spray hid the top of the rock, and now fell, and bubbled with black sand. They were watching the whirlpool, when out from the hole in

---

* There is a picture of this monster attacking a man in a boat. The picture was painted centuries before the time of Ulysses.

the cliff sprang the six heads of Scylla, and up into the air went six of Ulysses' men, each calling to him, as they were swept within her hole in the rock, where she devoured them. 'This was the most pitiful thing,' Ulysses said, 'that my eyes have seen, of all my sorrows in searching out the paths of the sea.'

The ship swept through the roaring narrows between the rock of Scylla and the whirlpool of Charybdis, into the open sea, and the men, weary and heavy of heart, bent over their oars, and longed for rest.

Now a place of rest seemed near at hand, for in front of the ship lay a beautiful island, and the men could hear the bleating of sheep and the lowing of cows as they were being herded into their stalls. But Ulysses remembered that, in the Land of the Dead, the ghost of the blind prophet had warned him of one thing. If his men killed and ate the cattle of the Sun, in the sacred island of Thrinacia, they would all perish. So Ulysses told his crew of this prophecy, and bade them row past the island. Eurylochus was angry and said that the men were tired, and could row no further, but must land, and take supper, and sleep comfortably on shore. On hearing Eurylochus, the whole crew shouted and said that they would go no further that night, and Ulysses had no power to compel them. He could only make them swear not to touch the cattle of the Sun God, which they promised readily enough, and so went ashore, took supper, and slept.

In the night a great storm arose: the clouds and driving mist blinded the face of the sea and sky, and for a whole month the wild south wind hurled the waves on the coast, and no ship of these times could venture out in the tempest. Meanwhile the crew ate up all the stores in the ship, and finished the wine, so that they were driven to catch sea birds and fishes, of which they took but few, the sea being so rough upon the rocks. Ulysses went up into the island alone, to pray to the Gods, and when he had prayed he found a sheltered place, and there he fell asleep.

Eurylochus took the occasion, while Ulysses was away, to bid the crew seize and slay the sacred cattle of the Sun God, which no man might touch, and this they did, so that, when Ulysses wakened, and came near the ship, he smelled the roast meat, and knew what had been done. He rebuked the men, but, as the cattle were dead, they kept eating them for six days; and then the storm ceased, the wind fell, the sun shone, and they set the sails, and away they went. But this evil deed was punished, for when they were out of sight of land, a great thunder cloud overshadowed them, the wind broke the mast, which crushed the head of the helmsman, the lightning struck the ship in the centre; she reeled, the men fell overboard, and the heads of the crew floated a moment, like cormorants, above the waves.

But Ulysses had kept hold of a rope, and, when the vessel righted, he walked the deck till a wave stripped off all the tackling, and loosened the sides from the keel. Ulysses had only time to lash the broken mast with a rope to the keel, and sit on this raft with his feet in the water, while the South Wind rose again furiously, and drove the raft back till it came under the rock where was the whirlpool of Charybdis. Here Ulysses would have been drowned, but he caught at the root of a fig tree that grew on the rock, and there he hung, clinging with his toes to the crumbling stones till the whirlpool boiled up again, and up came the timbers. Down on the timbers Ulysses dropped, and so sat rowing with his hands, and the wind drifted him at last to a shelving beach of an island.

Here dwelt a kind of fairy, called Calypso, who found Ulysses nearly dead on the beach, and was kind to him, and kept him in her cave, where he lived for seven long years, always desiring to leave the beautiful fairy and return to Ithaca and his wife Penelope. But no ship of men ever came near that isle, which is the central place of all the seas, and he had no ship, and no men to sail and row. Calypso was very kind, and very beautiful, being the daughter of the wizard Atlas, who holds the two pillars that keep earth and sea asunder. But Ulysses was longing to see if it were but the smoke going up from the houses of rocky Ithaca, and he had a desire to die.

– 4 –

HOW TELEMACHUS WENT TO SEEK HIS FATHER

WHEN ULYSSES HAD LIVED NEARLY SEVEN years in the island of Calypso, his son Telemachus, whom he had left in Ithaca as a little child, went forth to seek for his father. In Ithaca he and his mother, Penelope, had long been very unhappy. As Ulysses did not come home after the war, and as nothing was heard about him from the day when the Greeks sailed from Troy, it was supposed that he must be dead. But Telemachus was still but a boy of twelve years old, and the father of Ulysses, Laertes, was very old, and had gone to a farm in the country, where he did nothing but take care of his garden. There was thus no king in Ithaca, and the boys, who had been about ten years old when Ulysses went to Troy, were now grown up, and, as their fathers had gone to the war, they did just as they pleased. Twelve of them wanted to marry Penelope, and they, with about a hundred others as wild as themselves, from the neighbouring islands, by way of paying court to Penelope ate and drank all day at her house. They killed the cattle, sheep and swine; they drank the wine, and amused themselves with Penelope's maidens, of whom she had many. Nobody could stop them; they would never go away, they said, till Penelope chose one of them to be her husband, and king of the island, though Telemachus was the rightful prince.

Penelope at last promised that she would choose one of them when she had finished a great shroud of linen, to be the death shroud of old Laertes when he died. All day she wove it, but at night, when her wooers had gone (for they did not sleep in her house), she unwove it again. But one of her maidens told this to the wooers, so she had to finish the shroud, and now they pressed her more than ever to make her choice. But she kept hoping that Ulysses was still alive, and would return, though, if he did, how was he to turn so many strong young men out of his house?

The Goddess of Wisdom, Athene, had always favoured Ulysses, and now she spoke up among the Gods, where they sat, as men say, in their holy heaven. Not by winds is it shaken, nor wet with rain, nor does the snow come thither, but clear air is spread about it cloudless, and the white light floats over it. Athene told how good, wise, and brave Ulysses was, and how he was kept in the isle of Calypso, while men ruined his wealth and wooed his wife. She said that she would herself go to Ithaca, and make Telemachus appeal to all the people of the country, showing how evilly he was treated, and then sail abroad to seek news of his father. So Athene spoke, and flashed down from Olympus to Ithaca, where she took the shape of a mortal man, Mentes, a chief of the Taphians. In front of the doors she found the proud wooers playing at draughts and other games while supper was being made ready. When Telemachus, who was standing apart, saw the stranger, he went to him, and led him into the house, and treated him kindly, while the wooers ate and drank, and laughed noisily.

Then Telemachus told Athene (or, as he supposed, the stranger), how evilly he was used, while his father's white bones might be wasting on an unknown shore or rolling in the billows of the salt sea. Athene said, or Mentes said, that he himself was an old friend of Ulysses, and had touched at Ithaca on his way to Cyprus to buy copper. 'But Ulysses,' he said, 'is not dead; he will certainly come home, and that speedily. You are so like him, you must be his son.' Telemachus replied that he was, and Mentes was full of anger, seeing how the wooers insulted him, and told him first to complain to an assembly of all the people, and then to take a ship, and go seeking news of Ulysses.

Then Athene departed, and next day Telemachus called an assembly, and spoke to the people, but though they were sorry for him they could not help him. One old man, however, a prophet, said that Ulysses would certainly come home, but the wooers only threatened and insulted him. In the evening Athene came again, in the appearance of Mentor, not the same man as Mentes, but an Ithacan, and a friend of Ulysses. She encouraged Telemachus to take a ship, with twenty oarsmen, and he told the wooers that he was going to see Menelaus and Nestor, and ask tidings of his father. They only mocked him, but he made all things ready for his voyage without telling his mother. It was old Eurycleia, who had been his nurse and his father's nurse, that brought him wine and food for his journey; and at night, when the sea wind wakens in summer, he and Mentor went on board, and all night they sailed, and at noon next day they reached Pylos on the sea sands, the city of Nestor the Old.

Nestor received them gladly, and so did his sons, Pisistratus and Thrasymedes, who fought at Troy, and next day, when Mentor had gone, Pisistratus and Telemachus drove together, up hill and down dale, a two days' journey, to Lacedaemon, lying beneath Mount Taygetus on the bank of the clear river Eurotas.

Not one of the Greeks had seen Ulysses since the day when they all sailed from Troy, yet Menelaus, in a strange way, was able to tell Telemachus that his father still lived, and was with Calypso on a lonely island, the centre of all the seas. We shall see how Menelaus knew this. When Telemachus and Pisistratus came, he was giving a feast, and called them to his table. It would not have been courteous to ask them who they were till they had been bathed and clothed in fresh raiment, and had eaten and drunk. After dinner, Menelaus saw how much Telemachus admired his house, and the flashing of light from the walls, which were covered with bronze panels, and from the cups of gold, and the amber and ivory and silver. Such things Telemachus had never seen in Ithaca. Noticing his surprise, Menelaus said that he had brought many rich things from Troy, after eight years wandering to Cyprus, and Phoenicia, and Egypt, and even to Libya, on the north coast of Africa. Yet he said that, though he was rich and fortunate, he was unhappy when he remembered the brave men who had died for his sake at Troy. But above all he was miserable for the loss of the best of them all, Ulysses, who was so long unheard of, and none knew whether, at that hour, he was alive or dead. At these words Telemachus hid his face in his purple mantle and shed tears, so that Menelaus guessed who he was, but he said nothing.

Then came into the hall, from her own fragrant chamber, Helen of the fair hands, as beautiful as ever she had been, her bower maidens carrying her golden distaff, with which she span, and a silver basket to hold her wool, for the white hands of Helen were never idle.

Helen knew Telemachus by his likeness to his father, Ulysses, and when she said this to Menelaus, Pisistratus overheard her, and told how Telemachus had come to them seeking for news of his father. Menelaus was much moved in his heart, and Helen no less, when they saw the son of Ulysses, who had been the most trusty of all their friends. They could not help shedding tears, for Pisistratus remembered his dear brother Antilochus, whom Memnon slew in battle at Troy, Memnon the son of the bright Dawn. But Helen wished to comfort them, and she brought a drug of magical virtue, which Polydamna, the wife of Thon, King of Egypt had given to her. This drug lulls all pain and anger, and brings forgetfulness of every sorrow, and Helen poured it from a golden vial into the mixing bowl of gold, and they drank the wine and were comforted.

Then Helen told Telemachus what great deeds Ulysses did at Troy, and how he crept into the town disguised as a beggar, and came to her house, when he stole the Luck of Troy. Menelaus told how Ulysses kept him and the other princes quiet in the horse of tree, when Deiphobus made Helen call to them all in the very voices of their own wives, and to Telemachus it was great joy to hear of his father's courage and wisdom.

Next day Telemachus showed to Menelaus how hardly he and his mother were treated by the proud wooers, and Menelaus prayed that Ulysses might come back to Ithaca, and slay the wooers every one. 'But as to what you ask me,' he said, 'I will tell you all that I have heard about your father. In my wanderings after I sailed from Troy the storm winds kept me for three weeks in the island called Pharos, a day's voyage from the mouth of the river Aegyptus' (which is the old name of the Nile). 'We were almost starving, for our food was done, and my crew went round the shores, fishing with hook and line. Now in that isle lives a Goddess, the daughter of Proteus, the Old Man of the Sea. She advised me that if I could but catch her father when he came out of the sea to sleep on the shore he would tell me everything that I needed to know. At noonday he was used to come out, with all his flock of seals round him, and to sleep among them on the sands. If I could seize him, she said, he would turn into all manner of shapes in my hands: beasts, and serpents, and burning fire; but at last he would appear in his own shape, and answer all my questions.

'So the Goddess spoke, and she dug hiding-places in the sands for me and three of my men, and covered us with the skins of seals. At noonday the Old Man came out with his seals, and counted them, beginning with us, and then he lay down and fell asleep. Then we leaped up and rushed at him and gripped him fast. He turned into the shapes of a lion, and of a leopard, of a snake, and a huge boar; then he was running water, and next he was a tall, blossoming tree. But we held him firmly, and at last he took his own shape, and told me that I should never have a fair wind till I had sailed back into the river Aegyptus and sacrificed there to the Gods in heaven. Then I asked him for news about my brother, Agamemnon, and he told me how my brother was slain in his own hall, and how Ajax was drowned in the sea. Lastly, he told me about Ulysses: how he was kept on a lonely island by the fairy Calypso, and was unhappy, and had no ship and no crew to escape and win home.'

This was all that Menelaus could tell Telemachus, who stayed with Menelaus for a month. All that time the wooers lay in wait for him, with a ship, in a narrow strait which they thought he must sail through on his way back to Ithaca. In that strait they meant to catch him and kill him.

– 5 –

HOW ULYSSES ESCAPED FROM THE ISLAND OF CALYPSO

NOW THE DAY AFTER MENELAUS TOLD Telemachus that Ulysses was still a living man, the Gods sent Hermes to Calypso. So Hermes bound on his feet his fair golden sandals, that wax not old, and bear him, alike over wet sea and dry land, as swift as the wind. Along the crests of the waves he flew, like the cormorant that chases fishes through the sea deeps, with his plumage wet in the sea brine. He reached the island, and went up to the cave of Calypso, wherein dwelt the nymph of the braided tresses, and he found her within. And on the hearth there was a great fire burning, and from afar, through the isle, was smelt the fragrance of cleft cedar blazing, and of sandal wood. And the nymph within was singing with a sweet voice as she fared to and fro before the loom, and wove with a shuttle of gold. All round about the cave there was a wood blossoming, alder and poplar and sweet smelling cypress. Therein roosted birds long of wing – owls and falcons and chattering sea-crows, which have their business in the waters. And lo! there, about the hollow cave, trailed a gadding garden vine, all rich with clusters. And fountains, four set orderly, were running with clear water hard by one another, turned each to his own course. Around soft meadows bloomed of violets and parsley; yea, even a deathless God who came thither might wonder at the sight and be glad at heart.

There the messenger, the slayer of Argos, stood and wondered. Now when he had gazed at all with wonder, he went into the wide cave; nor did Calypso, that fair Goddess, fail to know him when she saw him face to face; for the Gods used not to be strange one to another, not though one have his habitation far away. But he found not Ulysses, the great-hearted, within the cave, who sat weeping on the shore even as aforetime, straining his soul with tears and groans and griefs, and as he wept he looked wistfully over the unharvested deep. And Calypso, that fair Goddess, questioned Hermes, when she had made him sit on a bright shining star: 'Wherefore, I pray thee, Hermes of the golden wand, hast thou come hither, worshipful and welcome, whereas as of old thou wert not wont to visit me? Tell me all thy thought; my heart is set on fulfilling it, if fulfil it I may, and if it hath been fulfilled in the counsel of fate. But now follow me further, that I may set before thee the entertainment of strangers.'

Therewith the Goddess spread a table with ambrosia and set it by him, and mixed the ruddy nectar. So the messenger, the slayer of Argos, did eat and drink. Now after he had supped and comforted his soul with food, at the last he answered, and spake to her on this wise: 'Thou makest question of me on my coming, a Goddess of a God, and I will tell thee this my saying truly, at thy command. 'Twas Zeus that bade me come hither, by no will of mine; nay, who of his free will would speed over such a wondrous space of sea whereby is no city of mortals that do sacrifice to the Gods. He saith that thou hast with thee a man most wretched beyond his fellows, beyond those men that round the city of Priam for nine years fought, and in the tenth year sacked the city and departed homeward. Yet on the way they sinned against Athene, and she raised upon them an evil blast and long waves of the sea. Then all the rest of his good company was lost, but it came to pass that the wind bare and the wave brought him hither. And now Zeus biddeth thee send him hence with what speed thou mayest, for it is not ordained that he die away from his friends, but rather it is his fate to look on them even yet, and to come to his high-roofed home and his own country.'

So spake he, and Calypso, that fair Goddess, shuddered and spake unto him: 'Hard are ye Gods and jealous exceeding, who ever grudge Goddesses openly to mate with men. Him I saved as he went all alone bestriding the keel of a bark, for that Zeus had crushed and cleft his swift ship with a white bolt in the midst of the wine-dark deep. There all the rest of his good company was lost, but it came to pass that the wind bare and the wave brought him hither. And him have I loved and cherished, and I said that I would make him to know not death and age for ever. But I will give him no despatch, not I, for I have no ships by me with oars, nor company to bear him on his way over the broad back of the sea. Yet will I be forward to put this in his mind, and will hide nought, that all unharmed he may come to his own country.'

Then the messenger, the slayer of Argos, answered her: 'Yea, speed him now upon his path and have regard unto the wrath of Zeus, lest haply he be angered and bear hard on thee hereafter.'

Therewith the great slayer of Argos departed, but the lady nymph went on her way to the great-hearted Ulysses, when she had heard the message of Zeus.

And there she found him sitting on the shore, and his eyes were never dry of tears, and his sweet life was ebbing away as he mourned for his return. In the daytime he would sit on the rocks and on the beach, straining his soul with tears and groans and griefs, and through his tears he would look wistfully over the unharvested deep. So, standing near him, that fair Goddess spake to him: 'Hapless man, sorrow no more I pray thee in this isle, nor let thy good life waste away, for even now will I send thee hence with all my heart. Nay, arise and cut long beams, and fashion a wide raft with the axe, and lay deckings high thereupon, that it may bear thee over the misty deep. And I will place therein bread and water, and red wine to thy heart's desire, to keep hunger far away. And I will put raiment upon thee, and send a fair gale, that so thou mayest come all unharmed to thine own country, if indeed it be the good pleasure of the Gods who hold wide heaven, who are stronger than I am both to will and to do.'

Then Ulysses was glad and sad: glad that the Gods took thought for him, and sad to think of crossing alone the wide unsailed seas. Calypso said to him: 'So it is indeed thy wish to get thee home to thine own dear country even in this hour? Good fortune go with thee even so! Yet didst thou know in thine heart what thou art ordained to suffer, or ever thou reach thine own country, here, even here, thou wouldst abide with me and keep this house, and wouldst never taste of death, though thou longest to see thy wife, for whom thou hast ever a desire day by day. Not, in sooth, that I avow me to be less noble than she in form or fashion, for it is in no wise meet that mortal women should match them with immortals in shape and comeliness.'

And Ulysses of many counsels answered, and spake unto her: 'Be not wroth with me, Goddess and Queen. Myself I know it well, how wise Penelope is meaner to look upon than thou in comeliness and stature. But she is mortal, and thou knowest not age nor death. Yet, even so, I wish and long day by day to fare homeward and see the day of my returning. Yea, and if some God shall wreck me in the wine-dark deep, even so I will endure, with a heart within me patient of affliction. For already have I suffered full much, and much have I toiled in perils of waves and war; let this be added to the tale of those.'

Next day Calypso brought to Ulysses carpenters' tools, and he felled trees, and made a great raft, and a mast, and sails out of canvas. In five days he had finished his raft and launched it, and Calypso placed in it skins full of wine and water, and flour and many pleasant things to eat, and so they kissed for that last time and took farewell, he going alone on the wide sea, and she turning lonely to her own home. He might have lived for ever with the beautiful fairy, but he chose to live and die, if he could, with his wife Penelope.

– 6 –

HOW ULYSSES WAS WRECKED, YET REACHED PHAEACIA

As long as the fair wind blew Ulysses sat and steered his raft, never seeing land or any ship of men. He kept his eye at night on the Great Bear, holding it always on his left hand, as Calypso taught him. Seventeen days he sailed, and on the eighteenth day he saw the shadowy mountain peaks of an island called Phaeacia. But now the Sea God saw him, and remembered how Ulysses had blinded his son the Cyclops. In anger he raised a terrible storm: great clouds covered the sky, and all the winds met. Ulysses wished that he had died when the Trojans gathered round him as he defended the dead body of Achilles. For, had he died then, he would have been burned and buried by his friends, but if he were now drowned his ghost would always wander alone on the fringes of the Land of the Dead, like the ghost of Elpenor.

As he thought thus, the winds broke the mast of his raft, and the sail and yardarm fell into the sea, and the waves dragged him deep down. At last he rose to the surface and swam after his raft, and climbed on to it, and sat there, while the winds tossed the raft about like a feather. The Sea Goddess, Ino, saw him and pitied him, and rose from the water as a seagull rises after it has dived. She spoke to him, and threw her bright veil to him, saying, 'Wind this round your breast, and throw off your clothes. Leap from the raft and swim, and, when you reach land, cast the veil back into the sea, and turn away your head.'

Ulysses caught the veil, and wound it about his breast, but he determined not to leave the raft while the timbers held together. Even as he thought thus, the timbers were driven asunder by the waves, and he seized a plank, and sat astride it as a man rides a horse. Then the winds fell, all but the North Wind, which drifted Ulysses on for two days and nights. On the third day all was calm, and the land was very near, and Ulysses began to swim towards it, through a terrible surf, which crashed and foamed on sheer rocks, where all his bones would be broken. Thrice he clasped a rock, and thrice the back wash of the wave dragged him out to sea. Then he swam outside of the breakers, along the line of land, looking for a safe place, and at last he came to the mouth of the river. Here all was smooth, with a shelving beach, and his feet touched bottom. He staggered out of the water and swooned away as soon as he was on dry land. When he came to himself he unbound the veil of Ino, and cast it into the sea, and fell back, quite spent, among the reeds of the river, naked and starving. He crept between two thick olive trees that grew close together and made a shelter against the wind, and he covered himself all over thickly with fallen dry leaves, till he grew warm again and fell into a deep sleep.

While Ulysses slept, alone and naked in an unknown land, a dream came to beautiful Nausicaa, the daughter of the King of that country, which is called Phaeacia. The dream was in the shape of a girl who was a friend of Nausicaa, and it said: 'Nausicaa, how has your mother such a careless daughter? There are many beautiful garments in the house that need to be washed, against your wedding day, when, as is the custom, you must give mantles and tunics to the guests. Let us go a washing to the river tomorrow, taking a car to carry the raiment.'

When Nausicaa wakened next day she remembered the dream, and went to her father, and asked him to lend her a car to carry the clothes. She said nothing about her marriage day, for though many young princes were in love with her, she was in love with none of them. Still, the clothes must be washed, and her father lent her a waggon with a high frame, and mules to drive. The clothes were piled in the car, and food was packed in a basket, every sort of dainty thing, and Nausicaa took the reins and drove slowly while many girls followed her, her friends of her own age. They came to a deep clear pool, that overflowed into shallow paved runs of water, and there they washed the clothes, and trod them down in the runlets. Next they laid them out to dry in the sun and wind on the pebbles, and then they took their meal of cakes and other good things.

When they had eaten they threw down their veils and began to play at ball, at a game like rounders. Nausicaa threw the ball at a girl who was running, but missed her, and the ball fell into the deep swift river. All the girls screamed and laughed, and the noise they made wakened Ulysses where he lay in the little wood. 'Where am I?' he said to himself; 'is this a country of fierce and savage men? A sound of girls at play rings round me. Can they be fairies of the hill tops and the rivers, and the water meadows?' As he had no clothes, and the voices seemed to be voices of women, Ulysses broke a great leafy bough which hid all his body, but his feet were bare, his face was wild with weariness, and cold, and hunger, and his hair and beard were matted and rough with the salt water.

The girls, when they saw such a face peering over the leaves of the bough, screamed, and ran this way and that along the beach. But Nausicaa, as became the daughter of the King, stood erect and unafraid, and as Ulysses dared not go near and kneel to her, he spoke from a distance and said: 'I pray thee, O Queen, whether thou art a Goddess or a mortal! If indeed thou art a Goddess of them that keep the wide heaven, to Artemis, then, the daughter of great Zeus, I mainly liken thee for beauty and stature and shapeliness. But if thou art one of the daughters of men who dwell on earth, thrice blessed are thy father and thy lady mother, and thrice blessed thy brethren. Surely their souls ever glow with gladness for thy sake each time they see thee entering the dance, so fair a flower of maidens. But he is of heart the most blessed beyond all other who shall prevail with gifts of wooing, and lead thee to his home. Never have mine eyes beheld such an one among mortals, neither man nor woman; great awe comes upon me as I look on thee. Yet in Delos once I saw as goodly a thing: a young sapling of a palm tree springing by the altar of Apollo. For thither, too, I went, and much people with me, on that path where my sore troubles were to be. Yea! and when I looked thereupon, long time I marvelled in spirit – for never grew there yet so goodly a shoot from ground – even in such wise as I wonder at thee, lady, and am astonished and do greatly fear to touch thy knees, though grievous sorrow is upon me.

'Yesterday, on the twentieth day, I escaped from the wine-dark deep, but all that time continually the wave bare me, and the vehement winds drave from the isle Ogygia. And now some God has cast me on this shore that here too, methinks, some evil may betide me; for I think not that trouble will cease; the Gods ere that time will yet bring many a thing to pass. But, Queen, have pity on me, for, after many trials and sore, to thee first of all am I come, and of the other folk, who hold this city and land, I know no man. Nay, show me the town; give me an old garment to cast about me, if thou hadst, when thou earnest here, any wrap for the linen. And may the Gods grant thee all thy heart's desire: a husband and a home, and a mind at one with his may they give – a good gift, for there is nothing mightier and nobler than when man and wife are of one heart and mind in a house, a grief to their foes, and to their friends great joy, but their own hearts know it best.'

Then Nausicaa of the white arms answered him, and said: 'Stranger, as thou seemest no evil man nor foolish – and it is Olympian Zeus himself that giveth weal to men, to the good and to the evil, to each one as he will, and this thy lot doubtless is of him, and so thou must in anywise endure it – now, since thou hast come to our city and our land, thou shalt not lack raiment nor aught else that is the due of a hapless suppliant when he has met them who can befriend him. And I will show thee the town, and name the name of the people. The Phaeacians hold this city and land, and I am the daughter of Alcinous, great of heart, on whom all the might and force of the Phaeacians depend.'

Thus she spake, and called to her maidens of the fair tresses: 'Halt, my maidens, whither flee ye at the sight of a man? Ye surely do not take him for an enemy? That mortal breathes not, and never will be born, who shall come with war to the land of the Phaeacians, for they are very dear to the Gods. Far apart we live in the wash of the waves, the outermost of men, and no other mortals are conversant with us. Nay, but this man is some helpless one come hither in his wanderings, whom now we must kindly entreat, for all strangers and beggars are from Zeus, and a little gift is dear. So, my maidens, give the stranger meat and drink, and bathe him in the river, where there is a shelter from the winds.'

So she spake, but they halted and called each to the other, and they brought Ulysses to the sheltered place, and made him sit down, as Nausicaa bade them, the daughter of Alcinous, high of heart. Beside him they laid a mantle and a doublet for raiment, and gave him soft olive oil in the golden cruse, and bade him wash in the streams of the river. Then goodly Ulysses spake among the maidens, saying: 'I pray you stand thus apart while I myself wash the brine from my shoulders, and anoint me with olive oil, for truly oil is long a stranger to my skin. But in your sight I will not bathe, for I am ashamed to make me naked in the company of fair-tressed maidens.'

Then they went apart and told all to their lady. But with the river water the goodly Ulysses washed from his skin the salt scurf that covered his back and broad shoulders, and from his head he wiped the crusted brine of the barren sea. But when he had washed his whole body, and anointed him with olive oil, and had clad himself in the raiment that the unwedded maiden gave him, then Athene, the daughter of Zeus, made him greater and more mighty to behold, and from his head caused deep curling locks to flow, like the hyacinth flower. And, as when some skilful man overlays gold upon silver – one that Hephaestus and Pallas Athene have taught all manner of craft, and full of grace is his handiwork – even so did Athene shed grace about his head and shoulders.

Then to the shore of the sea went Ulysses apart,

and sat down, glowing in beauty and grace, and the princess marvelled at him, and spake among her fair-tressed maidens, saying: 'Listen, my white-armed maidens, and I will say somewhat. Not without the will of all the Gods who hold Olympus has this man come among the godlike Phaeacians. Erewhile he seemed to me uncomely, but now he is like the Gods that keep the wide heaven. Would that such an one might be called my husband, dwelling here, and that it might please him here to abide! But come, my maidens, give the stranger meat and drink.'

Thus she spake, and they gave ready ear and hearkened, and set beside Ulysses meat and drink, and the steadfast goodly Ulysses did eat and drink eagerly, for it was long since he had tasted food.

Now Nausicaa of the white arms had another thought. She folded the raiment and stored it in the goodly wain, and yoked the mules, strong of hoof, and herself climbed into the car. Then she called on Ulysses, and spake and hailed him: 'Up now, stranger, and rouse thee to go to the city, that I may convey thee to the house of my wise father, where, I promise thee, thou shalt get knowledge of all the noblest of the Phaeacians. But do thou even as I tell thee, and thou seemest a discreet man enough. So long as we are passing along the fields and farms of men, do thou fare quickly with the maidens behind the mules and the chariot, and I will lead the way. But when we set foot within the city, whereby goes a high wall with towers, and there is a fair haven on either side of the town, and narrow is the entrance, and curved ships are drawn up on either hand of the mole, thou shalt find a fair grove of Athene, a poplar grove, near the road, and a spring wells forth therein, and a meadow lies all around.

'There is my father's land, and his fruitful close, within the sound of a man's shout from the city. Sit thee down there and wait until such time as we may have come into the city, and reached the house of my father. But when thou deemest that we are got to the palace, then go up to the city of the Phaeacians, and ask for the house of my father, Alcinous, high of heart. It is easily known, and a young child could be thy guide, for nowise like it are builded the houses of the Phaeacians, so goodly is the palace of the hero Alcinous. But when thou art within the shadow of the halls and the court, pass quickly through the great chamber till thou comest to my mother, who sits at the hearth in the light of the fire, weaving yarn of sea-purple stain, a wonder to behold. Her chair is leaned against a pillar, and her maidens sit behind her. And there my father's throne leans close to hers, wherein he sits and drinks his wine, like an immortal. Pass thou by him, and cast thy hands about my mother's knees that thou mayest see quickly and with joy the day of thy returning, even if thou art from a very far country. If but her heart be kindly disposed towards thee, then is there hope that thou shalt see thy friends, and come to thy well-builded house, and to thine own country.'

She spake and smote the mules with the shining whip, and quickly they left behind them the streams of the river; and well they trotted and well they paced, and she took heed to drive in such wise that the maidens and Ulysses might follow on foot, and cunningly she plied the lash Then the sun set, and they came to the famous grove, the sacred place of Athene; so there the goodly Ulysses sat him down. Then straightway he prayed to the daughter of mighty Zeus: 'Listen to me, child of Zeus, lord of the aegis, unwearied maiden; hear me even now, since before thou heardest not when I was smitten on the sea, when the renowned earth-shaker smote me. Grant me to come to the Phaeacians as one dear and worthy of pity.'

So he spake in prayer, and Pallas Athene heard him; but she did not yet appear to him face to face, for she had regard unto her father's brother, who furiously raged against the Godlike Ulysses till he should come to his own country.

While Nausicaa and her maidens went home,

Ulysses waited near the temple till they should have arrived, and then he rose and walked to the city, wondering at the harbour, full of ships, and at the strength of the walls. The Goddess Athene met him, disguised as a mortal girl, and told him again how the name of the king was Alcinous, and his wife's name was Arete: she was wise and kind, and had great power in the city. The Goddess caused Ulysses to pass unseen among the people till he reached the palace, which shone with bronze facings to the walls, while within the hall were golden hounds and golden statues of young men holding torches burning to give light to those who sat at supper. The gardens were very beautiful, full of fruit trees, and watered by streams that flowed from two fountains. Ulysses stood and wondered at the beauty of the gardens, and then walked, unseen, through the hall, and knelt at the feet of Queen Arete, and implored her to send him in a ship to his own country.

A table was brought to him, and food and wine were set before him, and Alcinous, as his guests were going home, spoke out and said that the stranger was to be entertained, whoever he might be, and sent safely on his way. The guests departed, and Arete, looking at Ulysses, saw that the clothes he wore were possessions of her house, and asked him who he was, and how he got the raiment? Then he told her how he had been shipwrecked, and how Nausicaa had given him food, and garments out of those which she had been washing. Then Arete said that Nausicaa should have brought Ulysses straight to her house; but Ulysses answered: 'Chide not, I pray you, the blameless damsel,' and explained that he himself was shy, and afraid that Nausicaa's parents might not like to see her coming with an unknown stranger. King Alcinous answered that he was not jealous and suspicious. To a stranger so noble as Ulysses he would very gladly see his daughter married, and would give him a house and plenty of everything. But if the stranger desired to go to his own country, then a ship should be made ready for him. Thus courteous was Alcinous, for he readily saw that Ulysses, who had not yet told his name, was of noble birth, strong and wise. Then all went to bed, and Ulysses had a soft bed and a warm, with blankets of purple.

Next day Alcinous sent two-and-fifty young men to prepare a ship, and they moored her in readiness out in the shore water; but the chiefs dined with Alcinous, and the minstrel sang about the Trojan war, and so stirred the heart of Ulysses, that he held his mantle before his face and wept. When Alcinous saw that, he proposed that they should go and amuse themselves with sports in the open air; races, wrestling, and boxing. The son of Alcinous asked Ulysses if he would care to take part in the games, but Ulysses answered that he was too heavy at heart. To this a young man, Euryalus, said that Ulysses was probably a captain of a merchant ship, a tradesman, not a sportsman.

At this Ulysses was ill pleased, and replied that while he was young and happy, he was well skilled in all sports, but now he was heavy and weak with war and wandering. Still, he would show what he could do. Then he seized a heavy weight, much heavier than any that the Phaeacians used in putting the stone. He whirled it up, and hurled it far – far beyond the furthest mark that the Phaeacians had reached when putting a lighter weight. Then he challenged any man to run a race with him or box with him, or shoot at a mark with him. Only his speed in running did he doubt, for his limbs were stiffened by the sea. Perhaps Alcinous saw that it would go ill with any man who matched himself against the stranger, so he sent for the harper, who sang a merry song, and then he made the young men dance and play ball, and bade the elder men go and bring rich presents of gold and garments for the wanderer. Alcinous himself gave a beautiful coffer and chest, and a great golden cup, and Arete tied up all the gifts in the coffer, while the damsels took Ulysses to the bath, and bathed him and anointed him with oil.

As he left the bath he met Nausicaa, standing at the entrance of the hall. She bade him goodbye, rather sadly, saying: 'Farewell, and do not soon forget me in your own country, for to me you owe the ransom of your life.' 'May God grant to me to see my own country, lady,' he answered, 'for there I will think of you with worship, as I think of the blessed Gods, all my days, for to you, lady, I owe my very life.' These were the last words they spoke to each other, for Nausicaa did not sit at meat in the hall with the great company of men. When they had taken supper, the blind harper sang again a song about the deeds of Ulysses at Troy, and again Ulysses wept, so that Alcinous asked him: 'Hast thou lost a dear friend or a kinsman in the great war?' Then Ulysses spoke out: 'I am Ulysses, Laertes' son, of whom all men have heard tell.' While they sat amazed, he began, and told them the whole story of his adventures, from the day when he left Troy till he arrived at Calypso's island; he had already told them how he was shipwrecked on his way thence to Phaeacia.

All that wonderful story he told to their pleasure, and Euryalus made amends for his rude words at the games, and gave Ulysses a beautiful sword of bronze, with an ivory hilt set with studs of gold. Many other gifts were given to him, and were carried and stored on board the ship which had been made ready, and then Ulysses spoke goodbye to the Queen, saying: 'Be happy, oh Queen, till old age and death come to you, as they come to all. Be joyful in your house with your children and your people, and Alcinous the King.' Then he departed, and lay down on sheets and cloaks in the raised deck of the ship, and soundly he slept while the fifty oars divided the waters of the sea, and drove the ship to Ithaca.

– 7 –

HOW ULYSSES CAME TO HIS OWN COUNTRY, AND FOR SAFETY DISGUISED HIMSELF AS AN OLD BEGGAR MAN

WHEN ULYSSES AWOKE, HE FOUND himself alone, wrapped in the linen sheet and the bright coverlet, and he knew not where he was. The Phaeacians had carried him from the ship as he slept, and put him on shore, and placed all the rich gifts that had been given him under a tree, and then had sailed away. There was a morning mist that hid the land, and Ulysses did not know the haven of his own island, Ithaca, and the rock whence sprang a fountain of the water fairies that men call Naiads. He thought that the Phaeacians had set him in a strange country, so he counted all his goods, and then walked up and down sadly by the seashore. Here he met a young man, delicately clad, like a king's son, with a double mantle, such as kings wear, folded round his shoulders, and a spear in his hand. 'Tell me pray,' said Ulysses, 'what land is this, and what men dwell here?'

The young man said: 'Truly, stranger, you know little, or you come from far away. This isle is Ithaca, and the name of it is known even in Troyland.'

Ulysses was glad, indeed, to learn that he was at home at last; but how the young men who had grown up since he went away would treat him, all alone as he was, he could not tell. So he did not let out that he was Ulysses the King, but said that he was a Cretan. The stranger would wonder why a Cretan had come alone to Ithaca, with great riches, and yet did not know that he was there. So he pretended that, in Crete, a son of Idomeneus had tried to rob him of all the spoil he took at Troy, and that he had killed this prince, and packed his wealth and fled on board a ship of the Phoenicians, who promised to land him at Pylos. But the wind had borne them out of their way, and they had all landed and slept on shore, here; but the Phoenicians had left him asleep and gone off in the dawn.

On this the young man laughed, and suddenly appeared as the great Goddess, Pallas Athene. 'How clever you are,' she said; 'yet you did not know me, who helped you in Troyland. But much trouble lies before you, and you must not let man or woman know who you really are, your enemies are so many and powerful.'

'You never helped me in my dangers on the sea,' said Ulysses, 'and now do you make mock of me, or is this really mine own country?'

'I had no mind,' said the Goddess, 'to quarrel with my brother the Sea God, who had a feud against you for the blinding of his son, the Cyclops. But come, you shall see this is really Ithaca,' and she scattered the white mist, and Ulysses saw and knew the pleasant cave of the Naiads, and the forests on the side of the mountain called Neriton. So he knelt down and kissed the dear earth of his own country, and prayed to the Naiads of the cave. Then the Goddess helped him to hide all his gold, and bronze, and other presents in a secret place in the cavern; and she taught him how, being lonely as he was, he might destroy the proud wooers of his wife, who would certainly desire to take his life.

The Goddess began by disguising Ulysses, so that his skin seemed wrinkled, and his hair thin, and his eyes dull, and she gave him dirty old wraps for clothes, and over all a great bald skin of a stag, like that which he wore when he stole into Troy disguised as a beggar. She gave him a staff, too, and a wallet to hold scraps of broken food. There was not a man or a woman that knew Ulysses in this disguise. Next, the Goddess bade him go across the island to his own swineherd, who remained faithful to him, and to stay there among the swine till she brought home Telemachus, who was visiting Helen and Menelaus in Lacedaemon. She fled away to Lacedaemon, and Ulysses climbed the hills that lay between the cavern and the farm where the swineherd lived.

When Ulysses reached the farmhouse, the swineherd, Eumaeus, was sitting alone in front of his door, making himself a pair of brogues out of the skin of an ox. He was a very honest man, and, though he was a slave, he was the son of a prince in his own country. When he was a little child some Phoenicians came in their ship to his father's house and made friends with his nurse, who was a Phoenician woman. One of them, who made love to her, asked her who she was, and she said that her father was a rich man in Sidon, but that pirates had carried her away and sold her to her master. The Phoenicians promised to bring her back to Sidon, and she fled to their ship, carrying with her the child whom she nursed, little Eumaeus; she also stole three cups of gold. The woman died at sea, and the pirates sold the boy to Laertes, the father of Ulysses, who treated him kindly. Eumaeus was fond of the family which he served, and he hated the proud wooers for their insolence.

When Ulysses came near his house the four great dogs rushed out and barked at him; they would have bitten, too, but Eumaeus ran up and threw stones at them, and no farm dog can face a shower of stones. He took Ulysses into his house, gave him food and wine, and told him all about the greed and pride of the wooers. Ulysses said that the master of Eumaeus would certainly come home, and told a long story about himself. He was a Cretan, he said, and had fought at Troy, and later had been shipwrecked, but reached a country called Thesprotia, where he learned that Ulysses was alive, and was soon to leave Thesprotia and return to Ithaca.

Eumaeus did not believe this tale, and supposed that the beggar man only meant to say what he would like to hear. However, he gave Ulysses a good dinner of his own pork, and Ulysses amused him and his fellow slaves with stories about the Siege of Troy, till it was bedtime.

In the meantime Athene had gone to Lacedaemon to the house of Menelaus, where Telemachus was lying awake. She told him that Penelope, his mother, meant to marry one of the wooers, and advised him to sail home at once, avoiding the strait between Ithaca and another isle, where his enemies were lying in wait to kill him. When he reached Ithaca he must send his oarsmen to the town, but himself walk alone across the island to see the swineherd. In the morning Telemachus and his friend, Pisistratus, said goodbye to Menelaus and Helen, who wished to make him presents, and so went to their treasure house. Now when they came to the place where the treasures were stored, then Atrides took a double cup, and bade his son, Megapenthes, to bear a mixing bowl of silver. And Helen stood by the coffers, wherein were her robes of curious needlework which she herself had wrought. So Helen, the fair lady, lifted one and brought it out – the widest and most beautifully embroidered of all – and it shone like a star, and lay far beneath the rest.

Then they went back through the house till they came to Telemachus; and Menelaus, of the fair hair, spake to him, saying: 'Telemachus, may Zeus the thunderer, and the lord of Hera, in very truth bring about thy return according to the desire of thy heart. And of the gifts, such as are treasures stored in my house, I will give thee the goodliest and greatest of price. I will give thee a mixing bowl beautifully wrought; it is all of silver, and the lips thereof are finished with gold, the work of Hephaestus; and the hero Phaedimus, the King of the Sidonians, gave it to me when his house sheltered me, on my coming thither. This cup I would give to thee.'

Therewith the hero Atrides set the double cup

in his hands. And the strong Megapenthes bare the shining silver bowl and set it before him. And Helen came up, beautiful Helen, with the robe in her hands, and spake and hailed him: 'Lo! I, too, give thee this gift, dear child, a memorial of the hands of Helen, against the day of thy desire, even of thy bridal, for thy bride to wear it. But, meanwhile, let it lie by thy dear mother in her chamber. And may joy go with thee to thy well-builded house and thine own country.'

Just when Telemachus was leaving her palace door, an eagle stooped from the sky and flew away with a great white goose that was feeding on the grass, and the farm servants rushed out shouting, but the eagle passed away to the right hand, across the horses of Pisistratus.

Then Helen explained the meaning of this omen. 'Hear me, and I will prophesy as the immortals put it into my heart, and as I deem it will be accomplished. Even as yonder eagle came down from the hill, the place of his birth and kin, and snatched away the goose that was fostered in the house, even so shall Ulysses return home after much trial and long wanderings and take vengeance; yea! or even now is he at home and sowing the seeds of evil for all the wooers.' We are told no more about Helen of the fair hands, except that she and Menelaus never died, but were carried by the Gods to the beautiful Elysian plain, a happy place where war and trouble never came, nor old age, nor death. After that she was worshipped in her own country as if she had been a Goddess, kind, gentle, and beautiful.

Telemachus thanked Helen for prophesying good luck, and he drove to the city of Nestor, on the sea, but was afraid to go near the old king, who would have kept him and entertained him, while he must sail at once for Ithaca. He went to his own ship in the harbour, and, while his crew made ready to sail, there came a man running hard, and in great fear of the avenger of blood. This was a second-sighted man, called Theoclymenus, and he implored Telemachus to take him to Ithaca, for he had slain a man in his own country, who had killed one of his brothers, and now the brothers and cousins of that man were pursuing him to take his life. Telemachus made him welcome, and so sailed north to Ithaca, wondering whether he should be able to slip past the wooers, who were lying in wait to kill him. Happily the ship of Telemachus passed them unseen in the night, and arrived at Ithaca. He sent his crew to the town, and was just starting to walk across the island to the swineherd's house, when the second-sighted man asked what *he* should do. Telemachus told Piraeus, one of his friends, to take the man home and be kind to him, which he gladly promised to do, and then he set off to seek the swineherd.

The swineherd, with Ulysses, had just lit a fire to cook breakfast, when they saw the farm dogs frolicking round a young man who was walking towards the house. The dogs welcomed him, for he was no stranger, but Telemachus. Up leaped the swineherd in delight, and the bowl in which he was mixing wine and water fell from his hands. He had been unhappy for fear the wooers who lay in wait for Telemachus should kill him, and he ran and embraced the young man as gladly as a father welcomes a son who has long been in a far country. Telemachus, too, was anxious to hear whether his mother had married one of the wooers, and glad to know that she still bore her troubles patiently.

When Telemachus stepped into the swineherd's house Ulysses arose from his seat, but Telemachus bade the old beggar man sit down again, and a pile of brushwood with a fleece thrown over it was brought for himself. They breakfasted on what was ready, cold pork, wheaten bread, and wine in cups of ivy wood, and Eumaeus told Telemachus that the old beggar gave himself out as a wanderer from Crete. Telemachus answered that he could not take strangers into his mother's house, for he was unable to protect them against the violence of the wooers, but he would give the wanderer clothes and shoes and a sword, and he might stay at the farm. He sent the swineherd to tell his mother, Penelope, that he had returned in safety, and Eumaeus started on his journey to the town.

At this moment the farm dogs, which had been taking their share of the breakfast, began to whine, and bristle up, and slunk with their tails between their legs to the inmost corner of the room. Telemachus could not think why they were afraid, or of what, but Ulysses saw the Goddess Athene, who appeared to him alone, and the dogs knew that something strange and terrible was coming to the door. Ulysses went out, and Athene bade him tell Telemachus who he really was, now that they were alone, and she touched Ulysses with her golden wand, and made him appear like himself, and his clothes like a king's raiment.

Telemachus, who neither saw nor heard Athene, wondered greatly, and thought the beggar man must be some God, wandering in disguise. But Ulysses said, 'No God am I, but thine own father,' and they embraced each other and wept for joy.

At last Ulysses told Telemachus how he had come home in a ship of the Phaeacians, and how his treasure was hidden in the cave of the Naiads, and asked him how many the wooers were, and how they might drive them from the house. Telemachus replied that the wooers were one hundred and eight, and that Medon, a servant of his own, took part with them, there was also the minstrel of the house, whom they compelled to sing at their feasts. They were all strong young men, each with his sword at his side, but they had with them no shields, helmets, and breastplates. Ulysses said that, with the help of the Goddess, he hoped to get the better of them, many as they were. Telemachus must go to the house, and Ulysses would come next day, in the disguise of an old beggar. However ill the wooers might use him, Telemachus must take no notice, beyond saying that they ought to behave better. Ulysses, when he saw a good chance, would give Telemachus a sign to take away the shields, helmets, and weapons that hung on the walls of the great hall, and to hide them in a secret place. If the wooers missed them, he must say – first, that the smoke of the fire was spoiling them; and, again, that they were better out of the reach of the wooers, in case they quarrelled over their wine. Telemachus must keep two swords, two spears, and two shields for himself and Ulysses to use, if they saw a chance, and he must let neither man nor woman know that the old beggar man was his father.

While they were talking, one of the crew of

Telemachus and the swineherd went to Penelope and told her how her son had landed. On hearing this the wooers held a council as to how they should behave to him: Antinous was for killing him, but Amphinomus and Eurymachus were for waiting, and seeing what would happen. Before Eumaeus came back from his errand to Penelope, Athene changed Ulysses into the dirty old beggar again.

- 8 -

ULYSSES COMES DISGUISED AS A BEGGAR TO HIS OWN PALACE

NEXT MORNING TELEMACHUS WENT home, and comforted his mother, and told her how he had been with Nestor and Menelaus, and seen her cousin, Helen of the fair hands, but this did not seem to interest Penelope, who thought that her beautiful cousin was the cause of all her misfortunes. Then Theoclymenus, the second-sighted man whom Telemachus brought from Pylos, prophesied to Penelope that Ulysses was now in Ithaca, taking thought how he might kill the wooers, who were then practising spear-throwing at a mark, while some of them were killing swine and a cow for breakfast.

Meanwhile Ulysses, in disguise, and the swineherd were coming near the town, and there they met the goatherd, Melanthius, who was a friend of the wooers, and an insolent and violent slave. He insulted the old beggar, and advised him not to come near the house of Ulysses, and kicked him off the road. Then Ulysses was tempted to slay him with his hands, but he controlled himself lest he should be discovered, and he and Eumaeus walked slowly to the palace. As they lingered outside the court, lo! a hound raised up his head and pricked his ears, even where he lay: Argos, the hound of Ulysses, of the hardy heart, which of old himself had bred. Now in time past the young men used to lead the hound against wild goats and deer and hares; but, as then, he lay despised (his master being afar) in the deep dung of mules and kine, whereof an ample bed was spread before the doors till the slaves of Ulysses should carry it away to dung therewith his wide demesne. There lay the dog Argos, full of vermin. Yet even now, when he was aware of Ulysses standing by, he wagged his tail and dropped both his ears, but nearer to his master he had not now the strength to draw. But Ulysses looked aside and wiped away a tear that he easily hid from Eumaeus, and straightway he asked him, saying: 'Eumaeus, verily this is a great marvel: this hound lying here in the dung. Truly he is goodly of growth, but I know not certainly if he have speed with this beauty, or if he be comely only, like men's trencher dogs that their lords keep for the pleasure of the eye.'

Then answered the swineherd Eumaeus: 'In very truth this is the dog of a man that has died in a far land. If he were what once he was in limb and in the feats of the chase, when Ulysses left him to go to Troy, soon wouldst thou marvel at the sight of his swiftness and his strength. There was no beast that could flee from him in the deep places of the wood when he was in pursuit; for even on a track he was the keenest hound. But now he is holden in an evil case, and his lord hath perished far from his own country, and the careless women take no charge of him.'

Therewith he passed within the fair-lying house, and went straight to the hall, to the company of the proud wooers. But upon Argos came death even in the hour that he beheld Ulysses again, in the twentieth year.

Thus the good dog knew Ulysses, though Penelope did not know him when she saw him, and tears came into Ulysses' eyes as he stood above the body of the hound that loved him well. Eumaeus went into the house, but Ulysses sat down where it was the custom for beggars to sit, on the wooden threshold outside the door of the hall. Telemachus saw him, from his high seat under the pillars on each side of the fire, in the middle of the room, and bade Eumaeus carry a loaf and a piece of pork to the beggar, who laid them in his wallet between his feet, and ate. Then he thought he would try if there were one courteous man among the wooers, and he entered the hall and began to beg among them. Some gave him crusts and bones, but Antinous caught up a footstool and struck him hard on the shoulder. 'May death come upon Antinous before his wedding day!' said Ulysses, and even the other wooers rebuked him for striking a beggar.

Penelope heard of this, and told Eumaeus to bring the beggar to her; she thought he might have news of her husband. But Ulysses made Eumaeus say that he had been struck once in the hall, and would not come to her till after sunset, when the wooers left the house. Then Eumaeus went to his own farmhouse, after telling Telemachus that he would come next day, driving swine for the wooers to eat.

Ulysses was the new beggar in Ithaca: he soon found that he had a rival, an old familiar beggar, named Iras. This man came up to the palace, and was angry when he saw a newcomer sitting in the doorway, 'Get up,' he said, 'I ought to drag you away by the foot: begone before we quarrel!' 'There is room enough for both of us,' said Ulysses, 'do not anger me.' Iras challenged him to fight, and the wooers thought this good sport, and they made a ring, and promised that the winner should be beggar-in-chief, and have the post to himself. Ulysses asked the wooers to give him fair play, and not to interfere, and then he stripped his shoulders, and kilted up his rags, showing strong arms and legs. As for Iras he began to tremble, but Antinous forced him to fight, and the two put up their hands. Iras struck at the shoulder of Ulysses, who hit him with his right fist beneath the ear, and he fell, the blood gushing from his mouth, and his heels dramming in the ground, and Ulysses dragged him from the doorway and propped him against the wall of the court, while the wooers laughed. Then Ulysses spoke gravely to Amphinomus, telling him that it would be wise in him to go home, for that if Ulysses came back it might not be so easy to escape his hands.

After sunset Ulysses spoke so fiercely to the maidens of Penelope, who insulted him, that they ran to their own rooms, but Eurymachus threw a footstool at him. He slipped out of the way, and the stool hit the cupbearer and knocked him down, and all was disorder in the hall. The wooers themselves were weary of the noise and disorder, and went home to the houses in the town where they slept. Then Telemachus and Ulysses, being left alone, hid the shields and helmets and spears that hung on the walls of the hall in an armoury within the house, and when this was done Telemachus went to sleep in his own chamber, in the courtyard, and Ulysses waited till Penelope should come into the hall.

Ulysses sat in the dusky hall, where the wood in the braziers that gave light had burned low, and waited to see the face of his wife, for whom he had left beautiful Calypso. The maidens of Penelope came trooping, laughing, and cleared away the food and the cups, and put faggots in the braziers. They were all giddy girls, in love with the handsome wooers, and one of them, Melantho, bade Ulysses go away, and sleep at the blacksmith's forge, lest he should be beaten with a torch. Penelope heard Melantho, whom she had herself brought up, and she rebuked her, and ordered a chair to be brought for Ulysses. When he was seated, she asked him who he was, and he praised her beauty, for she was still very fair, but did not answer her question. She insisted that he should tell her who he was, and he said that he was a Cretan prince, the younger brother of Idomeneus, and that he did not go to fight in Troyland. In Crete he stayed, and met Ulysses, who stopped there on his way to Troy, and he entertained Ulysses for a fortnight. Penelope wept when she heard that the stranger had seen her husband, but, as false stories were often told to her by strangers who came to Ithaca, she asked how Ulysses was dressed, and what manner of men were with him.

The beggar said that Ulysses wore a double mantle of purple, clasped with a gold brooch fastened by two safety pins (for these were used at that time), and on the face of the brooch was a figure of a hound holding a struggling fawn in his forepaws. (Many such brooches have been found in the graves in Greece.) Beneath his mantle Ulysses wore a shining smock, smooth and glittering like the skin of an onion. Probably it was made of silk: women greatly admired it. With him was a squire named Eurybates, a brown, round-shouldered man.

On hearing all this Penelope wept again and said that she herself had given Ulysses the brooch and the garments. She now knew that the beggar had really met Ulysses, and he went on to tell her that, in his wanderings, he had heard how Ulysses was still alive, though he had lost all his company, and that he had gone to Dodona in the west of Greece to ask for advice from the oak tree of Zeus, the whispering oak tree, as to how he should come home, openly or secretly. Certainly, he said, Ulysses would return that year.

Penelope was still unable to believe in such good news, but she bade Eurycleia, the old nurse, wash the feet of the beggar in warm water, so a foot-bath was brought. Ulysses turned his face away from the firelight, for the nurse said that he was very like her master. As she washed his legs she noticed the long scar of the wound made by the boar, when he hunted with his cousins, long ago, before he was married. The nurse knew him now, and spoke to him in a whisper, calling him by his name. But he caught her throat with his hand, and asked why she would cause his death, for the wooers would slay him if they knew who he was. Eurycleia called him her child, and promised that she would be silent, and then she went to fetch more hot water, for she had let his foot fall into the bath and upset it when she found the scar.

When she had washed him, Penelope told the beggar that she could no longer refuse to marry one of the wooers. Ulysses had left a great bow in the house, the old bow of King Eurytus, that few could bend, and he had left twelve iron axes, made with a round opening in the blade of each. Axes of this shape have been found at Lacedaemon, where Helen lived, so we know what the axes of Ulysses were like. When he was at home he used to set twelve of them in a straight line, and shoot an arrow through the twelve holes in the blades. Penelope therefore intended, next day, to bring the bow and the axes to the wooers, and to marry any one of them who could string the bow, and shoot an arrow through the twelve axes.

'I think,' said the beggar, 'that Ulysses will be

here before any of the wooers have bent his bow.' Then Penelope went to her upper chamber, and Ulysses slept in an outer gallery of the house on piled-up sheepskins.

There Ulysses lay, thinking how he might destroy all the wooers, and the Goddess Athene came and comforted him, and, in the morning, he rose and made his prayer to Zeus, asking for signs of his favour. There came, first a peal of thunder, and then the voice of a woman, weak and old, who was grinding corn to make bread for the wooers. All the other women of the mill had done their work and were asleep, but she was feeble and the round upper stone of the quern, that she rolled on the corn above the under stone, was too heavy for her.

She prayed, and said, 'Father Zeus, King of Gods and men, loudly hast thou thundered. Grant to me my prayer, unhappy as I am. May this be the last day of the feasting of the wooers in the hall of Ulysses: they have loosened my knees with cruel labour in grinding barley for them: may they now sup their last!' Hearing this prayer Ulysses was glad, for he thought it a lucky sign. Soon the servants were at work, and Eumaeus came with swine, and was as courteous to the beggar as Melanthius, who brought some goats, was insolent. The cowherd, called Philoetius, also arrived; he hated the wooers, and spoke friendly to the beggar. Last appeared the wooers, and went in to their meal, while Telemachus bade the beggar sit on a seat just within the hall, and told the servants to give him as good a share of the food as any of them received. One wooer, Ctesippus, said: 'His fair share this beggar man has had, as is right, but I will give him a present over and above it!' Then he picked up the foot of an ox, and threw it with all his might at Ulysses, who merely moved aside, and the ox-foot struck the wall.

Telemachus rebuked him, and the wooers began to laugh wildly and to weep, they knew not why, but Theoclymenus, the second-sighted man, knew that they were all fey men, that is, doomed to die, for such men are gay without reason. 'Unhappy that you are,' cried Theoclymenus, 'what is coming upon you? I see shrouds covering you about your knees and about your faces, and tears are on your cheeks, and the walls and the pillars of the roof are dripping blood, and in the porch and the court are your fetches, shadows of yourselves, hurrying hellward, and the sun is darkened.'

On this all the wooers laughed, and advised him to go out of doors, where he would see that the sun was shining. 'My eyes and ears serve me well,' said the second-sighted man, 'but out I will go, seeking no more of your company, for death is coming on every man of you.' Then he arose and went to the house of Piraeus, the friend of Telemachus. The wooers laughed all the louder, as fey men do, and told Telemachus that he was unlucky in his guests: one a beggar, the other a madman. But Telemachus kept watching his father while the wooers were cooking a meal that they did not live to enjoy.

Through the crowd of them came Penelope, holding in her hand the great bow of Eurytus, and a quiver full of arrows, while her maidens followed, carrying the chest in which lay the twelve iron axes. She stood up, stately and scornful, among the wooers, and told them that, as marry she must, she would take the man who could string the bow and shoot the arrow through the axes. Telemachus said that he would make the first trial, and that, if he succeeded, he would not allow any man of the wooers to take his mother away with him from her own house. Then thrice he tried to string the bow, and the fourth time he would have strung it, but Ulysses made a sign to him, and he put it down. 'I am too weak,' he said, 'let a stronger man achieve this adventure.' So they tried each in turn, beginning with the man who sat next the great mixing bowl of wine, and so each rising in his turn.

First their prophet tried, Leiodes the Seer, who sat next the bowl, but his white hands were too weak, and he prophesied, saying that the bow would be the death of all of them. Then Antinous bade the goatherd light a fire, and bring grease to heat the bow, and make it more supple. They warmed and greased the bow, and one after another tried to bend it. Eumaeus and the cowherd went out into the court, and Ulysses followed them. 'Whose side would you two take,' he asked, 'if Ulysses came home? Would you fight for him or for the wooers?' 'For Ulysses!' they both cried, 'and would that he was come indeed!' 'He is come, and I am he!' said Ulysses. Then he promised to give them lands of their own if he was victorious, and he showed them the scar on his thigh that the boar dealt with his white tusk, long ago. The two men kissed him and shed tears of joy, and Ulysses said that he would go back first into the hall, and that they were to follow him. He would ask to be allowed to try to bend the bow, and Eumaeus, whatever the wooers said, must place it in his hands, and then see that the women were locked up in their own separate hall. Philoetius was to fasten the door leading from the courtyard into the road. Ulysses then went back to his seat in the hall, near the door, and his servants followed.

Eurymachus was trying in vain to bend the bow, and Antinous proposed to put off the trial till next day, and then sacrifice to the God Apollo, and make fresh efforts. They began to drink, but Ulysses asked to be allowed to try if he could string the bow. They told him that wine had made him impudent, and threatened to put him in a ship and send him to King Echetus, an ogre, who would cut him to pieces. But Penelope said that the beggar must try his strength; not that she would marry him, if he succeeded. She would only give him new clothes, a sword, and a spear, and send him wherever he wanted to go. Telemachus cried out that the bow was his own; he would make a present of it to the beggar if he chose; and he bade his mother join her maidens, and work at her weaving. She was amazed to hear her son speak like the master of the house, and she went upstairs with her maidens to her own room.

Eumaeus was carrying the bow to Ulysses, when the wooers made such an uproar that he laid it down, in fear for his life. But Telemachus threatened to punish him if he did not obey his master, so he placed the bow in the hands of Ulysses, and then went and told Eurycleia to lock the women servants up in their own separate hall. Philoetius slipped into the courtyard, and made the gates fast with a strong rope, and then came back, and watched Ulysses, who was turning the bow this way and that, to see if the horns were still sound, for horns were then used in bow making. The wooers were mocking him, but suddenly he bent and strung the great bow as easily as a harper fastens a new string to his harp. He tried the string, and it twanged like the note of a swallow. He took up an arrow that lay on the table (the others were in the quiver beside him), he fitted it to the string, and from the chair where he sat he shot it through all the twelve axe-heads. 'Your guest has done you no dishonour, Telemachus,' he said, 'but surely it is time to eat,' and he nodded. Telemachus drew his sword, took a spear in his left hand, and stood up beside Ulysses.

– 9 –
THE SLAYING OF THE WOOERS

ULYSSES LET ALL HIS RAGS FALL DOWN, and with one leap he reached the high threshold, the door being behind him, and he dropped the arrows from the quiver at his feet. 'Now,' he said, 'I will strike another mark that no man yet has stricken!' He aimed the arrow at Antinous, who was drinking out of a golden cup. The arrow passed clean through the throat of Antinous; he fell, the cup rang on the ground, and the wooers leaped up, looking round the walls for shields and spears, but the walls were bare.

'Thou shalt die, and vultures shall devour thee,' they shouted, thinking the beggar had let the arrow fly by mischance.

'Dogs!' he answered, 'ye said that never should I come home from Troy; ye wasted my goods, and insulted my wife, and had no fear of the Gods, but now the day of death has come upon you! Fight or flee, if you may, but some shall not escape!'

'Draw your blades!' cried Eurymachus to the others; 'draw your blades, and hold up the tables as shields against this man's arrows. Have at him, and drive him from the doorway.' He drew his own sword, and leaped on Ulysses with a cry, but the swift arrow pierced his breast, and he fell and died. Then Amphinomus rushed towards Ulysses, but Telemachus sent his spear from behind through his shoulders. He could not draw forth the spear, but he ran to his father, and said, 'Let me bring shields, spears, and helmets from the inner chamber, for us, and for the swineherd and cowherd.' 'Go!' said Ulysses, and Telemachus ran through a narrow doorway, down a gallery to the secret chamber, and brought four shields, four helmets, and eight spears, and the men armed themselves, while Ulysses kept shooting down the wooers. When his arrows were spent he armed himself, protected by the other three. But the goatherd, Melanthius, knew a way of reaching the armoury, and he climbed up, and brought twelve helmets, spears, and shields to the wooers.

Ulysses thought that one of the women was showering down the weapons into the hall, but the swineherd and cowherd went to the armoury, through the doorway, as Telemachus had gone, and there they caught Melanthius, and bound him like a bundle, with a rope, and, throwing the rope over a rafter, dragged him up, and fastened him there, and left him swinging. Then they ran back to Ulysses, four men keeping the doorway against all the wooers that were not yet slain. But the Goddess Athene appeared to Ulysses, in the form of Mentor, and gave him courage. He needed it, for the wooers, having spears, threw them in volleys, six at a time, at the four. They missed, but the spears of the four slew each his man. Again the wooers threw, and dealt two or three slight wounds, but the spears of the four were winged with death. They charged, striking with spear and sword, into the crowd, who lost heart, and flew here and there, crying for mercy and falling at every blow. Ulysses slew the prophet, Leiodes, but Phemius, the minstrel, he spared, for he had done no wrong, and Medon, a slave, crept out from beneath an ox hide, where he had been lying, and asked Telemachus to pity him, and Ulysses sent him and the minstrel into the courtyard, where they sat trembling. All the rest of the wooers lay dead in heaps, like heaps of fish on the sea shore, when they have been netted, and drawn to land.

Then Ulysses sent Telemachus to bring Eurycleia, who, when she came and saw the wooers dead, raised a scream of joy, but Ulysses said 'it is an unholy thing to boast over dead men'. He bade Telemachus and the servants carry the corpses into the courtyard, and he made the women wash and clean the hall, and the seats, and tables, and the pillars. When all was clean, they took Melanthius and slew him, and then they washed themselves, and the maidens who were faithful to Penelope came out of their rooms, with torches in their hands, for it was now night, and they kissed Ulysses with tears of joy. These were not young women, for Ulysses remembered all of them.

Meanwhile old Eurycleia ran to tell Penelope all the good news: up the stairs to her chamber she ran, tripping, and falling, and rising, and laughing for joy. In she came and awakened Penelope, saying: 'Come and see what you have long desired: Ulysses in his own house, and all the wicked wooers slain by the sword.' 'Surely you are mad, dear nurse,' said Penelope, 'to waken me with such a wild story. Never have I slept so sound since Ulysses went to that ill Ilios, never to be named. Angry would I have been with any of the girls that wakened me with such a silly story; but you are old: go back to the women's working room.' The good nurse answered: 'Indeed, I tell you no silly tale. Indeed he is in the hall; he is that poor guest whom all men struck and insulted, but Telemachus knew his father.'

Then Penelope leaped up gladly, and kissed the nurse, but yet she was not sure that her husband had come, she feared that it might be some God disguised as a man, or some evil man pretending to be Ulysses. 'Surely Ulysses has met his death far away,' she said, and though Eurycleia vowed that she herself had seen the scar dealt by the boar, long ago, she would not be convinced. 'None the less,' she said, 'let us go and see my son, and the wooers lying dead, and the man who slew them.' So they went down the stairs and along a gallery on the ground floor that led into the courtyard, and so entered the door of the hall, and crossed the high stone threshold on which Ulysses stood when he shot down Antinous. Penelope went up to the hearth and sat opposite Ulysses, who was leaning against one of the four tall pillars that supported the roof; there she sat and gazed at him, still wearing his rags, and still not cleansed from the blood of battle. She did not know him, and was silent, though Telemachus called her hard of belief and cold of heart.

'My child,' she said, 'I am bewildered, and can hardly speak, but if this man is Ulysses, he knows things unknown to any except him and me.' Then Ulysses bade Telemachus go to the baths and wash, and put on fresh garments, and bade the maidens bring the minstrel to play music, while they danced in the hall. In the town the friends and kinsfolk of the wooers did not know that they were dead, and when they heard the music they would not guess that anything strange had happened. It was necessary that nobody should know, for, if the kinsfolk of the dead men learned the truth, they would seek to take revenge, and might burn down the house. Indeed, Ulysses was still in great danger, for the law was that the brothers and cousins of slain men must slay their slayers, and the dead were many, and had many clansmen.

Now Eurynome bathed Ulysses himself, and anointed him with oil, and clad him in new raiment, so that he looked like himself again, full of strength and beauty. He sat down on his own high seat beside the fire, and said: 'Lady, you are the fairest and most cruel Queen alive. No other woman would harden her heart against her husband, come home through many dangers after so many years. Nurse,' he cried to Eurycleia, 'strew me a bed to lie alone, for her heart is hard as iron.'

Now Penelope put him to a trial. 'Eurycleia,' she said, 'strew a bed for him outside the bridal chamber that he built for himself, and bring the good bedstead out of that room for him.'

'How can any man bring out that bedstead?' said Ulysses, 'did I not make it with my own hands, with a standing tree for the bedpost? No man could move that bed unless he first cut down the tree trunk.'

Then at last Penelope ran to Ulysses and threw her arms round his neck, kissing him, and said: 'Do not be angry, for always I have feared that some strange man of cunning would come and deceive me, pretending to be my lord. But now you have told me the secret of the bed, which no mortal has ever seen or knows but you and I, and my maiden whom I brought from my own home, and who kept the doors of our chamber.' Then they embraced, and it seemed as if her white arms would never quite leave their hold on his neck.

Ulysses told her many things, all the story of his wanderings, and how he must wander again, on land, not on the sea, till he came to the country of men who had never seen salt. 'The Gods will defend you and bring you home to your rest in the end,' said Penelope, and then they went to their own chamber, and Eurynome went before them with lighted torches in her hands, for the Gods had brought them to the haven where they would be.

– 10 –

THE END

WITH THE COMING OF THE GOLDEN dawn Ulysses awoke, for he had still much to do. He and Telemachus and the cowherd and Eumaeus put on full armour, and took swords and spears, and walked to the farm where old Laertes, the father of Ulysses, lived among his servants and worked in his garden. Ulysses sent the others into the farmhouse to bid the old housekeeper get breakfast ready, and he went alone to the vines, being sure that his father was at work among them.

There the old man was, in his rough gardening clothes, with leather gloves on, and patched leather leggings, digging hard. His servants had gone to gather loose stones to make a rough stone dyke, and he was all alone. He never looked up till Ulysses went to him, and asked him whose slave he was, and who owned the garden. He said that he was a stranger in Ithaca, but that he had once met the King of the island, who declared that one Laertes was his father.

Laertes was amazed at seeing a warrior all in

mail come into his garden, but said that he was the father of Ulysses, who had long been unheard of and unseen. 'And who are you?' he asked. 'Where is your own country?' Ulysses said that he came from Sicily, and that he had met Ulysses five years ago, and hoped that by this time he had come home.

Then the old man sat down and wept, and cast dust on his head, for Ulysses had not arrived from Sicily in five long years; certainly he must be dead. Ulysses could not bear to see his father weep, and told him that he was himself, come home at last, and that he had killed all the wooers.

But Laertes asked him to prove that he really was Ulysses, so he showed the scar on his leg, and, looking round the garden, he said: 'Come, I will show you the very trees that you gave me when I was a little boy running about after you, and asking you for one thing or another, as children do. These thirteen pear trees are my very own; you gave them to me, and mine are these fifty rows of vines, and these forty fig trees.'

Then Laertes was fainting for joy, but Ulysses caught him in his arms and comforted him. But, when he came to himself, he sighed, and said: 'How shall we meet the feud of all the kin of the slain men in Ithaca and the other islands?' 'Be of good courage, father,' said Ulysses. 'And now let us go to the farmhouse and breakfast with Telemachus.'

So Laertes first went to the baths, and then put on fresh raiment, and Ulysses wondered to see him look so straight and strong. 'Would I were as strong as when I took the castle of Nericus, long ago,' said the old man, 'and would that I had been in the fight against the wooers!' Then all the old man's servants came in, overjoyed at the return of Ulysses, and they breakfasted merrily together.

By this time all the people in the town knew that the wooers had been slain, and they crowded to the house of Ulysses in great sorrow, and gathered their dead and buried them, and then met in the market place. The father of Antinous, Eupeithes, spoke, and said that they would all be dishonoured if they did not slay Ulysses before he could escape to Nestor's house in Pylos. It was in vain that an old prophet told them that the young men had deserved their death. The most of the men ran home and put on armour, and Eupeithes led them towards the farm of Laertes, all in shining mail. But the Gods in heaven had a care for Ulysses, and sent Athene to make peace between him and his subjects.

She did not come too soon, for the avengers were drawing near the farmhouse, which had a garrison of only twelve men: Ulysses, Laertes, Telemachus, the swineherd, the cowherd, and servants of Laertes. They all armed themselves, and not choosing to defend the house, they went boldly out to meet their enemies. They encouraged each other, and Laertes prayed to Athene, and then threw his spear at Eupeithes. The spear passed clean through helmet and through head, and Eupeithes fell with a crash, and his armour rattled as he fell. But now Athene appeared, and cried: 'Hold your hands, ye men of Ithaca, that no more blood may be shed, and peace may be made.' The foes of Ulysses, hearing the terrible voice of the Goddess, turned and fled, and Ulysses uttered his war-cry, and was rushing among them, when a thunderbolt fell at his feet, and Athene bade him stop, lest he should anger Zeus, the Lord of Thunder. Gladly he obeyed, and peace was made with oaths and with sacrifice, peace in Ithaca and the islands.

Here ends the story of Ulysses, Laertes' son, for we do not know anything about his adventures when he went to seek a land of men who never heard of the sea, nor eat meat savoured with salt.

THE FLEECE OF GOLD

– I –

THE CHILDREN OF THE CLOUD

WHOLE TROY STILL STOOD FAST, AND before King Priam was born, there was a king called Athamas, who reigned in a country beside the Grecian sea. Athamas was a young man, and was unmarried; because none of the princesses who then lived seemed to him beautiful enough to be his wife. One day he left his palace and climbed high up into a mountain, following the course of a little river. He came to a place where a great black rock stood on one side of the river, jutting into the stream. Round the rock the water flowed deep and dark. Yet, through the noise of the river, the King thought he heard laughter and voices like the voices of girls. So he climbed very quietly up the back of the rock, and, looking over the edge, there he saw three beautiful maidens bathing in a pool, and splashing each other with the water. Their long yellow hair covered them like cloaks and floated behind them on the pool. One of them was even more beautiful than the others, and as soon as he saw her the King fell in love with her, and said to himself, 'This is the wife for me.'

As he thought this, his arm touched a stone, which slipped from the top of the rock where he lay, and went leaping, faster and faster as it fell, till it dropped with a splash into the pool below. Then the three maidens heard it, and were frightened, thinking someone was near. So they rushed out of the pool to the grassy bank where their clothes lay, lovely soft clothes, white and grey, and rosy-coloured, all shining with pearl drops, and diamonds like dew.

In a moment they had dressed, and then it was as if they had wings, for they rose gently from the ground, and floated softly up and up the windings of the brook. Here and there among the green tops of the mountain-ash trees the King could just see the white robes shining and disappearing, and shining again, till they rose far off like a mist, and so up and up into the sky, and at last he only followed them with his eyes, as they floated like clouds among the other clouds across the blue. All day he watched them, and at sunset he saw them sink, golden and rose-coloured and purple, and go down into the dark with the setting sun.

The King went home to his palace, but he was

very unhappy, and nothing gave him any pleasure. All day he roamed about among the hills, and looked for the beautiful girls, but he never found them, and all night he dreamed about them, till he grew thin and pale and was like to die.

Now, the way with sick men then was that they made a pilgrimage to the temple of a God, and in the temple they offered sacrifices. Then they hoped that the God would appear to them in a dream, or send them a true dream at least, and tell them how they might be made well again. So the King drove in his chariot a long way, to the town where this temple was. When he reached it, he found it a strange place. The priests were dressed in dogs' skins, with the heads of the dogs drawn down over their faces, and there were live dogs running all about the shrines, for they were the favourite beasts of the God, whose name was Asclepius. There was an image of him, with a dog crouched at his feet, and in his hand he held a serpent, and fed it from a bowl.

The King sacrificed before the God, and when night fell he was taken into the temple, and there were many beds strewn on the floor and many people lying on them, both rich and poor, hoping that the God would appear to them in a dream, and tell them how they might be healed. There the King lay, like the rest, and for long he could not close his eyes. At length he slept, and he dreamed a dream. But it was not the God of the temple that he saw in his dream; he saw a beautiful lady, she seemed to float above him in a chariot drawn by doves, and all about her was a crowd of chattering sparrows, and he knew that she was Aphrodite, the Queen of Love. She was more beautiful than any woman in the world, and she smiled as she looked at the King, and said, 'Oh, King Athamas, you are sick for love! Now this you must do: go home and on the first night of the new moon, climb the hills to that place where you saw the Three Maidens. In the dawn they will come again to the river, and bathe in the pool. Then do you creep out of the wood, and steal the clothes of her you love, and she will not be able to fly away with the rest, and she will be your wife.'

Then she smiled again, and her doves bore her away, and the King woke, and remembered the dream, and thanked the lady in his heart, for he knew that she was a Goddess, the Queen of Love.

Then he drove home, and did all that he had been told to do. On the first night of the new moon, when she shines like a thin gold thread in the sky, he left his palace, and climbed up through the hills, and hid in the wood by the edge of the pool. When the dawn began to shine silvery, he heard voices, and saw the three girls come floating through the trees, and alight on the river bank, and undress, and run into the water. There they bathed, and splashed each other with the water, laughing in their play. Then he stole to the grassy bank, and seized the clothes of the most beautiful of the three; and they heard him move, and rushed out to their clothes. Two of them were clad in a moment, and floated away up the glen, but the third crouched sobbing and weeping under the thick cloak of her yellow hair. Then she prayed the King to give her back her soft grey and rose-coloured raiment, but he would not till she had promised to be his wife. And he told her how long he had loved her, and how the Goddess had sent him to be her husband, and at last she promised, and took his hand, and in her shining robes went down the hill with him to the palace. But he felt as if he walked on the air, and she scarcely seemed to touch the ground with her feet. She told him that her name was Nephele, which meant 'a cloud', in their language, and that she was one of the Cloud Fairies who bring the rain, and live on the hilltops, and in the high lakes, and water springs, and in the sky.

So they were married, and lived very happily, and had two children, a boy called Phrixus, and a daughter named Helle. The two children had a beautiful pet, a Ram with a fleece all of gold, which was given them by the young God called Hermes, a beautiful God, with wings on his shoon – for these were the very Shoon of Swiftness, that he lent afterwards to the boy, Perseus, who slew the Gorgon, and took her head. This Ram the children used to play with, and they would ride on his back, and roll about with him on the flowery meadows.

They would all have been happy, but for one thing. When there were clouds in the sky, and when there was rain, then their mother, Nephele, was always with them; but when the summer days were hot and cloudless, then she went away, they did not know where. The long dry days made her grow pale and thin, and, at last, she would vanish altogether, and never come again, till the sky grew soft and grey with rain.

King Athamas grew weary of this, for often his wife would be long away. Besides there was a very beautiful girl called Ino a dark girl, who had come in a ship of Phoenician merchantmen, and had stayed in the city of the King when her friends sailed from Greece. The King saw her, and often she would be at the palace, playing with the children when their mother had disappeared with the Clouds, her sisters.

This Ino was a witch, and one day she put a drug into the King's wine, and when he had drunk it, he quite forgot Nephele, his wife, and fell in love with Ino. At last he married her, and they had two children, a boy and a girl, and Ino wore the crown, and was Queen, and gave orders that Nephele should never be allowed to enter the palace any more. So Phrixus and Helle never saw their mother, and they were dressed in ragged old skins of deer, and were ill fed, and were set to do hard work in the house, while the children of Ino wore gold crowns in their hair, and were dressed in fine raiment, and had the best of everything.

One day when Phrixus and Helle were in the field, herding the sheep (for now they were treated like peasant children, and had to work for their bread), they met an old woman, all wrinkled, and poorly clothed, and they took pity on her, and brought her home with them. Queen Ino saw her, and as she wanted a nurse for her own children, she took her in to be the nurse, and the old woman had charge of the children, and lived in the house, and she was kind to Phrixus and Helle. But neither of them knew that she was their own mother, Nephele, who had disguised herself as an old woman and a servant, that she might be with her children.

Phrixus and Helle grew strong and tall, and more beautiful than Ino's children, so she hated them, and determined, at last, to kill them. They all slept at night in one room, but Ino's children had gold crowns in their hair, and beautiful coverlets on their beds. One night, Phrixus was half-awake, and he heard the old nurse come, in the dark, and put something on his head, and on his sister's, and change their coverlets. But he was so drowsy that he half thought it was a dream, and he lay and fell asleep. In the dead of night, the wicked stepmother, Ino, crept into the room with a dagger in her hand, and she stole up to the bed of Phrixus, and felt his hair, and his coverlet. Then she went softly to the bed of Helle, and felt her coverlet, and her hair with the gold crown on it. So she supposed these to be her own children, and she kissed them in the dark, and went to the beds of the other two children. She felt their heads, and they had no crowns on, so she killed them, supposing that they were Phrixus and Helle. Then she crept downstairs and went back to bed.

In the morning, there lay the stepmother Ino's children cold and dead, and nobody knew who had killed them. Only the wicked Queen knew, and she, of course, would not tell of herself, but if she hated Phrixus and Helle before, now she hated them a hundred times worse than ever. But the old nurse was gone; nobody ever saw her there again, and everybody but the Queen thought that *she* had killed the two children. Everywhere the King sought for her, to burn her alive, but he never found her, for she had gone back to her sisters, the Clouds.

And the Clouds were gone, too! For six long months, from winter to harvest time, the rain never fell. The country was burned up, the trees grew black and dry, there was no water in the streams, the corn turned yellow and died before it was come into the ear. The people were starving, the cattle and sheep were perishing, for there was no grass. And every day the sun rose hot and red, and went blazing through the sky without a cloud.

Here the wicked stepmother, Ino, saw her chance. The King sent messengers to Pytho, to consult the prophetess, and to find out what should be done to bring back the clouds and the rain. Then Ino took the messengers, before they set out on their journey, and gave them gold, and threatened also to kill them, if they did not bring the message she wished from the prophetess. Now this message was that Phrixus and Helle must be burned as a sacrifice to the Gods.

So the messengers went, and came back dressed in mourning. And when they were brought before the King, at first they would tell him nothing. But he commanded them to speak, and then they told him, not the real message from the prophetess, but what Ino had bidden them to say: that Phrixus and Helle must be offered as a sacrifice to appease the Gods.

The King was very sorrowful at this news, but he could not disobey the Gods. So poor Phrixus and

Helle were wreathed with flowers, as sheep used to be when they were led to be sacrificed, and they were taken to the altar, all the people following and weeping, and the Golden Ram went between them, as they walked to the temple. Then they came within sight of the sea, which lay beneath the cliff where the temple stood, all glittering in the sun, and the happy white sea-birds flying over it.

Here the Ram stopped, and suddenly he spoke to Phrixus, for the God gave him utterance, and said: 'Lay hold of my horn, and get on my back, and let Helle climb up behind you, and I will carry you far away.'

Then Phrixus took hold of the Ram's horn, and Helle mounted behind him, and grasped the Golden Fleece, and suddenly the Ram rose in the air, and flew above the people's heads, far away over the sea.

Far away to the eastward he flew, and deep below them they saw the sea, and the islands, and the white towers and temples, and the fields, and ships. Eastwards always he went, towards the rising sun, and Helle grew dizzy and weary. At last a deep sleep came over her, and she let go her hold of the Fleece, and fell from the Ram's back, down and down, into the narrow seas, that run between Europe and Asia, and there she was drowned. And that strait is called Helle's Ford, or Hellespont, to this day.

But Phrixus and the Ram flew on up the narrow seas, and over the great sea which the Greeks called the Euxine and we call the Black Sea, till they reached a country named Colchis. There the Ram alighted, so tired and weary that he died, and Phrixus had his beautiful Golden Fleece stripped off, and hung on an oak tree in a dark wood. And there it was guarded by a monstrous dragon, so that nobody dared to go near it. And Phrixus married the King's daughter, and lived long, till he died also, and a King called Aeëtes, the brother of the enchantress, Circe, ruled that country. Of all the things he had, the rarest was the Golden Fleece, and it became a proverb that nobody could take that Fleece away, nor deceive the dragon who guarded it.

– 2 –

THE SEARCH FOR THE FLEECE

SOME YEARS AFTER THE GOLDEN RAM DIED in Colchis, far across the sea, a certain King reigned in Iolcos in Greece, and his name was Pelias. He was not the rightful king, for he had turned his stepbrother, King Aeson, from the throne, and taken it for himself. Now, Aeson had a son, a boy called Jason, and he sent him far away from Pelias, up into the mountains. In these hills there was a great cave, and in that cave lived Chiron the Wise, who, the story says, was half a horse. He had the head and breast of a man, but a horse's body and legs. He was famed for knowing more about everything than anyone else in all Greece. He knew about the stars, and the plants of earth, which were good for medicine and which were poisonous. He was the best archer with the bow, and the best player of the harp; he could sing songs and tell stories of old times, for he was the last of a people, half horse and half man, who had dwelt in ancient days on the hills. Therefore the Kings in Greece sent their sons to him to be taught shooting, singing, and telling the truth, and that was all the teaching they had then, except that they learned to hunt, fish, and fight, and throw spears, and toss the hammer and the stone. There Jason lived with Chiron and the boys in the cave, and many of the boys became famous.

There was Orpheus who played the harp so sweetly that wild beasts followed his minstrelsy, and even the trees danced after him, and settled where he stopped playing. There was Mopsus who could understand what the birds say to each other; and there was Butes, the handsomest of men; and Tiphys, the best steersman of a ship; and Castor, with his brother Polydeuces, the boxer. Heracles, too, the strongest man in the whole world, was there; and Lynceus, whom they called Keen-Eye, because he could see so far, and could see even the dead men in their graves under the earth. There was Euphemus, so swift and light-footed that he could run upon the grey sea and never wet his feet; and there were Calais and Zetes, the two sons of the North Wind, with golden wings upon their feet. There also was Peleus, who later married Thetis of the silver feet, Goddess of the Sea Foam, and was the father of Achilles. Many others were there whose names it would take too long to tell. They all grew up together in the hills good friends, healthy, and brave, and strong. And they all went out to their own homes at last; but Jason had no home to go to, for his uncle, Pelias, had taken it, and his father was a wanderer.

So at last he wearied of being alone, and he said goodbye to his teacher, and went down through the hills toward Iolcos, his father's old home, where his wicked uncle Pelias was reigning. As he went, he came to a great, flooded river, running red from bank to bank, rolling the round boulders along. And there on the bank was an old woman sitting.

'Cannot you cross, mother?' said Jason; and she said she could not, but must wait until the flood fell, for there was no bridge.

'I'll carry you across,' said Jason, 'if you will let me carry you.'

So she thanked him, and said it was a kind deed, for she was longing to reach the cottage where her little grandson lay sick.

Then he knelt down, and she climbed upon his back, and he used his spear for a staff, and stepped into the river. It was deeper than he thought, and stronger, but at last he staggered out on the farther bank, far below where he went in. And then he set the old woman down.

'Bless you, my lad, for a strong man and a brave!'

she said, 'and my blessing go with you to the world's end.'

Then he looked and she was gone he did not know where, for she was the greatest of the Goddesses, Hera, the wife of Zeus, who had taken the shape of an old woman, to try Jason, whether he was kind and strong, or rude and churlish. From this day her grace went with him, and she helped him in all dangers.

Then Jason went down limping to the city, for he had lost one shoe in the flood. And when he reached the town he went straight up to the palace, and through the court, and into the open door, and up the hall, where the King was sitting at his table among his men. There Jason stood, leaning on his spear.

When the King saw him he turned white with terror. For he had been told by the prophetess of Pytho that a man with only one shoe would come someday and take away his kingdom. And here was the half-shod man of whom the prophecy had spoken.

But Pelias still remembered to be courteous, and he bade his men lead the stranger to the baths, and there the attendants bathed him, pouring hot water over him. And they anointed his head with oil, and clothed him in new raiment, and brought him back to the hall, and set him down at a table beside the King, and gave him meat and drink.

When he had eaten and was refreshed, the king said: 'Now it is time to ask the stranger who he is, and who his parents are, and whence he comes to Iolcos?'

And Jason answered, 'I am Jason, son of the rightful King, Aeson, and I am come to take back my kingdom.'

The King grew pale again, but he was cunning, and he leaped up and embraced the lad, and made much of him, and caused a gold circlet to be twisted in his hair. Then he said he was old, and weary of judging the people. 'And weary work it is,' he said, 'and no joy therewith shall any King have. For there is a curse on the country, that shall not be taken away till the Fleece of Gold is brought home, from the land of the world's end. The ghost of Phrixus stands by my bedside every night, wailing and will not be comforted, till the Fleece is brought home again.'

When Jason heard that he cried, 'I shall take the curse away, for by the splendour of Lady Hera's brow, I shall bring the Fleece of Gold from the land of the world's end before I sit on the throne of my father.'

Now this was the very thing that the King wished, for he thought that if once Jason went after the Fleece, certainly he would never come back living to Iolcos. So he said that it could never be done, for the land was far away across the sea, so far that the birds could not come and go in one year, so great a sea was that and perilous. Also, there was a dragon that guarded the Fleece of Gold, and no man could face it and live.

But the idea of fighting a dragon was itself a temptation to Jason, and he made a great vow by the water of Styx, an oath the very Gods feared to break, that certainly he would bring home that Fleece to Iolcos. And he sent out messengers all over Greece, to all his old friends, who were with him in the Centaur's cave, and bade them come and help him, for that there was a dragon to kill, and that there would be fighting. And they all came, driving in their chariots down dales and across hills: Heracles, the strong man, with the bow that none other could bend; and Orpheus with his harp, and Castor and Polydeuces, and Zetes and Calais of the golden wings, and Tiphys, the steersman, and young Hylas, still a boy, and as fair as a girl, who always went with Heracles the strong.

These came, and many more, and they set shipbuilders to work, and oaks were felled for beams, and ashes for oars, and spears were made, and arrows feathered, and swords sharpened. But in the prow of the ship they placed a bough of an oak tree from the forest of Zeus in Dodona where the trees can speak, and that bough spoke, and prophesied things to come. They called the ship *Argo*, and they launched her, and put bread, and meat, and wine on board, and hung their shields outside the bulwarks. Then they said goodbye to their friends, went aboard, sat down at the oars, set sail, and so away eastward to Colchis, in the land of the world's end.

All day they rowed, and at night they beached the ship, as was then the custom, for they did not sail at night, and they went on shore, and took supper, and slept, and next day to the sea again. And old Chiron, the man-horse, saw the swift ship from his mountain heights, and ran down to the beach; there he stood with the waves of the gray sea breaking over his feet, waving with his mighty hands, and wishing his boys a safe return. And his wife stood beside him, holding in her arms the little son of one of the ship's company, Achilles, the son of Peleus of the Spear, and of Thetis the Goddess of the Sea Foam.

So they rowed ever eastward, and ere long they came to a strange isle where dwelt men with six hands apiece, unruly giants. And these giants lay in wait for them on cliffs above the river's mouth where the ship was moored, and before the dawn they rolled down great rocks on the crew. But Heracles drew his huge bow, the bow for which he slew Eurytus, King of Oechalia, and wherever a giant showed hand or shoulder above the cliff, he pinned him through with an arrow, till all were slain. After that they still held eastward, passing many islands, and towns of men, till they reached Mysia, and the Asian shore. Here they landed, with bad luck. For while they were cutting reeds and grass to strew their beds on the sands, young Hylas, beautiful Hylas, went off with a pitcher in his hand to draw water. He came to a beautiful spring, a deep, clear, green pool, and there the water fairies lived, whom men called Nereids. There were Eunis, and Nycheia with her April eyes, and when they saw the beautiful Hylas, they longed to have him always with them, to live in the crystal caves beneath the water, for they had never seen anyone so beautiful. As he stooped with his pitcher and dipped it into the stream, they caught him softly in their arms, and drew him down below, and no man ever saw him any more, but he dwelt with the water fairies.

But Heracles the strong, who loved him like a younger brother, wandered all over the country crying '*Hylas! Hylas!*' and the boy's voice answered so faintly from below the stream that Heracles never heard him. So he roamed alone in the forests, and the rest of the crew thought he was lost.

Then the sons of the North Wind were angry, and bade them set sail without him, and sail they did, leaving the strong man behind. Long afterwards, when the Fleece was won, Heracles met the sons of the North Wind, and slew them with his arrows. And he buried them, and set a great stone on each grave, and one of these is ever stirred, and shakes when the North Wind blows. There they lie, and their golden wings are at rest.

Still they sped on, with a west wind blowing, and they came to a country whose King was strong, and thought himself the best boxer then living, so he came down to the ship and challenged anyone of that crew; and Polydeuces, the boxer, took up the challenge. All the rest, and the people of the country, made a ring, and Polydeuces and huge King Amycus stepped into the midst, and put up their hands. First they moved round each other cautiously, watching for a chance, and then, as the sun shone forth in the Giant's face, Polydeuces leaped in and struck him between the eyes with his left hand, and, strong as he was, the Giant staggered and fell. Then his friends picked him up, and sponged his face with water, and all the crew of *Argo* shouted with joy. He was soon on his feet again, and rushed at Polydeuces, hitting out so hard that he would have killed him if the blow had gone home. But Polydeuces just moved his head a little on one side, and the blow went by, and, as the Giant slipped, Polydeuces planted one in his mouth and another beneath his ear, and was away before the Giant could recover.

There they stood, breathing heavily, and glaring at each other, till the Giant made another rush, but Polydeuces avoided him, and struck him several blows quickly in the eyes, and now the Giant was almost blind. Then Polydeuces at once ended the combat by a right-hand blow on the temple. The Giant fell, and lay as if he were dead. When he came to himself again, he had no heart to go on, for his knees shook, and he could hardly see. So Polydeuces made him swear never to challenge strangers again as long as he lived, and then the crew of *Argo* crowned Polydeuces with a wreath of poplar leaves, and they took supper, and Orpheus sang to them, and they slept, and next day they came to the country of the unhappiest of Kings.

His name was Phineus, and he was a prophet; but, when he came to meet Jason and his company, he seemed more like the ghost of a beggar than a crowned King. For he was blind, and very old, and he wandered like a dream, leaning on a staff, and feeling the wall with his hand. His limbs all trembled, he was but a thing of skin and bone, and foul and filthy to see. At last he reached the doorway of the house where Jason was, and sat down, with his purple cloak fallen round him, and he held up his skinny hands, and welcomed Jason, for, being a prophet, he knew that now he should be delivered from his wretchedness.

He lived, or rather lingered, in all this misery because he had offended the Gods, and had told men what things were to happen in the future beyond what the Gods desired that men should know. So they blinded him, and they sent against him hideous monsters with wings and crooked claws, called Harpies, which fell upon him at his meat, and carried it away before he could put it to his mouth. Sometimes they flew off with all the meat; sometimes they left a little, that he might not quite starve, and die, and be at peace, but might live in misery. Yet what they left was made so foul, and of such evil savour, that even a starving man could scarcely take it within his lips. Thus this King was the most miserable of all men living.

He welcomed the heroes, and, above all, Zetes and Calais, the sons of the North Wind, for they, he knew, would help him. And they all went into his wretched, naked hall, and sat down at the tables, and the servants brought meat and drink and placed it before them, the latest and last supper of the Harpies. Then down on the meat swooped the Harpies, like lightning or wind, with clanging brazen wings, and iron claws, and the smell of a battlefield where men lie dead; down they swooped, and flew shrieking away with the food. But the two sons of the North Wind drew their short swords, and rose in the air on their golden wings, and followed where the Harpies fled, over many a sea and many a land, till they came to a distant isle, and there they slew the Harpies with their swords. And that isle was called 'Turn Again', for there the sons of the North Wind turned, and it was late in the night when they came back to the hall of Phineus, and to their companions.

Here Phineus was telling Jason and his company how they might win their way to Colchis and the world's end, and the wood of the Fleece of Gold. 'First,' he said, 'you shall come in your ship to the Rocks Wandering, for these rocks wander like living things in the sea, and no ship has ever sailed between them. They open, like a great mouth, to let ships pass, and when she is between their lips they clash again, and crush her in their iron jaws. By this way even winged things may never pass; nay, not even the doves that bear ambrosia to Father Zeus, the Lord of Olympus, but the rocks ever catch one even of these. So, when you come near them, you must let loose a dove from the ship, and let her go before you to try the way. And if she flies safely between the rocks from one sea to the other sea, then row with all your might when the rocks open again. But if the rocks close on the bird, then return, and do not try the adventure. But, if you win safely through, then hold right on to the mouth of the river Phasis, and there you shall see the towers of Aeëtes, the King, and the grove of the Fleece of Gold. And then do as well as you may.'

So they thanked him, and the next morning they set sail, till they came to a place where the Rocks Wandering wallowed in the water, and all was foam; but when the Rocks leaped apart the stream ran swift, and the waves roared beneath the rocks, and the wet cliffs bellowed. Then Euphemus took the dove in his hands, and set her free, and she flew straight at the pass where the rocks met, and sped right through, and the rocks gnashed like gnashing teeth, but they caught only a feather from her tail.

Then slowly the rocks opened again, like a wild beast's mouth that opens, and Tiphys, the helmsman, shouted, 'Row on, hard all!' and he held the ship straight for the pass. Then the oars bent like bows in the hands of men, and the good ship leaped at the stroke. Three strokes they pulled, and at each the ship leaped, and now they were within the black jaws of the rocks, the water boiling round them, and so dark it was that overhead they could see the stars, but the oarsmen could not see the daylight behind them, and the steersman could not see the daylight in front. Then the great tide rushed in between the rocks like a rushing river, and lifted the ship as if it were lifted by a hand, and through the strait she passed like a bird, and the rocks clashed, and only broke the carved wood of the ship's stern. And the ship reeled into the seething sea beyond, and all the men of Jason bowed their heads over their oars, half-dead with the fierce rowing.

Then they set all sail, and the ship sped merrily on, past the shores of the inner sea, past bays and towns, and river mouths, and round green hills, the tombs of men slain long ago. And, behold, on the top of one mound stood a tall man, clad in rusty armour, and with a broken sword in his hand, and on his head a helmet with a blood-red crest. Thrice he waved his hand, and thrice he shouted aloud, and was no more seen, for this was the ghost of Sthenelus, Actaeon's son, whom an arrow had slain there long since, and he had come forth from his tomb to see men of his own blood, and to greet Jason and his company. So they anchored there, and slew sheep in sacrifice, and poured blood and wine on the grave of Sthenelus. There Orpheus left a harp, placing it in the bough of a tree, that the wind might sing in the chords, and make music to Sthenelus below the earth.

Then they sailed on, and at evening they saw

above their heads the snowy crests of Mount Caucasus, flushed in the sunset; and high in the air they saw, as it were, a black speck that grew greater and greater, and fluttered black wings, and then fell sheer down like a stone. Then they heard a dreadful cry from a valley of the mountain, for there Prometheus was fastened to the rock, and the eagles fed upon him, because he stole fire from the Gods, and gave it to men. All the heroes shuddered when they heard his cry; but not long after Heracles came that way, and he slew the eagle with his bow, and set Prometheus free.

But at nightfall they came into the wide mouth of the river Phasis, that flows through the land of the world's end, and they saw the lights burning in the palace of Aeëtes the King. So now they were come to the last stage of their journey, and there they slept, and dreamed of the Fleece of Gold.

– 3 –

THE WINNING OF THE FLEECE

NEXT MORNING THE HEROES AWOKE, AND left the ship moored in the river's mouth, hidden by tall reeds, for they took down the mast, lest it should be seen. Then they walked towards the city of Colchis, and they passed through a strange and horrible wood. Dead men, bound together with cords, were hanging from the branches, for the Colchis people buried women, but hung dead men from the branches of trees. Then they came to the palace, where King Aeëtes lived, with his young son Absyrtus, and his daughter Chalciope, who had been the wife of Phrixus, and his younger daughter, Medea, who was a witch, and the priestess of Brimo, a dreadful Goddess. Now Chalciope came out and welcomed Jason, for she knew the heroes were of her dear husband's country. And beautiful Medea, the dark witch-girl, came forth and saw Jason, and as soon as she saw him she loved him more than her father and her brother and all her father's house. For his bearing was gallant, and his armour golden, and long yellow hair fell over his shoulders, and over the leopard skin that he wore above his armour. Medea turned white and then red, and cast down her eyes, but Chalciope took the heroes to the baths, and gave them food, and they were brought to Aeëtes, who asked them why they came, and they told him that they desired the Fleece of Gold, and he was very angry, and told them that only to a better man than himself would he give up that Fleece. If any wished to prove himself worthy of it he must tame two bulls which breathed flame from their nostrils, and must plough four acres with these bulls, and next he must sow the field with thc teeth of a dragon, and these teeth when sown would immediately grow up into armed men. Jason said that, as it must be, he would try this adventure, but he went sadly enough back to the ship and did not notice how kindly Medea was looking after him as he went.

Now, in the dead of night, Medea could not sleep, because she was so sorry for the stranger, and she knew that she could help him by her magic. But she remembered how her father would burn her for a witch if she helped Jason, and a great shame, too, came on her that she should prefer a stranger to her own people. So she arose in the dark, and stole just as she was to her sister's room, a white figure roaming like a ghost in the palace. At her sister's door she turned back in shame, saying, 'No, I will never do it,' and she went back again to her chamber, and came again, and knew not what to do; but at last she returned to her own bower, and threw herself on her bed, and wept. Her sister heard her weeping, and came to her and they cried together, but softly, that no one might hear them. For Chalciope was as eager to help the Greeks for love of Phrixus, her dead husband, as Medea was for the love of Jason.

At last Medea promised to carry to the temple of the Goddess of whom she was a priestess, a drug that would tame the bulls which dwelt in the field of that temple. But still she wept and wished that she were dead, and had a mind to slay herself; yet, all the time, she was longing for the dawn, that she might go and see Jason, and give him the drug, and see his face once more, if she was never to see him again. So, at dawn she bound up her hair, and bathed her face, and took the drug, which was pressed from a flower. That flower first blossomed when the eagle shed the blood of Prometheus on the earth. The virtue of the juice of the flower was this, that if a man anointed himself with it, he could not that day be wounded by swords, and fire could not burn him. So she placed it in a vial beneath her girdle, and she went with other girls, her friends, to the temple of the Goddess. Now Jason had been warned by Chalciope to meet her there, and he was coming with Mopsus who knew the speech of birds. But Mopsus heard a crow that sat on a poplar tree speaking to another crow, saying: 'Here comes a silly prophet, and sillier than a goose. He is walking with a young man to meet a maid, and does not know that, while he is there to hear, the maid will not say a word that is in her heart. Go away, foolish prophet; it is not you she cares for.'

Then Mopsus smiled, and stopped where he was; but Jason went on, where Medea was pretending to play with the girls, her companions. When she saw Jason she felt as if she could neither go forward, nor go back, and she was very pale. But Jason told her not to be afraid, and asked her to help him, but for long she could not answer him; however, at the last, she gave him the drug, and taught him how to use it. 'So shall you carry the Fleece to Iolcos, far away, but what is it to me where you go when you have gone from here? Still remember the name of me, Medea, as I shall remember you. And may there come to me some voice, or some bird bearing the message, whenever you have quite forgotten me.'

But Jason answered, 'Lady, let the winds blow what voice they will, and what that bird will, let him bring. But no wind or bird shall ever bear the news that I have forgotten you, if you will cross the sea with me, and be my wife.'

Then she was glad, and yet she was afraid, at the thought of that dark voyage, with a stranger, from her father's home and her own. So they parted, Jason to the ship, and Medea to the palace. But in the morning Jason anointed himself and his armour with the drug, and all the heroes struck at him with spears and swords, but the swords would not bite on him nor on his armour. He felt so strong and light that he leaped in the air with joy, and the sun shone on his glittering shield. Now they all went up together to the field where the bulls were breathing flame. There already was Aeëtes, with Medea, and all the Colchians had come to see Jason die. A plough had been brought to which he was to harness the bulls. Then he walked up to them, and they blew fire at him that flamed all round him, but the magic drug protected him. He took a horn of one bull in his right hand, and a horn of the other in his left, and dashed their heads together so mightily that they fell.

When they rose, all trembling, he yoked them to the plough, and drove them with his spear, till all the field was ploughed in straight ridges and furrows. Then he dipped his helmet in the river, and drank water, for he was weary; and next he sowed the dragon's teeth on the right and left. Then you might see spear-points, and sword points, and crests of helmets break up from the soil like shoots of corn, and presently the earth was shaken like sea waves, as armed men leaped out of the furrows, all furious for battle, and all rushed to slay Jason. But he, as Medea had told him to do, caught up a great rock, and threw it among them, and he who was struck by the rock said to his neighbour, 'You struck me; take that!' and ran his spear through that man's breast, but before he could draw it out another man had cleft his helmet with a stroke, and so it went: an hour of striking and shouting, while the sparks of fire sprang up from helmet and breastplate and shield. The farrows ran red with blood, and wounded men crawled on hands and knees to strike or stab those that were yet standing and fighting. So axes and sword and spear flashed and fell, till now all the men were down but one, taller and stronger than the rest. Round him he looked, and saw only Jason standing there, and he staggered towards him, bleeding, and lifting his great axe above his head. But Jason only stepped aside from the blow which would have cloven him to the waist, the last blow of the Men of the Dragon's Teeth, for he who struck fell, and there he lay and died.

Then Jason went to the King, where he sat looking darkly on, and said, 'O King, the field is ploughed, the seed is sown, the harvest is reaped. Give me now the Fleece of Gold, and let me be gone.' But the King said, 'Enough is done. Tomorrow is a new day. Tomorrow shall you win the Fleece.'

Then he looked sidewise at Medea, and she knew that he suspected her, and she was afraid.

Aeëtes went and sat brooding over his wine with the captains of his people; and his mood was bitter, both for loss of the Fleece, and because Jason had won it not by his own prowess, but by the magic aid of Medea. As for Medea herself, it was the King's purpose to put her to a cruel death, and this she needed not her witchery to know, and a fire was in her eyes, and terrible sounds were ringing in her ears, and it seemed she had but two choices: to drink poison and die, or to flee with the heroes in the ship *Argo*. But at last flight seemed better than death. So she hid all her engines of witchcraft in the folds of her gown, and she kissed her bed where she would never sleep again, and the posts of the door, and she caressed the very walls with her hand in that last farewell. And she cut a long lock of her yellow hair, and left it in the room, a keepsake to her mother dear, in memory of her maiden days. 'Goodbye, my mother,' she said, 'this long lock I leave thee in place of me; goodbye, a long goodbye, to me who am going on a long journey; goodbye, my sister Chalciope, goodbye! dear house, goodbye!'

Then she stole from the house, and the bolted doors leaped open at their own accord at the swift spell Medea murmured. With her bare feet she ran down the grassy paths, and the daisies looked black against the white feet of Medea. So she sped to the temple of the Goddess, and the moon overhead looked down on her. Many a time had she darkened the moon's face with her magic song, and now the Lady Moon gazed white upon her, and said, 'I am not, then, the only one that wanders in the night for love, as I love Endymion the sleeper, who sleeps on the crest of the Latmian hill, and beholds me in his dreams. Many a time hast thou darkened my face with thy songs, and made night black with thy sorceries, and now thou too art in love! So go thy way, and bid thy heart endure, for a sore fate is before thee!'

But Medea hastened on till she came to the high river bank, and saw the heroes, merry at their wine in the light of a blazing fire. Thrice she called aloud, and they heard her, and came to her, and she said, 'Save me, my friends, for all is known, and my death is sure. And I will give you the Fleece of Gold for the price of my life.'

Then Jason swore that she should be his wife, and more dear to him than all the world. So she went aboard their boat, and swiftly they rowed up stream to the dark wood where the dragon who never sleeps lay guarding the Fleece of Gold. There she landed, and Jason, and Orpheus with his harp, and through the wood they went, but that old serpent saw them coming, and hissed so loud that women wakened in Colchis town, and children cried to their mothers. But Orpheus struck softly on his harp, and he sang a hymn to Sleep, bidding him come and cast a slumber on the dragon's wakeful eyes. This was the song he sang:

'Sleep! King of Gods and men!
Come to my call again,
Swift over field and fen,
  Mountain and deep:
Come, bid the waves be still;
Sleep, streams on height and hill;
Beasts, birds, and snakes, thy will
  Conquereth, Sleep!
Come on thy golden wings,
Come ere the swallow sings,
Lulling all living things,
  Fly they or creep!
Come with thy leaden wand,
Come with thy kindly hand,
Soothing on sea or land
  Mortals that weep.

Come from the cloudy west,
Soft over brain and breast,
Bidding the Dragon rest,
  Come to me, Sleep!'

This was Orpheus's song, and he sang so sweetly that the bright, small eyes of the dragon closed, and all his hard coils softened and uncurled. Then Jason set his foot on the dragon's neck and hewed off his head, and lifted down the Golden Fleece from the sacred oak tree, and it shone like a golden cloud at dawn. He waited not to wonder at it, but he and Medea and Orpheus hurried through the wet wood paths to the ship, and threw it on board, cast a cloak over it, and bade the heroes sit down to the oars, half of them, but the others to take their shields and stand each beside the oarsmen, to guard them from the arrows of the Colchians. Then he cut the stern cables with his sword, and softly they rowed, under the bank, down the dark river to the sea. But the hissing of the dragon had already awakened the Colchians, and lights were flitting by the palace windows, and Aeëtes was driving in his chariot with all his men down to the banks of the river. Then their arrows fell like hail about the ship, but they rebounded from the shields of the heroes, and the swift ship sped over the bar, and leaped as she felt the first waves of the salt sea.

And now the Fleece was won. But it was weary work bringing it home to Greece, and Medea and Jason did a deed which angered the Gods. They slew her brother Absyrtus, who followed after them with a fleet, and cut him limb from limb, and when Aeëtes came with his ships, and saw the dead limbs, he stopped, and went home, for his heart was broken. The Gods would not let the Greeks return by the way they had come, but by strange ways where never another ship has sailed. Up the Ister (the Danube) they rowed, through countries of savage men, till the *Argo* could go no further, by reason of the narrowness of the stream. Then they hauled her overland, where no man knows, but they launched her on the Elbe at last, and out into a sea where never sail had been seen. Then they were driven wandering out into Ocean, and to a fairy, far-off isle where Lady Circe dwelt. Circe was the sister of King Aeëtes, both were children of the Sun God, and Medea hoped that Circe would be kind to her, as she could not have heard of the slaying of Absyrtus. Medea and Jason went up through the woods of the isle to the house of Circe, and had no fear of the lions and wolves and bears that guarded the house. These knew that Medea was an enchantress, and they fawned on her and Jason and let them pass. But in the house they found Circe clad in dark mourning raiment, and all her long black hair fell wet and dripping to her feet, for she had seen visions of terror and sin, and therefore she had purified herself in salt water of the sea. The walls of her chamber, in the night, had shone as with fire, and dripped as with blood, and a voice of wailing had broken forth, and the spirit of dead Absyrtus had cried in her ears.

When Medea and Jason entered her hall, Circe bade them sit down, and called her bower maidens, fairies of woods and waters, to strew a table with a cloth of gold, and set on it food and wine. But Jason and Medea ran to the hearth, the sacred place of the house to which men that have done murder flee, and there they are safe, when they come in their flight to the house of a stranger. They cast ashes from the hearth on their heads, and Circe knew that they had slain Absyrtus. Yet she was of Medea's near kindred, and she respected the law of the hearth. Therefore she did the rite of purification, as was the custom, cleansing blood with blood, and she burned in the fire a cake of honey, and meal, and oil, to appease the Furies who revenge the deaths of kinsmen by the hands of kinsmen.

When all was done, Jason and Medea rose from their knees, and sat down on chairs in the hall, and Medea told Circe all her tale, except the slaying of Absyrtus.

'More and worse than you tell me you have done,' said Circe, 'but you are my brother's daughter.'

Then she advised them of all the dangers of their way home to Greece, how they must shun the Sirens, and Scylla and Charybdis, and she sent a messenger, Iris, the Goddess of the Rainbow, to bid Thetis help them through the perils of the sea, and bring them safe to Phaeacia, where the Phaeacians would send them home.

'But you shall never be happy, nor know one good year in all your lives,' said Circe, and she bade them farewell.

They went by the way that Ulysses went on a later day; they passed through many perils, and came to Iolcos, where Pelias was old, and made Jason reign in his stead.

But Jason and Medea loved each other no longer, and many stories, all different from each other, are told concerning evil deeds that they wrought, and certainly they left each other, and Jason took another wife, and Medea went to Athens. Here she lived in the palace of Aegeus, an unhappy King who had been untrue to his own true love, and therefore the Gods took from him courage and strength. But about Medea at Athens the story is told in the next tale, the tale of Theseus, Aegeus's son.

THESEUS

– I –

THE WEDDING OF AETHRA

LONG BEFORE ULYSSES WAS BORN, THERE lived in Athens a young King, strong, brave, and beautiful, named Aegeus. Athens, which later became so great and famous, was then but a little town, perched on the top of a cliff which rises out of the plain, two or three miles from the sea. No doubt the place was chosen so as to be safe against pirates, who then used to roam all about the seas, plundering merchant ships, robbing cities, and carrying away men, women, and children, to sell as slaves. The Athenians had then no fleet with which to put the pirates down, and possessed not so much land as would make a large estate in England: other little free towns held the rest of the surrounding country.

King Aegeus was young, and desired to take a wife, indeed a wife had been found for him. But he wanted to be certain, if he could, that he was to have sons to succeed him: so many misfortunes happen to kings who have no children. But how was he to find out whether he should have children or not?

At that time, and always in Greece before it was converted to Christianity, there were temples of the Gods in various places, at which it was supposed that men might receive answers to their questions. These temples were called oracles, or places where oracles were given, and the most famous of them was the temple of Apollo at Pytho, or Delphi, far to the north-west of Athens. Here was a deep ravine of a steep mountain, where the God Apollo was said to have shot a monstrous dragon with his arrows. He then ordered that a temple should be built here, and in this temple a maiden, being inspired by the God, gave her prophecies. The people who came to consult her made the richest presents to the priests, and the temple was full of cups and bowls of gold and silver, and held more wealth in its chambers than the treasure houses of the richest kings.

Aegeus determined to go to Delphi to ask his question: would he have sons to come after him? He did not tell his people where he was going; he left the kingdom to be governed by his brother Pallas, and he set out secretly at night, taking no servant. He did not wear royal dress, and he drove his own chariot, carrying for his offering only a small cup of silver, for he did not wish it to be known that he was a King, and told the priests that he was a follower of Peleus, King of Phthia. In answer to his question, the maiden sang two lines of verse, for she always prophesied in verse. Her reply was difficult to understand, as oracles often were, for the maiden seldom spoke out clearly, but in a kind of riddle that might be understood in more ways than one; so that, whatever happened, she could not be proved to have made a mistake.

Aegeus was quite puzzled by the answer he got. He did not return to Athens, but went to consult the prince of Troezen, named Pittheus, who was thought the wisest man then living. Pittheus did not know who Aegeus was, but saw that he seemed of noble birth, tall and handsome, so he received him very kindly, and kept him in his house for some time, entertaining him with feasts, dances, and hunting parties. Now Pittheus had a very lovely daughter, named Aethra. She and Aegeus fell in love with each other, so deeply that they desired to be married. It was the custom that the bridegroom should pay a price, a number of cattle, to the father of the bride, and Aegeus, of course, had no cattle to give. But it was also the custom, if the lover did some very brave and useful action, to reward him with the hand of his lady, and Aegeus had his opportunity. A fleet of pirates landed at Troezen and attacked the town, but Aegeus fought so bravely and led the men of Pittheus so well, that he not only slew the pirate chief, and defeated his men, but also captured some of his ships, which were full of plunder, gold, and bronze, and iron, and slaves. With this wealth Aegeus paid the bride price, as it was called, for Aethra, and they were married. Pittheus thought himself a lucky man, for he had no son, and here was a son-in-law who could protect his little kingdom, and wear the crown when he himself was dead.

Though Pittheus was believed to be very wise, in this matter he was very foolish. He never knew who Aegeus really was, that is the King of Athens, nor did poor Aethra know. In a short time Aegeus wearied of beautiful Aethra, who continued to love him dearly. He was anxious also to return to his kingdom, for he heard that his brother Pallas and his many sons were governing badly; and he feared that Pallas might keep the crown for himself, so he began to speak mysteriously to Aethra, talking about a long and dangerous journey which he was obliged to make, for secret reasons, and from which he might never return alive. Aethra wept bitterly, and sometimes thought, as people did in these days, that the beautiful stranger might be no man, but a God, and that he might return to Olympus, the home of the Gods, and forget her; for the Gods never tarried long with the mortal women who loved them.

At last Aegeus took Aethra to a lonely glen in the

woods, where, beside a little mountain stream, lay a great moss-grown boulder that an earthquake, long ago, had shaken from the rocky cliff above. 'The time is coming,' said Aegeus, 'when you and I must part, and only the Gods can tell when we shall meet again! It may be that you will bear a child, and, if he be a boy, when he has come to his strength you must lead him to this great stone, and let no man or woman be there but you two only. You must then bid him roll away the stone, and, if he has no strength to raise it, so must it be. But if he can roll it away, then let him take such things as he finds there, and let him consider them well, and do what the Gods put into his heart.'

Thus Aegeus spoke, and on the dawn of the third night after this day, when Aethra awoke from sleep, she did not find him by her side. She arose, and ran through the house, calling his name, but there came no answer, and from that time Aegeus was never seen again in Troezen, and people marvelled, thinking that he, who came whence no man knew, and was so brave and beautiful, must be one of the immortal Gods. 'Who but a God,' they said, 'would leave for no cause a bride, the flower of Greece for beauty, young, and loving; and a kingdom to which he was not born? Truly he must be Apollo of the silver bow, or Hermes of the golden wand.'

So they spoke among each other, and honoured Aethra greatly, but she pined and drooped with sorrow, like a tall lily flower, that the frost has touched in a rich man's garden.

– 2 –

THE BOYHOOD OF THESEUS

TIME WENT BY, AND AETHRA HAD A BABY, a son. This was her only comfort, and she thought that she saw in him a likeness to his father, whose true name she did not know. Certainly he was a very beautiful baby, well formed and strong, and, as soon as he could walk he was apt to quarrel with other children of his own age, and fight with them in a harmless way. He never was an amiable child, though he was always gentle to his mother. From the first he was afraid of nothing, and when he was about four or five he used to frighten his mother by wandering from home, with his little bow and arrows, and staying by himself in the woods. However, he always found his own way back again, sometimes with a bird or a snake that he had shot, and once dragging the body of a fawn that was nearly as heavy as himself. Thus his mother, from his early boyhood, had many fears for him, that he might be killed by some fierce wild boar in the woods, for he would certainly shoot at whatever beast he met;

or that he might kill some other boy in a quarrel, when he would be obliged to leave the country. The other boys, however, soon learned not to quarrel with Theseus (so Aethra had named her son), for he was quick of temper, and heavy of hand, and, as for the wild beasts, he was cool as well as eager, and seemed to have an untaught knowledge of how to deal with them.

Aethra was therefore very proud of her son, and began to hope that when he was older he would be able to roll away the great stone in the glen. She told him nothing about it when he was little, but, in her walks with him in the woods or on the sea shore, she would ask him to try his force in lifting large stones. When he succeeded she kissed and praised him, and told him stories of the famous strong man, Heracles, whose name was well known through all Greece. Theseus could not bear to be beaten at lifting any weight, and, if he failed, he would rise early and try again in the morning, for many men, as soon as they rise from bed, can lift weights which are too heavy for them later in the day.

When Theseus was seven years old, Aethra found for him a tutor, named Connidas, who taught him the arts of netting beasts and hunting, and how to manage the dogs, and how to drive a chariot, and wield sword and shield, and to throw the spear.

Other things Connidas taught him which were known to few men in Greece, for Connidas came from the great rich island of Crete. He had killed a man there in a quarrel, and fled to Troezen to escape the revenge of the man's brothers and cousins. In Crete many people could read and write, which in Greece, perhaps none could do, and Connidas taught Theseus this learning.

When he was fifteen years old, Theseus went, as was the custom of young princes, to the temple of Delphi, not to ask questions, but to cut his long hair, and sacrifice it to the God, Apollo. He cut the forelock of his hair, so that no enemy, in battle, might take hold of it, for Theseus intended to fight at close quarters, hand to hand, in war, not to shoot arrows and throw spears from a distance. By this time he thought himself a man, and was always asking where his father was, while Aethra told him how her husband had left her soon after their marriage, and that she had never heard of him since, but that some day Theseus might find out all about him for himself, which no other person would ever be able to do.

Aethra did not wish to tell Theseus too soon the secret of the great stone, which hid she knew not what. She saw that he would leave her and go to seek his father, if he was able to raise the stone and find out the secret, and she could not bear to lose him, now that day by day he grew more like his father, her lost lover. Besides, she wanted him not to try to raise the stone till he came to his strength. But when he was in his nineteenth year, he told her that he would now go all over Greece and the whole world seeking for his father. She saw that he meant what he said, and one day she led him alone to the glen where the great stone lay, and sat down with him there, now talking, and now silent as if she were listening to the pleasant song of the burn that fell from a height into a clear deep pool. Really she was listening to make sure that no hunter and no lovers were near them in the wood, but she only heard the songs of the water and the birds, no voices, or cry of hounds, or fallen twig cracking under a footstep.

At last, when she was quite certain that nobody was near, she whispered, and told Theseus how her husband, before he disappeared, had taken her to this place, and shown her the great moss-grown boulder, and said that, when his son could lift that stone away, he would find certain tokens, and that he must then do what the Gods put into his heart. Theseus listened eagerly, and said, 'If my father lifted that stone, and placed under it certain tokens, I also can lift it, perhaps not yet, but some day I shall be as strong a man as my father.' Then he set himself to move the stone, gradually putting out all his force, but it seemed rooted in the earth, though he tried it now on one side and now on another. At last he flung himself at his mother's feet, with his head in the grass, and lay without speaking. His breath came hard and quick, and his hands were bleeding. Aethra laid her hand on his long hair, and was silent. 'I shall not lose my boy this year,' she thought.

They were long in that lonely place, but at last Theseus rose, and kissed his mother, and stretched his arms. 'Not today!' he said, but his mother thought in her heart, 'Not for many a day, I hope!' Then they walked home to the house of Pittheus, saying little, and when they had taken supper, Theseus said that he would go to bed and dream of better fortune. So he arose, and went to his own chamber, which was built apart in the court of the palace, and soon Aethra too went to sleep, not unhappy, for her boy, she thought, would not leave her for a long time.

But in the night Theseus arose, and put on his shoes, and his smock, and a great double mantle. He girt on his sword of bronze, and went into the housekeeper's chamber, where he took a small skin of wine, and some food. These he placed in a wallet which he slung round his neck by a cord, and, lastly he stole out of the court, and walked to the lonely glen, and to the pool in the burn near which the great stone lay. Here he folded his purple mantle of fine wool round him, and lay down to sleep in the grass, with his sword lying near his hand.

When he awoke the clear blue morning light was round him, and all the birds were singing their song to the dawn. Theseus arose, threw off his mantle and smock, and plunged into the cold pool of the burn, and then he drank a little of the wine, and ate of the bread and cold meat, and set himself to move the stone. At the first effort, into which he put all his strength, the stone stirred. With the second he felt it rise a little way from the ground, and then he lifted with all the might in his heart and body, and rolled the stone clean over.

Beneath it there was nothing but the fresh turned soil, but in a hollow of the foot of the rock, which now lay uppermost, there was a wrapping of purple woollen cloth, that covered something. Theseus tore out the packet, unwrapped the cloth, and found within it a wrapping of white linen. This wrapping was in many folds, which he undid, and at last he found a pair of shoon, such as kings wear, adorned with gold, and also the most beautiful sword that he had ever seen. The handle was of clear rock crystal, and through the crystal you could see gold, inlaid with pictures of a lion hunt done in different shades of gold and silver. The sheath was of leather, with patterns in gold nails, and the blade was of bronze, a beautiful pattern ran down the centre to the point, the blade was straight, and double edged, supple, sharp, and strong. Never had Theseus seen so beautiful a sword, nor one so well balanced in his hand.

He saw that this was a King's sword; and he thought that it had not been wrought in Greece, for in Greece was no swordsmith that could do such work. Examining it very carefully he found characters engraved beneath the hilt, not letters such as the Greeks used in later times, but such Cretan signs as Connidas had taught him to read, for many a weary hour, when he would like to have been following the deer in the forest.

Theseus pored over these signs till he read:

Icmalius me made. Of Aegeus of Athens am I.

Now he knew the secret. His father was Aegeus, the King of Athens. Theseus had heard of him and knew that he yet lived, a sad life full of trouble. For Aegeus had no child by his Athenian wife, and the fifty sons of his brother Pallas (who were called the Pallantidae) despised him, and feasted all day in his hall, recklessly and fiercely, robbing the people, and Aegeus had no power in his own kingdom.

'Methinks that my father has need of me!' said Theseus to himself. Then he wrapped up the sword and shoon in the linen and the cloth of wool, and walked home in the early morning to the palace of Pittheus.

When Theseus came to the palace, he went straight to the upper chamber of his mother, where she was spinning wool with a distaff of ivory. When he laid before her the sword and the shoon, the distaff fell from her hand, and she hid her head in a fold of her robe. Theseus kissed her hands and comforted her, and she dried her eyes, and praised him for his strength. 'These are the sword and the shoon of your father,' she said, 'but truly the Gods have taken away his strength and courage. For all men say that Aegeus of Athens is not master in his own house; his brother's sons rule him, and with them Medea, the witch woman, that once was the wife of Jason.'

'The more he needs his son!' said Theseus. 'Mother, I must go to help him, and be the heir of his kingdom, where you shall be with me always, and rule the people of Cecrops that fasten the locks of their hair with grasshoppers of gold.'

'So may it be, my child,' said Aethra, 'if the Gods go with you to protect you. But you will sail to Athens in a ship with fifty oarsmen, for the ways by land are long, and steep, and dangerous, beset by cruel giants and monstrous men.'

'Nay, mother,' said Theseus, 'by land must I go, for I would not be known in Athens, till I see how matters fall out; and I would destroy these giants and robbers, and give peace to the people, and win glory among men. This very night I shall set forth.'

He had a sore and sad parting from his mother, but under cloud of night he went on his way, girt with the sword of Aegeus, his father, and carrying in his wallet the shoon with ornaments of gold.

– 3 –

ADVENTURES OF THESEUS

THESEUS WALKED THROUGH THE NIGHT, and slept for most of the next day at a shepherd's hut. The shepherd was kind to him, and bade him beware of one called the Maceman, who guarded a narrow path with a sheer cliff above, and a sheer precipice below. 'No man born may deal with the Maceman,' said the shepherd, 'for his great club is of iron, that cannot be broken, and his strength is as the strength of ten men, though his legs have no force to bear his body. Men say that he is the son of the lame God, Hephaestus, who forged his iron mace; there is not the like of it in the world.'

'Shall I fear a lame man?' said Theseus, 'and is it not easy, even if he be so terrible a fighter, for me to pass him in the darkness, for I walk by night?'

The shepherd shook his head. 'Few men have passed Periphetes the Maceman,' said he, 'and wiser are they who trust to swift ships than to the upland path.'

'You speak kindly, father,' said Theseus, 'but I am minded to make the upland paths safe for all men.'

So they parted, and Theseus walked through the sunset and the dusk, always on a rising path, and the further he went the harder it was to see the way, for the path was overgrown with grass, and the shadows were deepening. Night fell, and Theseus hardly dared to go further, for on his left hand was a wall of rock, and on his right hand a cliff sinking sheer and steep to the sea. But now he saw a light in front of him, a red light flickering, as from a great fire, and he could not be content till he knew why that fire was lighted. So he went on, slowly and warily, till he came in full view of the fire which covered the whole of a little platform of rock; on one side the blaze shone up the wall of cliff on his left hand, on the other was the steep fall to the sea. In front of this fire was a great black bulk; Theseus knew not what it might be. He walked forward till he saw that the black bulk was that of a monstrous man, who sat with his back to the fire. The man nodded his heavy head, thick with red unshorn hair, and Theseus went up close to him.

'Ho, sir,' he cried, 'this is my road, and on my road I must pass!'

The seated man opened his eyes sleepily.

'Not without my leave,' he said, 'for I keep this way, I and my club of iron.'

'Get up and begone!' said Theseus.

'That were hard for me to do,' said the monstrous man, 'for my legs will not bear the weight of my body, but my arms are strong enough.'

'That is to be seen!' said Theseus, and he drew his sword, and leaped within the guard of the iron club that the monster, seated as he was, swung lightly to this side and that, covering the whole width of the path. The Maceman swung the club at Theseus, but Theseus sprang aside, and in a moment, before the monster could recover his stroke, drove through his throat the sword of Aegeus, and he fell back dead.

'He shall have his rights of fire, that his shadow may not wander outside the House of Hades,' said Theseus to himself, and he toppled the body of the Maceman into his own great fire. Then he went back some way, and wrapping himself in his mantle, he slept till the sun was high in heaven, while the fire had sunk into its embers, and Theseus lightly sprang over them, carrying with him the Maceman's iron club. The path now led downwards, and a burn that ran through a green forest kept him company on the way, and brought him to pleasant farms and houses of men.

They marvelled to see him, a young man, carrying the club of the Maceman. 'Did you find him asleep?' they asked, and Theseus smiled and said, 'No, I found him awake. But now he sleeps an iron sleep, from which he will never waken, and his body had due burning in his own watchfire.' Then the men and women praised Theseus, and wove for him a crown of leaves and flowers, and sacrificed sheep to the Gods in heaven, and on the meat they dined, rejoicing that now they could go to Troezen by the hill path, for they did not love ships and the sea.

When they had eaten and drunk, and poured out the last cup of wine on the ground, in honour of Hermes, the God of Luck, the country people asked Theseus where he was going? He said that he was going to walk to Athens, and at this the people looked sad. 'No man may walk across the neck of land where Ephyre is built,' they said, 'because above it Sinis the Pine-Bender has his castle, and watches the way.'

'And who is Sinis, and why does he bend pine trees?' asked Theseus.

'He is the strongest of men, and when he catches a traveller, he binds him hand and foot, and sets him between two pine trees. Then he bends them down till they meet, and fastens the traveller to the boughs of each tree, and lets them spring apart, so that the man is riven asunder.'

'Two can play at that game,' said Theseus, smiling, and he bade farewell to the kind country people, shouldered the iron club of Periphetes, and went singing on his way. The path led him over moors, and past farmhouses, and at last rose towards the crest of the hill whence he would see the place where two seas would have met, had they not been sundered by the neck of land which is now called the Isthmus of Corinth. Here the path was very narrow, with thick forests of pine trees on each hand, and 'here', thought Theseus to himself, 'I am likely to meet the Pine-Bender.'

Soon he knew that he was right, for he saw the ghastly remains of dead men that the pine trees bore like horrible fruit, and presently the air was darkened overhead by the waving of vultures and ravens that prey upon the dead. 'I shall fight the better in the shade,' said Theseus, and he loosened the blade of the sword in its sheath, and raised the club of Periphetes aloft in his hand.

Well it was for him that he raised the iron club, for, just as he lifted it, there flew out from the thicket something long, and slim, and black, that fluttered above his head for a moment, and then a loop at the end of it fell, round the head of Theseus, and was drawn tight with a sudden jerk. But the loop fell also above and round the club, which Theseus held firm, pushing away the loop, and so pushed it off that it did not grip his neck. Drawing with his left hand his bronze dagger, he cut through the leather lasso with one stroke, and bounded into the bushes from which it had flown. Here he found a huge man, clad in the skin of a lion, with its head fitting to his own like a mask. The man lifted a club made of the trunk of a young pine tree, with a sharp-edged stone fastened into the head of it like an axe-head. But, as the monster raised his long weapon it struck on a strong branch of a tree above him, and was entangled in the boughs, so that Theseus had time to thrust the head of the iron club full in his face, with all his force, and the savage fell with a crash like a falling oak among the bracken. He was one of the last of an ancient race of savage men, who dwelt in Greece before the Greeks, and he fought as they had fought, with weapons of wood and stone.

Theseus dropped with his knees on the breast of the Pine-Bender, and grasped his hairy throat with both his hands, not to strangle him, but to hold him sure and firm till he came to himself again. When at last the monster opened his eyes, Theseus gripped his throat the harder, and spoke, 'Pine-Bender, for thee shall pines be bent. But I am a man and not a monster, and thou shalt die a clean death before thy body is torn in twain to be the last feast of thy vultures.' Then, squeezing the throat of the wretch with his left hand, he drew the sword of Aegeus, and drove it into the heart of Sinis the Pine-Bender, and he gave a cry like a bull's, and his soul fled from him. Then Theseus bound the body of the savage with his own leather cord, and, bending down the tops of two pine trees, he did to the corpse as Sinis had been wont to do to living men.

Lastly he cleaned the sword-blade carefully, wiping it with grass and bracken, and thrusting it to the hilt through the soft fresh ground under the trees, and so went on his way till he came to a little stream that ran towards the sea from the crest of the hill above the town of Ephyre, which is now called Corinth. But as he cleansed himself in the clear water, he heard a rustle in the boughs of the wood, and running with sword drawn to the place whence the sound seemed to come, he heard the whisper of a woman. Then he saw a strange sight. A tall and very beautiful girl was kneeling in a thicket, in a patch of asparagus thorn, and was weeping, and praying, in a low voice, and in a childlike innocent manner, to the thorns, begging them to shelter and defend her.

Theseus wondered at her, and, sheathing his sword, came softly up to her, and bade her have no fear. Then she threw her arms about his knees, and raised her face, all wet with tears, and bade him take pity upon her, for she had done no harm.

'Who are you, maiden? You are safe with me,' said Theseus. 'Do you dread the Pine-Bender?'

'Alas, sir,' answered the girl, 'I am his daughter, Perigyne, and his blood is on your hands.'

'Yet I do not war with women,' said Theseus, 'though that has been done which was decreed by the Gods. If you follow with me, you shall be kindly used, and marry, if you will, a man of a good house, being so beautiful as you are.'

When she heard this, the maiden rose to her feet, and would have put her hand in his. 'Not yet,' said Theseus, kindly, 'till water has clean washed away that which is between thee and me. But wherefore, maiden, being in fear as you were, did you not call to the Gods in heaven to keep you, but to the asparagus thorns that cannot hear or help?'

'My father, sir,' she said, 'knew no Gods, but he came of the race of the asparagus thorns, and to them I cried in my need.'

Theseus marvelled at these words, and said, 'From this day you shall pray to Zeus, the Lord of Thunder, and to the other Gods.' Then he went forth from the wood, with the maiden following, and wholly cleansed himself in the brook that ran by the way.

So they passed down to the rich city of Ephyre, where the King received him gladly, when he heard of the slaying of the Maceman, Periphetes, and of Sinis the Pine-Bender. The Queen, too, had pity on

Perigyne, so beautiful she was, and kept her in her own palace. Afterwards Perigyne married a prince, Deiones, son of Eurytus, King of Oechalia, whom the strong man Heracles slew for the sake of his bow, the very bow with which Ulysses, many years afterwards, destroyed the wooers in his halls. The sons of Perigyne and Deiones later crossed the seas to Asia, and settled in a land called Caria, and they never burned or harmed the asparagus thorn to which Perigyne had prayed in the thicket.

Greece was so lawless in these days that all the road from Troezen northward to Athens was beset by violent and lawless men. They loved cruelty even more than robbery, and each of them had carefully thought out his particular style of being cruel. The cities were small, and at war with each other, or at war among themselves, one family fighting against another for the crown. Thus there was no chance of collecting an army to destroy the monstrous men of the roads, which it would have been easy enough for a small body of archers to have done. Later Theseus brought all into great order, but now, being but one man, he went seeking adventures.

On the border of a small country called Megara, whose people were much despised in Greece, he found a chance of advancing himself, and gaining glory. He was walking in the middle of the day along a narrow path at the crest of a cliff above the sea, when he saw the flickering of a great fire in the blue air, and steam going up from a bronze cauldron of water that was set on the fire. On one side of the fire was a foot-bath of glittering bronze. Hard by was built a bower of green branches, very cool on that hot day, and from the door of the bower stretched a great thick hairy pair of naked legs.

Theseus guessed, from what he had been told, that the owner of the legs was Sciron the Kicker. He was a fierce outlaw who was called the Kicker because he made all travellers wash his feet, and, as they were doing so, kicked them over the cliff. Some say that at the foot of the cliff dwelt an enormous tortoise, which ate the dead and dying when they fell near his lair, but as tortoises do not eat flesh, generally, this may be a mistake. Theseus was determined not to take any insolence from Sciron, so he shouted –

'Slave, take these dirty legs of yours out of the way of a Prince.'

'Prince!' answered Sciron, 'if my legs are dirty, the Gods are kind who have sent you to wash them for me.'

Then he got up, lazily, laughing and showing his ugly teeth, and stood in front of his bath with his heavy wooden club in his hand. He whirled it round his head insultingly, but Theseus was quicker than he, and again, as when he slew the Pine-Bender, he did not strike, for striking is slow compared to thrusting, but like a flash he lunged forward and drove the thick end of his iron club into the breast of Sciron. He staggered, and, as he reeled, Theseus dealt him a blow across the thigh, and he fell. Theseus seized the club which dropped from the hand of Sciron, and threw it over the cliff; it seemed long before the sound came up from the rocks on which it struck. 'A deep drop into a stony way, Sciron,' said Theseus, 'now wash my feet! Stand up, and turn your back to me, and be ready when I tell you.' Sciron rose, slowly and sulkily, and stood as Theseus bade him do.

Now Theseus was not wearing light shoes or sandals, like the golden sandals of Aegeus, which he carried in his wallet. He was wearing thick boots, with bronze nails in the soles, and the upper leathers were laced high up his legs, for the Greeks wore such boots when they took long walks on mountain roads. As soon as Theseus had trained Sciron to stand in the proper position, he bade him stoop to undo the lacings of his boots. As Sciron stooped, Theseus gave him one tremendous kick, that lifted him over the edge of the cliff, and there was an end of Sciron.

Theseus left the marches of Megara, and walked singing on his way, above the sea, for his heart was light, and he was finding adventures to his heart's desire. Being so young and well trained, his foot and hand, in a combat, moved as swift as lightning, and his enemies were older than he, and, though very strong, were heavy with full feeding, and slow to move. Now it is speed that wins in a fight, whether between armies or single men, if strength and courage go with it.

At last the road led Theseus down from the heights to a great fertile plain, called the Thriasian plain, not far from Athens. There, near the sea, stands the famous old city of Eleusis. When Hades, the God of the Dead, carried away beautiful Persephone, the daughter of Demeter, the Goddess of Corn and all manner of grain, to his dark palace beside the stream of Ocean, it was to Eleusis that Demeter wandered. She was clad in mourning robes, and she sat down on a stone by the way, like a weary old woman. Now the three daughters of the King who then reigned in Eleusis came by, on the way to the well, to fetch water, and when they saw the old woman they set down their vessels and came round her, asking what they could do for her, who was so tired and poor. They said that they had a baby brother at home, who was the favourite of them all, and that he needed a nurse. Demeter was pleased with their kindness, and they left their vessels for water beside her, and ran home to their mother. Their long golden hair danced on their shoulders as they ran, and they came, out of breath, to their mother the Queen, and asked her to take the old woman to be their brother's nurse. The Queen was kind, too, and the old woman lived in their house, till Zeus, the chief God, made the God of the Dead send back Persephone, to be with her mother through spring, and summer, and early autumn, but in winter she must live with her husband in the dark palace beside the river of Ocean.

Then Demeter was glad, and she caused the grain to grow abundantly for the people of Eleusis, and taught them ceremonies, and a kind of play in which all the story of her sorrows and joy was acted. It was also taught that the souls of men do not die with the death of their bodies, any more than the seed of corn dies when it is buried in the dark earth, but that they live again in a world more happy and beautiful than ours. These ceremonies were called the Mysteries of Eleusis, and were famous in all the world.

Theseus might have expected to find Eleusis a holy city, peaceful and quiet. But he had heard, as he travelled, that in Eleusis was a strong bully, named Cercyon; he was one of the rough Highlanders of Arcadia, who lived in the hills of the centre of Southern Greece, which is called Peloponnesus. He is said to have taken the kingship, and driven out the descendants of the King whose daughters were kind to Demeter. The strong man used to force all strangers to wrestle with him, and, when he threw them, for he had never been thrown, he broke their backs.

Knowing this, and being himself fond of wrestling, Theseus walked straight to the door of the King's house, though the men in the town warned him, and the women looked at him with sad eyes. He found the gate of the courtyard open, with the altar of Zeus the high God smoking in the middle of it, and at the threshold two servants welcomed him, and took him to the polished bath, and women washed him, and anointed him with oil, and clothed him in fresh raiment, as was the manner in Kings' houses. Then they led him into the hall, and he walked straight up to the high seats between the four pillars beside the hearth, in the middle of the hall.

There Cercyon sat, eating and drinking, surrounded by a score of his clan, great, broad, red-haired men, but he himself was the broadest and the most brawny. He welcomed Theseus, and caused a table to be brought, with meat, and bread, and wine, and when Theseus had put away his hunger, began to ask him who he was and whence he came. Theseus told him that he had walked from Troezen, and was on his way to the court of King Peleus (the father of Achilles), in the north, for he did not want the news of his coming to go before him to Athens.

'You walked from Troezen?' said Cercyon. 'Did you meet or hear of the man who killed the Maceman and slew the Pine-Bender, and kicked Sciron into the sea?'

'I walk fast, but news flies faster,' said Theseus.

'The news came through my second-sighted man,' said Cercyon, 'there he is, in the corner,' and Cercyon threw the leg bone of an ox at his prophet, who just managed to leap out of the way. 'He seems to have foreseen that the bone was coming at him,' said Cercyon, and all his friends laughed loud. 'He told us this morning that a stranger was coming, he who had killed the three watchers of the way. From your legs and shoulders, and the iron club that you carry, methinks you are that stranger?'

Theseus smiled, and nodded upwards, which the Greeks did when they meant 'Yes!'

'Praise be to all the Gods!' said Cercyon. 'It is long since a good man came my way. Do they practise wrestling at Troezen?'

'Now and then,' said Theseus.

'Then you will try a fall with me? There is a smooth space strewn with sand in the courtyard.'

Theseus answered that he had come hoping that the King would graciously honour him by trying a fall. Then all the wild guests shouted, and out they all went and made a circle round the wrestling-place, while Theseus and Cercyon threw down their clothes and were anointed with oil over their bodies. To it they went, each straining forward and feeling for a grip, till they were locked, and then they swayed this way and that, their feet stamping the ground; and now one would yield a little, now the other, while the rough guests shouted, encouraging each of them. At last they rested and breathed, and now the men began to bet; seven oxen to three was laid on Cercyon, and taken in several places. Back to the wrestle they went, and Theseus found this by far the hardest of his adventures, for Cercyon was heavier than he, and as strong, but not so active. So Theseus for long did little but resist the awful strain of the arms of Cercyon, till, at last, for a moment Cercyon weakened. Then Theseus slipped his hip under the hip of Cercyon, and heaved him across and up, and threw him on the ground. He lighted in such a way that his neck broke, and there he lay dead.

'Was it fairly done?' said Theseus.

'It was fairly done!' cried the Highlanders of Arcadia; and then they raised such a wail for the dead that Theseus deemed it wise to put on his clothes and walk out of the court; and, leaping into a chariot that stood empty by the gate, for the servant in the chariot feared the club of iron, he drove away at full speed.

Though Cercyon was a cruel man and a wild, Theseus was sorry for him in his heart.

The groom in the chariot tried to leap out, but Theseus gripped him tight. 'Do not hurry, my friend,' said Theseus, 'for I have need of you. I am not stealing the chariot and horses, and you shall drive them back after we reach Athens.'

'But, my lord,' said the groom, 'you will never reach Athens.'

'Why not?' asked Theseus.

'Because of the man Procrustes, who dwells in a strong castle among the hills on the way. He is the maimer of all mortals, and has at his command a company of archers and spearmen, pirates from the islands. He meets every traveller, and speaks to him courteously, praying him to be his guest, and if any refuses the archers leap out of ambush and seize and bind him. With them no one man can contend. He has a bed which he says is a thing magical, for it is of the same length as the tallest or the shortest man who sleeps in it, so that all are fitted. Now the manner of it is this – there is an engine with ropes at the head of the bed, and a saw is fitted at the bed foot. If a man is too short, the ropes are fastened to his hands, and are strained till he is drawn to the full length of the bed. If he is too long the saw shortens him. Such a monster is Procrustes.

'Verily, my lord, King Cercyon was tomorrow to lead an army against him, and the King had a new device, as you may see, by which two great shields are slung along the side of this chariot, to ward off the arrows of the men of Procrustes.'

'Then you and I will wear the shields when we come near the place where Procrustes meets travellers by the way, and I think that tonight his own bed will be too long for him,' said Theseus.

To this the groom made no answer, but his body trembled.

Theseus drove swiftly on till the road began to climb the lowest spur of Mount Parnes, and then he drew rein, and put on one of the great shields that covered all his body and legs, and he bade the groom do the like. Then he drove slowly, watching the bushes and underwood beside the way. Soon he saw the smoke going up from the roof of a great castle high in the woods beside the road; and on the road there was a man waiting. Theseus, as he drove towards him, saw the glitter of armour in the underwood, and the setting sun shone red on a spear-point above the leaves. 'Here is our man,' he said to the groom, and pulled up his horses beside the stranger. He loosened his sword in the sheath, and leaped out of the chariot, holding the reins in his left hand, and bowed courteously to the man, who was tall, weak-looking, and old, with grey hair and a cleanshaven face, the colour of ivory. He was clad like a king, in garments of dark silk, with gold bracelets, and gold rings that clasped the leather gaiters on his legs, and he smiled and smiled, and rubbed his hands, while he looked to right and left, and not at Theseus.

'I am fortunate, fair sir,' said he to Theseus, 'for I love to entertain strangers, with whom goes the favour and protection of Zeus. Surely strangers are dear to all men, and holy! You, too, are not unlucky, for the night is falling, and the ways will be dark and dangerous. You will sup and sleep with me, and tonight I can give you a bed that is well spoken of, for its nature is such that it fits all men, the short and the tall, and you are of the tallest.'

'Tonight, fair sir,' quoth Theseus, 'your own bed will be full long for you.' And, drawing the sword of Aegeus, he cut sheer through the neck of Procrustes at one blow, and the head of the man flew one way, and his body fell another way.

Then with a swing of his hand Theseus turned his shield from his front to his back, and leaped into the chariot. He lashed the horses forward with a cry, while the groom also turned his own shield from front to back; and the arrows of the bowmen of Procrustes rattled on the bronze shields as the chariot flew along, or struck the sides and the seat of it. One arrow grazed the flank of a horse, and the pair broke into a wild gallop, while the yells of the bowmen grew faint in the distance. At last the horses slackened in their pace as they climbed a hill, and from the crest of it Theseus saw the lights in the city of Aphidnae.

'Now, my friend,' he said to the groom, 'the way is clear to Athens, and on your homeward road with the horses and the chariot you shall travel well guarded. By the splendour of Lady Athene's brow, I will burn that raven's nest of Procrustes!'

So they slept that night on safe beds at the house of the sons of Phytalus, who bore rule in Aphidnae. Here they were kindly welcomed, and the sons of Phytalus rejoiced when they heard how Theseus had made safe the ways, and slain the beasts that guarded them. 'We are your men,' they said, 'we and all our people, and our spears will encircle you when you make yourself King of Athens, and of all the cities in the Attic land.'

– 4 –

THESEUS FINDS HIS FATHER

NEXT DAY THESEUS SAID FAREWELL TO the sons of Phytalus, and drove slowly through the pleasant green woods that overhung the clear river Cephisus. He halted to rest his horses in a glen, and saw a very beautiful young man walking in a meadow on the other side of the river. In his hand he bore a white flower, and the root of it was black; in the other hand he carried a golden wand, and his upper lip was just beginning to darken, he was of the age when youth is most gracious. He came towards Theseus, and crossed the stream where it broke deep, and swift, and white, above a long pool, and it seemed to Theseus that his golden shoon did not touch the water.

'Come, speak with me apart,' the young man said; and Theseus threw the reins to the groom, and went aside with the youth, watching him narrowly, for he knew not what strange dangers might beset him on the way.

'Whither art thou going, unhappy one,' said the

youth, 'thou that knowest not the land? Behold, the sons of Pallas rule in Athens, fiercely and disorderly. Thy father is of no force, and in the house with him is a fair witch woman from a far country. Her name is Medea, the daughter of Aeëtes, the brother of Circe the Sorceress. She wedded the famous Jason, and won for him the Fleece of Gold, and slew her own brother Absyrtus. Other evils she wrought, and now she dwells with Aegeus, who fears and loves her greatly. Take thou this herb of grace, and if Medea offers you a cup of wine, drop this herb in the cup, and so you shall escape death. Behold, I am Hermes of the golden wand.'

Then he gave to Theseus the flower, and passed into the wood, and Theseus saw him no more; so then Theseus knelt down, and prayed, and thanked the Gods. The flower he placed in the breast of his garment, and, returning to his chariot, he took the reins, and drove to Athens, and up the steep narrow way to the crest of the rock where the temple of Athene stood and the palace of King Aegeus.

Theseus drove through to the courtyard, and left his chariot at the gate. In the court young men were throwing spears at a mark, while others sat at the house door, playing draughts, and shouting and betting. They were heavy, lumpish, red-faced young men, all rather like each other. They looked up and stared, but said nothing. Theseus knew that they were his cousins, the sons of Pallas, but as they said nothing to him he walked through them, iron club on shoulder, as if he did not see them, and as one tall fellow stood in his way, the tall fellow spun round from a thrust of his shoulder. At the hall door Theseus stopped and shouted, and at his cry two or three servants came to him.

'Look to my horses and man,' said Theseus; 'I come to see your master.' And in he went, straight up to the high chairs beside the fire in the centre. The room was empty, but in a high seat sat, fallen forward and half-asleep, a man in whose grey hair was a circlet of gold and a golden grasshopper. Theseus knew that it was his father, grey and still, like the fallen fire on the hearth. As the King did not look up, Theseus touched his shoulder, and then knelt down, and put his arms round the knees of the King. The King aroused himself with a start. 'Who? What want you?' he said, and rubbed his red, bloodshot eyes.

'A suppliant from Troezen am I, who come to your knees, oh, long, and bring you gifts.'

'From Troezen!' said the King sleepily, as if he were trying to remember something.

'From Aethra, your wife, your son brings your sword and your shoon,' said Theseus; and he laid the sword and the shoon at his father's feet.

The King rose to his feet with a great cry. 'You have come at last,' he cried, 'and the Gods have forgiven me and heard my prayers. But gird on the sword, and hide the shoon, and speak not the name of "wife", for there is one that hears.'

'One that has heard,' said a sweet silvery voice, and from behind a pillar came a woman, dark and pale, but very beautiful, clothed in a rich Eastern robe that shone and shifted from colour to colour. Lightly she threw her white arms round the neck of Theseus, lightly she kissed his cheeks, and a strange sweet fragrance hung about her. Then, holding him apart, with her hands on his shoulders, she laughed, and half-turning to Aegeus, who had fallen back into his chair, she said: 'My lord, did you think that you could hide anything from me?' Then she fixed her great eyes on the eyes of Theseus. 'We are friends?' she said, in her silvery voice.

'Lady, I love you even as you love my father, King Aegeus,' said Theseus.

'Even so much?' said the lady Medea. 'Then we must both drink to him in wine.' She glided to the great golden mixing-cup of wine that stood on a table behind Aegeus, and with her back to Theseus she ladled wine into a cup of strange coloured glass. 'Pledge me and the King,' she said, bringing the cup to Theseus. He took it, and from his breast he drew the flower of black root and white blossom that Hermes had given him, and laid it in the wine. Then the wine bubbled and hissed, and the cup burst and broke, and the wine fell on the floor, staining it as with blood.

Medea laughed lightly. 'Now we are friends indeed, for the Gods befriend you,' she said, 'and I swear by the Water of Styx that your friends are my friends, and your foes are my foes, always, to the end. The Gods are with you; and by the great oath of the Gods I swear, which cannot be broken; for I come of the kin of the Gods who live for ever.'

Now the father of the father of Medea was the Sun God.

Theseus took both her hands. 'I also swear,' he said, 'by the splendour of Zeus, that your friends shall be my friends, and that your foes shall be my foes, always, to the end.'

Then Medea sat by the feet of Aegeus and drew down his head to her shoulder, while Theseus took hold of his hand, and the King wept for joy. For the son he loved, and the woman whom he loved and feared, were friends, and they two were stronger than the sons of Pallas.

While they sat thus, one of the sons of Pallas – the Pallantidae they were called – slouched into the hall to see if dinner was ready. He stared, and slouched out again, and said to his brothers: 'The old man is sitting in the embraces of the foreign woman, and of the big stranger with the iron club!' Then they all came together, and growled out their threats and fears, kicking at the stones in the courtyard, and quarrelling as to what it was best for them to do.

Meanwhile, in the hall, the servants began to spread the tables with meat and drink, and Theseus was taken to the bath, and clothed in new raiment.

While Theseus was at the bath Medea told Aegeus what he ought to do. So when Theseus came back into the hall, where the sons of Pallas were eating and drinking noisily, Aegeus stood up, and called to Theseus to sit down at his right hand. He added, in a loud voice, looking all round the hall: 'This is my son, Theseus, the slayer of monsters, and his is the power in the house!'

The sons of Pallas grew pale with fear and anger, but not one dared to make an insolent answer. They knew that they were hated by the people of Athens, except some young men of their own sort, and they did not dare to do anything against the man who had slain Periphetes and Sinis, and Cercyon and Sciron, and, in the midst of his paid soldiers, had struck off the head of Procrustes. Silent all through dinner sat the sons of Pallas, and, when they had eaten, they walked out silently, and went to a lonely place, where they could make their plans without being overheard.

Theseus went with Medea into her fragrant chamber, and they spake a few words together. Then Medea took a silver bowl, filled it with water, and, drawing her dark silken mantle over her head, she sat gazing into the bowl. When she had gazed silently for a long time she said: 'Some of them are going towards Sphettus, where their father dwells, to summon his men in arms, and some are going to Gargettus on the other side of the city, to lie in ambush, and cut us off when they of Sphettus assail us. They will attack the palace just before the dawn. Now I will go through the town, and secretly call the trusty men to arm and come to defend the palace, telling them that the son of Aegeus, the man who cleared the ways, is with us. And do you take your chariot, and drive speedily to the sons of Phytalus, and bring all their spears, chariot men and footmen, and place them in ambush around the village of Gargettus, where one band of the Pallantidae will lie tonight till dawn. The rest you know.'

Theseus nodded and smiled. He drove at full speed to Aphidnae, where the sons of Phytalus armed their men, and by midnight they lay hidden in the woods round the village of Gargettus. When the stars had gone onward, and the second of the three watches of the night was nearly past, they set bands of men to guard every way from the little town, and Theseus with another band rushed in, and slew the men of the sons of Pallas around their fires, some of them awake, but most of them asleep. Those who escaped were taken by the bands who watched the ways, and when the sky was now clear at the earliest dawn, Theseus led his companions to the palace of Aegeus, where they fell furiously upon the rear of the men from Sphettus, who were besieging the palace of Aegeus.

The Sphettus company had broken in the gate of the court, and were trying to burn the house, while arrows flew thick from the bows of the trusty men of Athens on the palace roof. The Pallantids had set no sentinels, for they thought to take Theseus in the palace, and there to burn him, and win the kingdom for themselves. Then silently and suddenly the friends of Theseus stole into the courtyard, and, leaving some to guard the gate, they drew up in line, and charged the confused crowd of the Pallantids. Their spears flew thick among the enemy, and then they charged with the sword, while the crowd, in terror, ran this way and that way, being cut down at the gate, and dragged from the walls, when they tried to climb them. The daylight found the Pallantidae and their men lying dead in the courtyard, all the sort of them.

Then Theseus with the sons of Phytalus and their company marched through the town, proclaiming that the rightful prince was come, and that the robbers and oppressors were fallen, and all honest men rejoiced. They burned the dead, and buried their ashes and bones, and for the rest of that day they feasted in the hall of Aegeus. Next day Theseus led his friends back to Aphidnae, and on the next day they attacked and stormed the castle of Procrustes, and slew the pirates, and Theseus divided all the rich plunder among the sons of Phytalus and their company, but the evil bed they burned to ashes.

– 5 –

HERALDS COME FOR TRIBUTE

THE DAYS AND WEEKS WENT BY, AND Theseus reigned with his father in peace. The chief men came to Athens from the little towns in the country, and begged Theseus to be their lord, and they would be his men, and he would lead their people if any enemy came up against them. They would even pay tribute to be used for buying better arms, and making strong walls, and providing ships, for then the people of Athens had no navy. Theseus received them courteously, and promised all that they asked, for he did not know that soon he himself would be sent away as part of the tribute which the Athenians paid every nine years to King Minos of Crete.

Though everything seemed to be peaceful and happy through the winter, yet Theseus felt that all was not well. When he went into the houses of the town's people, where all had been merry and proud of his visits, he saw melancholy, silent mothers, and he missed the young people, lads and maidens. Many of them were said to have gone to visit friends in far-away parts of Greece. The elder folk, and the young people who were left, used to stand watching the sea all day, as if they expected something strange to come upon them from the sea, and Aegeus sat sorrowful over the fire, speaking little, and he seemed to be in fear.

Theseus was disturbed in his mind, and he did not choose to put questions to Aegeus or to the townsfolk. He and Medea were great friends, and one day when they were alone in her chamber, where a fragrant fire of cedar wood burned, he told her what he had noticed. Medea sighed, and said: 'The curse of the sons of Pallas is coming upon the people of Athens – such a curse and so terrible that not even you, Prince Theseus, can deal with it. The enemy is not one man or one monster only, but the greatest and most powerful King in the world.'

'Tell me all,' said Theseus, 'for though I am but one man, yet the ever-living Gods protect and help me.'

'The story of the curse is long,' said Medea. 'When your father Aegeus was young, after he returned to Athens from Troezen, he decreed that games should be held every five years, contests in running, boxing, wrestling, foot races, and chariot races. Not only the people of Athens, but strangers were allowed to take part in the games, and among the strangers came Androgeos, the eldest son of great Minos, King of Knossos, in the isle of Crete of the Hundred Cities, far away in the southern sea. Minos is the wisest of men, and the most high God, even Zeus, is his counsellor, and speaks to him face to face. He is the richest of men, and his ships are without number, so that he rules all the islands, and makes war, when he will, even against the King of Egypt. The son of Minos it was who came to the sports with three fair ships, and he was the strongest and swiftest of men. He won the foot race, and the prizes for boxing and wrestling, and for shooting with the bow, and throwing the spear, and hurling the heavy weight, and he easily overcame the strongest of the sons of Pallas.

'Then, being unjust men and dishonourable, they slew him at a feast in the hall of Aegeus, their own guest in the King's house they slew, a thing hateful to the Gods above all other evil deeds. His ships fled in the night, bearing the news to King Minos, and, a year after that day, the sea was black with his countless ships. His men landed, and they were so many, all glittering in armour of bronze, that none dared to meet them in battle. King Aegeus and all the elder men of the city went humbly to meet Minos, clad in mourning, and bearing in their hands boughs of trees, wreathed with wool, to show that they came praying for mercy. "Mercy ye shall have when ye have given up to me the men who slew my son," said Minos. But Aegeus could not give up the sons of Pallas, for long ago they had fled in disguise, and were lurking here and there, in all the uttermost parts of Greece, in the huts of peasants. Such mercy, then, the Athenians got as Minos was pleased to give. He did not burn the city, and slay the men, and carry the women captives. But he made Aegeus and the chief men swear that every nine years they would choose by lot seven of the strongest youths, and seven of the fairest maidens, and give them to his men, to carry away to Crete. Every nine years he sends a ship with dark sails, to bear away the captives, and this is the ninth year, and the day of the coming of the ship is at hand. Can you resist King Minos?'

'His ship we could burn, and his men we could slay,' said Theseus; and his hand closed on the hilt of his sword.

'That may well be,' said Medea, 'but in a year Minos would come with his fleet and his army, and burn the city; and the other cities of Greece, fearing him and not loving us, would give us no aid.'

'Then,' said Theseus, 'we must even pay the tribute for this last time; but in nine years, if I live, and the Gods help me, I shall have a fleet, and Minos must fight for his tribute. For in nine years Athens will be queen of all the cities round about, and strong in men and ships. Yet, tell me, how does Minos treat the captives from Athens, kindly or unkindly?'

'None has ever come back to tell the tale,' said Medea, 'but the sailors of Minos say that he places the captives in a strange prison called the Labyrinth. It is full of dark winding ways, cut in the solid rock, and therein the captives are lost and perish of hunger, or live till they meet a Thing called the Minotaur. This monster has the body of a strong man, and a man's legs and arms, but his head is the head of a bull, and his teeth are the teeth of a lion, and no man may deal with him. Those whom he meets he tosses, and gores, and devours. Whence this evil beast came I know, but the truth of it may not be spoken. It is not lawful for King Minos to slay the Horror, which to him is great shame and grief; neither may he help any man to slay it. Therefore, in his anger against the Athenians he swore that, once in every nine years, he would give fourteen of the Athenian men and maidens to the Thing, and that none of them should bear sword or spear, dagger or axe, or any other weapon. Yet, if one of the men, or all of them together, could slay the monster, Minos made oath that Athens should be free of him and his tribute.'

Theseus laughed and stood up. 'Soon,' he said, 'shall King Minos be free from the Horror, and Athens shall be free from the tribute, if, indeed, the Gods be with me. For me need no lot be cast; gladly I will go to Crete of my free will.'

'I needed not to be a prophetess, to know that you would speak thus,' said Medea. 'But one thing even I can do. Take this phial, and bear it in your breast, and, when you face the Minotaur, do as I shall tell you.' Then she whispered some words to Theseus, and he marked them carefully.

He went forth from Medea's bower; he walked to the crest of the hill upon which Athens is built, and there he saw all the people gathered, weeping, and looking towards the sea. Swiftly a ship with black sails was being rowed towards the shore, and her sides shone with the bronze shields of her crew, that were hung on the bulwarks.

'My friends,' cried Theseus, 'I know that ship, and wherefore she comes, and with her I shall sail to Crete and slay the Minotaur. Did I not slay Sinis and Sciron, Cercyon and Procrustes, and Periphetes? Let there be no drawing of lots. Where are seven men and seven maidens who will come with me, and meet these Cretans when they land, and sail back with them, and see this famous Crete, for the love of Theseus?'

Then there stepped forth seven young men of the best of Athens, tall, and strong, and fair, the ancestors of them who smote, a thousand years afterwards, the Persians at Marathon and in the strait of Salamis. 'We will live or die with you, Prince Theseus,' they said.

Next, one by one, came out of the throng, blushing, but with heads erect and firm steps, the seven maidens whom the seven young men loved. They, too, were tall, and beautiful, and stately, like the stone maidens called Caryatides who bear up the roofs of temples.

'We will live and die with you, Prince Theseus, and with our lovers,' they cried; and all the people gave such a cheer that King Aegeus heard it, and came from his palace, leaning on his staff, and Medea walked beside him.

'Why do you raise a glad cry, my children?' said Aegeus. 'Is not that the Ship of Death, and must we not cast lots for the tribute to King Minos?'

'Sir,' said Theseus, 'we rejoice because we go as free folk, of our own will, these men and maidens and I, to take such fortune as the Gods may give us, and to do as well as we may. Nay, delay us not, for from this hour shall Athens be free, without master or lord among Cretan men.'

'But, my son, who shall defend me, who shall guide me, when I have lost thee, the light of mine eyes, and the strength of my arm?' whimpered Aegeus.

'Is the King weeping alone, while the fathers and mothers of my companions have dry eyes?' said Theseus. 'The Gods will be your helpers, and the lady who is my friend, and who devised the slaying of the sons of Pallas. Hers was the mind, if the hand was my own, that wrought their ruin. Let her be your counsellor, for no other is so wise. But that ship is near the shore, and we must go.'

Then Theseus embraced Aegeus, and Medea kissed him, and the young men and maidens kissed their fathers and mothers, and said farewell. With Theseus at their head they marched down the hill, two by two; but Medea sent after them chariots laden with changes of raiment, and food, and skins of wine, and all things of which they had need. They were to sail in their own hired ship, for such was the custom, and the ship was ready with her oarsmen. But Theseus and the Seven, by the law of Minos, might carry no swords or other weapons of war. The ship had a black sail, but Aegeus gave to the captain a sail dyed scarlet with the juice of the scarlet oak, and bade him hoist it if he was bringing back Theseus safe, but, if not, to return under the black sail.

The captain, and the outlook man, and the crew, and the ship came all from the isle of Salamis, for as yet the Athenians had no vessels fit for long voyages – only fishing-boats. As Theseus and his company marched along they met the herald of King Minos, bearing a sacred staff, for heralds were holy, and to slay a herald was a deadly sin. He stopped when he met Theseus, and wondered at his beauty and strength. 'My lord,' said he, 'wherefore come you with the Fourteen? Know you to what end they are sailing?'

'That I know not, nor you, nor any man, but they and I are going to one end, such as the Gods may give us,' answered Theseus. 'Speak with me no more, I pray you, and go no nearer Athens, for there men's hearts are high today, and they carry swords.'

The voice and the eyes of Theseus daunted the herald, and he with his men turned and followed behind, humbly, as if they were captives and Theseus were conqueror.

– 6 –

THESEUS IN CRETE

AFTER MANY DAYS' SAILING, NOW THROUGH the straits under the beautiful peaks of the mountains that crowned the islands, and now across the wide sea far from sight of land, they beheld the crest of Mount Ida of Crete, and ran into the harbour, where a hundred ships lay at anchor, and a great crowd was gathered. Theseus marvelled at the ships, so many and so strong, and at the harbour with its huge walls, while he and his company landed. A hundred of the guardsmen of Minos, with large shields, and breastplates made of ribs of bronze, and helmets of bronze with horns on them, were drawn up on the pier. They surrounded the little company of Athenians, and they all marched to the town of Knossos, and the palace of the King.

If Theseus marvelled at the harbour he wondered yet more at the town. It was so great that it seemed endless, and round it went a high wall, and at every forty yards was a square tower with small square windows high up. These towers were exactly like those which you may see among the hills and beside the burns in the Border country, the south of Scotland and the north of England; towers built when England and Scotland were at war. But when they had passed through the gateway in the chief tower, the town seemed more wonderful than the walls, for in all things it was quite unlike the cities of Greece. The street, paved with flat paving stones, wound between houses like our own, with a ground floor (in this there were no windows) and with two or three storeys above, in which there were windows, with sashes, and with so many panes to each window, the panes were coloured red. Each window opened on a balcony, and the balconies were crowded with ladies in gay dresses like those which are now worn. Under their hats their hair fell in long plaits over their shoulders: they had very fine white blouses, short jackets, embroidered in bright coloured silk, and skirts with flounces. Laughing merrily they looked down at the little troop of prisoners, chatting, and some saying they were sorry for the Athenian girls. Others, seeing Theseus marching first, a head taller than the tallest guardsman, threw flowers that fell at his feet, and cried, 'Go on, brave Prince!' for they could not believe that he was one of the prisoners.

The crowd in the street being great, the march was stopped under a house taller than the rest; in the balcony one lady alone was seated, the others stood round her as if they were her handmaidens. This lady was most richly dressed, young, and very beautiful and stately, and was, indeed, the King's daughter, Ariadne. She looked grave and full of pity, and, as Theseus happened to glance upwards, their eyes met, and remained fixed on each other. Theseus, who had never thought much about girls before, grew pale, for he had never seen so beautiful a maiden: Ariadne also turned pale, and then blushed and looked away, but her eyes glanced down again at Theseus, and he saw it, and a strange feeling came into his heart.

The guards cleared the crowd, and they all marched on till they came to the palace walls and gate, which were more beautiful even than the walls of the town. But the greatest wonder of all was the palace, standing in a wide park, and itself far greater than such towns as Theseus had seen, Troezen, or Aphidnae, or Athens. There was a multitude of roofs of various heights, endless roofs, endless windows, terraces, and gardens: no King's palace of our times is nearly so great and strong. There were fountains and flowers and sweet-smelling trees in blossom, and, when the Athenians were led within the palace, they felt lost among the winding passages and halls.

The walls of them were painted with pictures of flying fishes, above a clear white sea, in which fish of many kinds were swimming, with the spray and bubbles flying from their tails, as the sea flows apart from the rudder of a ship. There were pictures of bull fights, men and girls teasing the bull, and throwing somersaults over him, and one bull had just tossed a girl high in the air. Ladies were painted in balconies, looking on, just such ladies as had watched Theseus and his company; and young men bearing tall cool vases full of wine were painted on other walls; and others were decorated with figures of bulls and stags, in hard plaster, fashioned marvellously, and standing out from the walls 'in relief', as it is called. Other walls, again, were painted with patterns of leaves and flowers.

The rooms were full of the richest furniture, chairs inlaid with ivory, gold, and silver, chests inlaid with painted porcelain in little squares, each square containing a separate bright coloured picture. There were glorious carpets, and in some passages stood rows of vases, each of them large enough to hold a man, like the pots in the story of Ali Baba and the Forty Thieves in the Arabian Nights. There were tablets of stone brought from Egypt, with images carved of Gods and Kings, and strange Egyptian writing, and there were cups of gold and silver – indeed, I could not tell you half the beautiful and wonderful things in the palace of Minos. We know that this is true, for the things themselves, all of them, or pictures of them, have been brought to light, dug out from under ground; and, after years of digging, there is still plenty of this wonderful palace to be explored.

The Athenians were dazzled, and felt lost and giddy with passing through so many rooms and passages, before they were led into the great hall named the Throne Room, where Minos was sitting in his gilded throne that is still standing. Around him stood his chiefs and princes, gloriously clothed in silken robes with jewels of gold; they left a lane between their ranks, and down this lane was led Theseus at the head of his little company. Minos, a dark-faced man, with touches of white in his hair and long beard, sat with his elbow on his knee, and his chin in his hand, and he fixed his eyes on the eyes of Theseus. Theseus bowed and then stood erect, with his eyes on the eyes of Minos.

'You are fifteen in number,' said Minos at last, 'my law claims fourteen.'

'I came of my own will,' answered Theseus, 'and of their own will came my company. No lots were cast.'

'Wherefore?' asked Minos.

'The people of Athens have a mind to be free, O King.'

'There is a way,' said Minos. 'Slay the Minotaur and you are free from my tribute.'

'I am minded to slay him,' said Theseus, and, as he spoke, there was a stir in the throng of chiefs, and priests, and princes, and Ariadne glided through them, and stood a little behind her father's throne, at one side. Theseus bowed low, and again stood erect, with his eyes on the face of Ariadne.

'You speak like a King's son that has not known misfortune,' said Minos.

'I have known misfortune, and my name is Theseus, Aegeus' son,' said Theseus.

'This is a new thing. When I saw King Aegeus he had no son, but he had many nephews.'

'No son that he wotted of,' said Theseus, 'but now he has no nephews, and one son.'

'Is it so?' asked Minos, 'then you have avenged me on the slayers of my own son, fair sir, for it was your sword, was it not, that delivered Aegeus from the sons of Pallas?'

'My sword and the swords of my friends, of whom seven stand before you.'

'I will learn if this be true,' said Minos.

'True!' cried Theseus, and his hand flew to the place where his sword-hilt should have been, but he had no sword.

King Minos smiled. 'You are young,' he said, 'I

will learn more of these matters. Lead these men and maidens to their own chambers in the palace,' he cried to his guard. 'Let each have a separate chamber, and all things that are fitting for princes. Tomorrow I will take counsel.'

Theseus was gazing at Ariadne. She stood behind her father, and she put up her right hand as if to straighten her veil, but, as she raised her hand, she swiftly made the motion of lifting a cup to the lips; and then she laid on her lips the fingers of her left hand, closing them fast. Theseus saw the token, and he bowed, as did all his company, to Minos and to the princess, and they were led upstairs and along galleries, each to a chamber more rich and beautiful than they had seen before in their dreams. Then each was taken to a bath, they were washed and clothed in new garments, and brought back to their chambers, where meat was put before them, and wine in cups of gold. At the door of each chamber were stationed two guards, but four guards were set at the door of Theseus. At nightfall more food was brought, and, for Theseus, much red wine, in a great vessel adorned with ropes and knobs of gold.

Theseus ate well, but he drank none, and, when he had finished, he opened the door of his chamber, and carried out all the wine and the cup. 'I am one,' he said, 'who drinks water, and loves not the smell of wine in his chamber.'

The guards thanked him, and soon he heard them very merry over the King's best wine, next he did not hear them at all, next – he heard them snoring!

Theseus opened the door gently and silently: the guards lay asleep across and beside the threshold. Something bright caught his eye, he looked up, a lamp was moving along the dark corridor, a lamp in the hand of a woman clad in a black robe; the light fell on her white silent feet, and on the feet of another woman who followed her.

Theseus softly slipped back into his chamber. The light, though shaded by the girl's hand, showed in the crevice between the door and the doorpost. Softly entered Ariadne, followed by an old woman that had been her nurse. 'You guessed the token?' she whispered. 'In the wine was a sleepy drug.'

Theseus, who was kneeling to her, nodded.

'I can show you the way to flee, and I bring you a sword.'

'I thank you, lady, for the sword, and I pray you to show me the way – to the Minotaur.'

Ariadne grew pale, and her hand flew to her heart.

'I pray you make haste. Flee I will not, nor, if the King have mercy on us, will I leave Crete till I have met the Minotaur: for he has shed the blood of my people.'

Ariadne loved Theseus, and knew well in her heart that he loved her. But she was brave, and she made no more ado; she beckoned to him, and stepped across the sleeping guardsmen that lay beside the threshold. Theseus held up his hand, and she stopped, while he took two swords from the men of the guard. One was long, with a strong straight narrow blade tapering to a very sharp point; the other sword was short and straight, with keen cutting double edges. Theseus slung them round his neck by their belts, and Ariadne walked down the corridor, Theseus following her, and the old nurse following him. He had taken the swords from the sleeping men lest, if Ariadne gave him one, it might be found out that she had helped him, and she knew this in her heart, for neither of them spoke a word.

Swiftly and silently they went, through galleries and corridors that turned and wound about, till Ariadne came to the door of her own chamber. Here she held up her hand, and Theseus stopped, till she came forth again, thrusting something into the bosom of her gown. Again she led the way, down a broad staircase between great pillars, into a hall, whence she turned, and passed down a narrower stair, and then through many passages, till she came into the open air, and they crossed rough ground to a cave in a hill. In the back of the cave was a door plated with bronze which she opened with a key. Here she stopped and took out of the bosom of her gown a coil of fine strong thread.

'Take this,' she said, 'and enter by that door, and first of all make fast the end of the coil to a stone, and so walk through the labyrinth, and, when you would come back, the coil shall be your guide. Take this key also, to open the door, and lock it from within. If you return place the key in a cleft in the wall within the outer door of the palace.'

She stopped and looked at Theseus with melancholy eyes, and he threw his arms about her, and they kissed and embraced as lovers do who are parting and know not if they may ever meet again.

At last she sighed and said, 'The dawn is near – farewell; the Gods be with you. I give you the watchword of the night, that you may pass the sentinels if you come forth alive,' and she told him the word. Then she opened the door and gave him the key, and the old nurse gave him the lamp which she carried, and some food to take with him.

– 7 –

THE SLAYING OF THE MINOTAUR

THESEUS FIRST FASTENED ONE END OF HIS coil of string to a pointed rock, and then began to look about him. The labyrinth was dark, and he slowly walked, holding the string, down the broadest path, from which others turned off to right or left. He counted his steps, and he had taken near three thousand steps when he saw the pale sky showing in a small circle cut in the rocky roof, above his head, and he saw the fading stars. Sheer walls of rock went up on either hand of him, a roof of rock was above him, but in the roof was this one open place, across which were heavy bars. Soon the daylight would come.

Theseus set the lamp down on a rock behind a corner, and he waited, thinking, at a place where a narrow dark path turned at right angles to the left. Looking carefully round he saw a heap of bones, not human bones, but skulls of oxen and sheep, hoofs of oxen, and shank bones. 'This,' he thought, 'must be the place where the food of the Minotaur is let down to him from above. They have not Athenian youths and maidens to give him every day! Beside his feeding place I will wait.' Saying this to himself, he rose and went round the corner of the dark narrow path cut in the rock to the left. He made his own breakfast, from the food that Ariadne had given him, and it occurred to his mind that probably the Minotaur might also be thinking of breakfast time.

He sat still, and from afar away within he heard a faint sound, like the end of the echo of a roar, and he stood up, drew his long sword, and listened keenly. The sound came nearer and louder, a strange sound, not deep like the roar of a bull, but more shrill and thin. Theseus laughed silently. A monster with the head and tongue of a bull, but with the chest of a man, could roar no better than that! The sounds came nearer and louder, but still with the thin sharp tone in them. Theseus now took from his bosom the phial of gold that Medea had given him in Athens when she told him about the Minotaur. He removed the stopper, and held his thumb over the mouth of the phial, and grasped his long sword with his left hand, after fastening the clue of thread to his belt.

The roars of the hungry Minotaur came nearer and nearer; now his feet could be heard padding along the echoing floor of the labyrinth. Theseus moved to the shadowy corner of the narrow path, where it opened into the broad light passage, and he crouched there; his heart was beating quickly. On came the Minotaur, up leaped Theseus, and dashed the contents of the open phial in the eyes of the monster; a white dust flew out, and Theseus leaped back into his hiding-place. The Minotaur uttered strange shrieks of pain; he rubbed his eyes with his monstrous hands; he raised his head up towards the sky, bellowing and confused; he stood tossing his head up and down; he turned round and round about, feeling with his hands for the wall. He was quite blind. Theseus drew his short sword, crept up, on naked feet, behind the monster, and cut through the back sinews of his legs at the knees. Down fell the Minotaur, with a crash and a roar, biting at the rocky floor with his lion's teeth, and waving his hands, and clutching at the empty air. Theseus waited for his chance, when the clutching hands rested, and then, thrice he drove the long sharp blade of bronze through the heart of the Minotaur. The body leaped, and lay still.

Theseus kneeled down, and thanked all the Gods, and promised rich sacrifices, and a new temple to Pallas Athene, the Guardian of Athens. When he had finished his prayer, he drew the short sword, and hacked off the head of the Minotaur. He sheathed both his swords, took the head in his hand, and followed the string back out of the daylit place, to the rock where he had left his lamp. With the lamp and the guidance of the string he easily found his way to the door, which he unlocked. He noticed that the thick bronze plates of the door were dinted and scarred by the points of the horns of the Minotaur, trying to force his way out.

He went out into the fresh early morning; all the birds were singing merrily, and merry was the heart of Theseus. He locked the door, and crossed to the palace, which he entered, putting the key in the place which Ariadne had shown him. She was there, with fear and joy in her eyes. 'Touch me not,' said Theseus, 'for I am foul with the blood of the Minotaur.' She brought him to the baths on the ground floor, and swiftly fled up a secret stair. In the bathroom Theseus made himself clean, and clad himself in fresh raiment which was lying ready for him. When he was clean and clad he tied a rope of byblus round the horns of the head of the Minotaur, and went round the back of the palace, trailing the head behind him, till he came to a sentinel. 'I would see King Minos,' he said, 'I have the password, *Androgeos!*'

The sentinel, pale and wondering, let him pass,

and so he went through the guards, and reached the great door of the palace, and there the servants wrapped the bleeding head in cloth, that it might not stain the floors. Theseus bade them lead him to King Minos, who was seated on his throne, judging the four guardsmen, that had been found asleep.

When Theseus entered, followed by the serving men with their burden, the King never stirred on his throne, but turned his grey eyes on Theseus. 'My lord,' said Theseus, 'that which was to be done is done.' The servants laid their burden at the feet of King Minos, and removed the top fold of the covering.

The King turned to the captain of his guard. 'A week in the cells for each of these four men,' said he, and the four guards, who had expected to die by a cruel death, were led away. 'Let that head and the body also be burned to ashes and thrown into the sea, far from the shore,' said Minos, and his servants silently covered the head of the Minotaur, and bore it from the throne room.

Then, at last, Minos rose from his throne, and took the hand of Theseus, and said, 'Sir, I thank you, and I give you back your company safe and free; and I am no more in hatred with your people. Let there be peace between me and them. But will you not abide with us awhile, and be our guests?'

Theseus was glad enough, and he and his company tarried in the palace, and were kindly treated. Minos showed Theseus all the splendour and greatness of his kingdom and his ships, and great armouries, full of all manner of weapons: the names and numbers of them are yet known, for they are written on tablets of clay, that were found in the storehouse of the King. Later, in the twilight, Theseus and Ariadne would walk together in the fragrant gardens where the nightingales sang, and Minos knew it, and was glad. He thought that nowhere in the world could he find such a husband for his daughter, and he deemed it wise to have the alliance of so great a King as Theseus promised to be. But, loving his daughter, he kept Theseus with him long, till the prince was ashamed of his delay, knowing that his father, King Aegeus, and all the people of his country, were looking for him anxiously.

Therefore he told what was in his heart to Minos, who sighed, and said, 'I knew what is in your heart, and I cannot say you nay. I give to you my daughter as gladly as a father may.' Then they spoke of things of state, and made firm alliance between Knossos and Athens while they both lived; and the wedding was done with great splendour, and, at last, Theseus and Ariadne and all their company went aboard, and sailed from Crete. One misfortune they had:

the captain of their ship died of a sickness while they were in Crete, but Minos gave them the best of his captains. Yet by reason of storms and tempests they had a long and terrible voyage, driven out of their course into strange seas. When at length they found their bearings, a grievous sickness fell on beautiful Ariadne. Day by day she was weaker, till Theseus, with a breaking heart, stayed the ship at an isle but two days' sail from Athens. There Ariadne was carried ashore, and laid in a bed in the house of the King of that island, and the physicians and the wise women did for her what they could. But she died with her hands in the hands of Theseus, and his lips on her lips. In that isle she was buried, and Theseus went on board his ship, and drew his cloak over his head, and so lay for two days, never moving nor speaking, and tasting neither meat nor drink. No man dared to speak to him, but when the vessel stopped in the harbour of Athens, he arose, and stared about him.

The shore was dark with people all dressed in mourning raiment, and the herald of the city came with the news that Aegeus the King was dead. For the Cretan captain did not know that he was to hoist the scarlet sail if Theseus came home in triumph, and Aegeus, as he watched the waters, had descried the dark sail from afar off, and, in his grief, had thrown himself down from the cliff, and was drowned. This was the end of the voyaging of Theseus.

Theseus wished to die, and be with Ariadne, in the land of Queen Persephone. But he was a strong man, and he lived to be the greatest of the Kings of Athens, for all the other towns came in, and were his subjects, and he ruled them well. His first care was to build a great fleet in secret harbours far from towns and the ways of men, for, though he and Minos were friends while they both lived, when Minos died the new Cretan King might oppress Athens.

Minos died, at last, and his son picked a quarrel with Theseus, who refused to give up a man that had fled to Athens because the new King desired to slay him, and news came to Theseus that a great navy was being made ready in Crete to attack him. Then he sent heralds to the King of a fierce people, called the Dorians, who were moving through the countries to the north-west of Greece, seizing lands, settling on them, and marching forward again in a few years. They were wild, strong, and brave, and they are said to have had swords of iron, which were better than the bronze weapons of the Greeks. The heralds of Theseus said to them, 'Come to our King, and he will take you across the sea, and show you plunder enough. But you shall swear not to harm his kingdom.'

This pleased the Dorians well, and the ships of Theseus brought them round to Athens, where Theseus joined them with many of his own men, and they did the oath. They sailed swiftly to Crete, where, as they arrived in the dark, the Cretan captains thought that they were part of their own navy, coming in to join them in the attack on Athens; for that Theseus had a navy the Cretans knew not; he had built it so secretly. In the night he marched his men to Knossos, and took the garrison by surprise, and burned the palace, and plundered it. Even now we can see that the palace has been partly burned, and hurriedly robbed by some sudden enemy.

The Dorians stayed in Crete, and were there in the time of Ulysses, holding part of the island, while the true Cretans held the greater part of it. But Theseus returned to Athens, and married Hippolyte, Queen of the Amazons. The story of their wedding festival is told in Shakespeare's play, *A Midsummer Night's Dream.* And Theseus had many new adventures, and many troubles, but he left Athens rich and strong, and in no more danger from the Kings of Crete. Though the Dorians, after the time of Ulysses, swept all over the rest of Greece, and seized Mycenae and Lacedaemon, the towns of Agamemnon and Menelaus, they were true to their oath to Theseus, and left Athens to the Athenians.

PERSEUS

– I –

THE PRISON OF DANAE

MANY YEARS BEFORE THE SIEGE OF TROY there lived in Greece two princes who were brothers and deadly enemies. Each of them wished to be King both of Argos (where Diomedes ruled in the time of the Trojan War), and of Tiryns. After long wars one of the brothers, Proetus, took Tiryns, and built the great walls of huge stones, and the palace, while the other brother, Acrisius, took Argos, and he married Eurydice, a Princess of the Royal House of Lacedaemon, where Menelaus and Helen were King and Queen in later times.

Acrisius had one daughter, Danae, who became the most beautiful woman in Greece, but he had no son. This made him very unhappy, for he thought that, when he grew old, the sons of his brother Proetus would attack him, and take his lands and city, if he had no son to lead his army. His best plan would have been to find some brave young prince, like Theseus, and give Danae to him for his wife, and their sons would be leaders of the men of Argos. But

Acrisius preferred to go to the prophetic maiden of the temple of Apollo at Delphi (or Pytho, as it was then called), and ask what chance he had of being the father of a son.

The maiden seldom had good news to give any man; but at least this time it was easy to understand what she said. She went down into the deep cavern below the temple floor, where it was said that a strange mist or steam flowed up out of the earth, and made her fall into a strange sleep, in which she could walk and speak, but knew not what she was singing, for she sang her prophecies. At last she came back, very pale, with her laurel wreath twisted awry, and her eyes open, but seeing nothing. She sang that Acrisius would never have a son; but that his daughter would bear a son, who would kill him.

Acrisius mounted his chariot, sad and sorry, and was driven homewards. On the way he never spoke a word, but was thinking how he might escape from the prophecy, and baffle the will of Zeus, the chief of the Gods. He did not know that Zeus himself had looked down upon Danae and fallen in love with her, nor did Danae know.

The only sure way to avoid the prophecy was to kill Danae, and Acrisius thought of doing this; but he loved her too much; and he was afraid that his people would rise against him, if he slew his daughter, the pride of their hearts. Still another fear was upon Acrisius, which will be explained later in the story. He could think of nothing better than to build a house all of bronze, in the court of his palace, a house sunk deep in the earth, but with part of the roof open to the sky, as was the way in all houses then; the light came in from above, and the smoke of the fire went out in the same way. This chamber Acrisius built, and in it he shut up poor Danae with the woman that had been her nurse. They saw nothing, hills or plains or sea, men or trees, they only saw the sun at midday, and the sky, and the free birds flitting across it. There Danae lay, and was weary and sad, and she could not guess why her father thus imprisoned her. He used to visit her often and seemed kind and sorry for her, but he would never listen when she implored him to sell her for a slave into a far country, so that, at least, she might see the world in which she lived.

Now on a day a mysterious thing happened; the old poet Pindar, who lived long after, in the time of the war between the Greeks and the King of Persia, says that a living stream of gold flowed down from the sky and filled the chamber of Danae. Some time after this Danae bore a baby, a son, the strongest and most beautiful of children. She and her nurse kept it secret, and the child was brought up in an inner chamber of the house of bronze. It was difficult to prevent so lively a child from making a noise in his play, and one day, when Acrisius was with Danae, the boy, now three or four years old, escaped from his nurse, and ran from her room, laughing and shouting. Acrisius rushed out, and saw the nurse catch the child, and throw her mantle over him. Acrisius seized the boy, who stood firm on his little legs, with his head high, frowning at his grandfather, and gazing in anger out of his large blue eyes. Acrisius saw that this child would be dangerous when he became a man, and in great anger he bade his guards take the nurse out, and strangle her with a rope, while Danae knelt weeping at his feet.

When they were alone he said to Danae: 'Who is the father of this child?' but she, with her boy on her arm, slipped past Acrisius, and out of the open door, and up the staircase, into the open air. She ran to the altar of Zeus, which was built in the court, and threw her arms round it, thinking that there no man dared to touch her. 'I cry to Zeus that is throned in the highest, the Lord of Thunder,' she said: 'for he and no other is the father of my boy, even Perseus.' The sky was bright and blue without a cloud, and Danae cried in vain. There came no flash of lightning nor roll of thunder.

'Is it even so?' said Acrisius, 'then let Zeus guard his own.' He bade his men drag Danae from the altar; and lock her again in the house of bronze; while he had a great strong chest made. In that chest he had the cruelty to place Danae and her boy, and he sent them out to sea in a ship, the sailors having orders to let the chest down into the waters when they were far from shore. They dared not disobey, but they put food and a skin of wine, and two skins of water in the chest, and lowered it into the sea, which was perfectly calm and still. It was their hope that some ship would come sailing by, perhaps a ship of Phoenician merchantmen, who would certainly save Danae and the child, if only that they might sell them for slaves.

King Acrisius himself was not ignorant that this might happen and that his grandson might live to be the cause of his death. But the Greeks believed that if any man killed one of his own kinsfolk, he would be pursued and driven mad by the Furies called the Erinyes, terrible winged women with cruel claws. These winged women drove Orestes, the son of Agamemnon, fleeing like a madman through the world, because he slew his own mother, Clytemnestra, to avenge his father, whom she and Aegisthus had slain. Nothing was so much dreaded as these Furies, and therefore Acrisius did not dare to slay his daughter and his grandson, Perseus, but only put them in the way of being drowned. He heard no more of them, and hoped that both of their bodies were rolling in the waves, or that their bones lay bleaching on some unknown shore. But he could not be certain – indeed, he soon knew better – and as long as he lived, he lived in fear that Perseus had escaped, and would come and slay him, as the prophetess had said in her song.

The chest floated on the still waters, and the sea birds swooped down to look at it, and passed by, with one waft of their wings. The sun set, and Danae watched the stars, the Bear and Orion with his belt, and wrapped her boy up warm, and he slept sound, for he never knew fear, in his mother's arms. The Dawn came in her golden throne, and Danae saw around her the blue sharp crests of the mountains of the islands that lay scattered like water lilies on the seas of Greece. If only the current would drift her to an island, she thought, and prayed in her heart to the Gods of Good Help, Pallas Athene, and Hermes of the Golden Wand. Soon she began to hope that the chest was drawing near an island. She turned her head in the opposite direction for a long while, and then looked forward again. She was much nearer the island, and could see the smoke going up from cottages among the trees. But she drifted on and drifted past the end of the isle, and on with the current, and so all day.

A weary day she had, for the boy was full of play, and was like to capsize the chest. She gave him some wine and water, and presently he fell asleep, and Danae watched the sea and the distant isles till night came again. It was dark, with no moon, and the darker because the chest floated into the shadow of a mountain, and the current drew it near the shore. But Danae dared not hope again; men would not be abroad, she thought, in the night. As she lay thus helpless, she saw a light moving on the sea, and she cried as loud as she could cry. Then the light stopped, and a man's shout came to her over the water, and the light moved swiftly towards her. It came from a brazier set on a pole in a boat, and now Danae could see the bright sparks that shone in the drops from the oars, for the boat was being rowed towards her, as fast as two strong men could pull.

Being weak from the heat of the sun that had beaten on her for two days, and tired out with hopes and fears, Danae fainted, and knew nothing till she felt cold water on her face. Then she opened her eyes, and saw kind eyes looking at her own, and the brown face of a bearded man, in the light of the blaze that fishermen carry in their boats at night, for the fish come to wonder at it, and the fishermen spear them.

There were many dead fish in the boat, into which Danae and the child had been lifted, and a man with a fish spear in his hand was stooping over her.

Then Danae knew that she and her boy were saved, and she lay, unable to speak, till the oarsmen had pulled their boat to a little pier of stone. There the man with the fish spear lifted her up lightly and softly set her on her feet on land, and a boatman handed to him the boy, who was awake, and was crying for food.

'You are safe, lady!' said the man with the spear, 'and I have taken fairer fish than ever swam the sea. I am called Dictys; my brother, Polydectes, is King of this island, and my wife is waiting for me at home, where she will make you welcome, and the boy thrice welcome, for the Gods have taken our only son.'

He asked no questions of Danae; it was reckoned ill manners to put questions to strangers and guests, but he lighted two torches at the fire in the boat, and bade his two men walk in front, to show the way, while he supported Danae, and carried the child on his shoulder. They had not far to go, for Dictys, who loved fishing of all things, had his house near the shore. Soon they saw the light shining up from the opening in the roof of the hall; and the wife of Dictys came running out, crying: 'Good sport?' when she heard their voices and footsteps.

'Rare sport,' shouted Dictys cheerily, and he led in Danae, and gave the child into the arms of his wife. Then they were taken to the warm baths, and dressed in fresh raiment. Food was set before them, and presently Danae and Perseus slept on soft beds, with coverlets of scarlet wool.

Dictys and his wife never asked Danae any questions about how and why she came floating on the sea through the night. News was carried quickly enough from the mainland to the islands by fishers in their boats and merchantmen, and pedlars. Dictys heard how the King of Argos had launched his daughter and her son on the sea, hoping that both would be drowned. All the people knew in the island, which was called Seriphos, and they hated the cruelty of Acrisius, and many believed that Perseus was the son of Zeus.

If the news from Argos reached Seriphos, we may guess that the news from Seriphos reached Argos, and that Acrisius heard how a woman as beautiful as a Goddess, with a boy of the race of the Gods, had drifted to the shore of the little isle. Acrisius knew, and fear grew about his heart, fear that was sharper as the years went on, while Perseus was coming to his manhood. Acrisius often thought of ways by which he might have his grandson slain; but none of them seemed safe. By the time when Perseus was fifteen, Acrisius dared not go out of doors, except among the spears of his armed guards, and he was so eaten up by fear that it would have been happier for him if he had never been born.

– 2 –

THE VOW OF PERSEUS

IT WAS FORTUNATE FOR PERSEUS THAT Dictys treated him and taught him like his own son, and checked him if he was fierce and quarrelsome, as so strong a boy was apt to be. He was trained in all the exercises of young men, the use of spear and sword, shield and bow; and in running, leaping, hunting, rowing, and the art of sailing a boat. There were no books in Seriphos, nobody could read or write; but Perseus was told the stories of old times, and of old warriors who slew monsters by sea and land. Most of the monsters had been killed, as Perseus was sorry to hear, for he desired to try his own luck with them when he came to be a man. But the most terrible of all, the Gorgons, who were hated by men and Gods, lived still, in an island near the Land of the Dead; but the way to that island was unknown. These Gorgons were two sisters, and a third woman; the two were hideous to look on, with hair and wings and claws of bronze, and with teeth like the white tusks of swine. Swinish they were, ugly and loathsome, feeding fearfully on the bodies of unburied men. But the third Gorgon was beautiful save for the living serpents that coiled in her hair. She alone of the three Gorgons was mortal, and could be slain, but who could slay her? So terrible were her eyes that men who had gone up against her were changed into pillars of stone.

This was one of the stories that Perseus heard when he was a boy; and there was a proverb that this or that hard task was 'as difficult to do as to slay the Gorgon'. Perseus, then, ever since he was a little boy, was wondering how he could slay the Gorgon and become as famous as the strong man Heracles, or the good knight Bellerophon, who slew the Chimaera. Perseus was always thinking of such famous men as these, and especially loved the story of Bellerophon, which is this.

In the city of Ephyre, now called Corinth, was a King named Glaucus, who had a son, Bellerophon. He was brought up far from home, in Argos, by King Proetus (the great-uncle of Perseus), who was his foster-father, and loved him well. Proetus was an old man, but his wife, Anteia, was young and beautiful, and Bellerophon also was beautiful and young, and, by little and little, Anteia fell in love with him, and could not be happy without him, but no such love was in Bellerophon's heart for her, who was his foster-mother. At last Anteia, forgetting all shame, told Bellerophon that she loved him, and hated her husband, and she asked him to fly with her to the seashore, where she had a ship lying ready, and they two would sail to some island far away, and be happy together.

Bellerophon knew not what to say; he could not wrong King Proetus, his foster-father. He stood speechless, his face was red with shame, but the face of Anteia grew white with rage.

'Dastard!' she said, 'thou shalt not live long in Argos to boast of my love and your own virtue!' She ran from him, straight to King Proetus, and flung herself at his feet. 'What shall be done, oh King,' she cried, 'to the man who speaks words of love dishonourable to the Queen of Argos?'

'By the splendour of Zeus,' cried Proetus, 'if he were my own foster-son he shall die!'

'Thou hast named him!' said Anteia, and she ran to her own upper chamber, and locked the door, and flung herself on the bed, weeping for rage as if her heart would break. Proetus followed her, but she would not unlock her door, only he heard her bitter weeping, and he went apart, alone, and took thought how he should be revenged on Bellerophon. He had no desire to slay him openly, for then the King of Ephyre would make war against him. He could not bring him to trial before the judges, for there was no witness against him except Anteia; and he did not desire to make his subjects talk about the Queen, for it was the glory of a woman, in those days, not to be spoken of in the conversation of men.

Therefore Proetus, for a day or two, seemed to favour Bellerophon more kindly than ever. Next he called him into his chamber, alone, and said that it was well for young men to see the world, to cross the sea and visit foreign cities, and win renown. The eyes of Bellerophon brightened at these words, not only because he desired to travel, but because he was miserable in Argos, where he saw every day the angry eyes of Anteia. Then Proetus said that the King of Lycia, in Asia far across the sea, was his father-in-law, and his great friend. To him he would send Bellerophon, and Proetus gave him a folded tablet, in which he had written many deadly signs. Bellerophon took the folded tablet, not looking, of course, at what was written in it, and away he sailed to Lycia. The King of that country received him well, and on the tenth day after his arrival asked him if he brought any token from King Proetus.

Bellerophon gave him the tablet, which he opened and read. The writing said that Bellerophon must die. Now at that time Lycia was haunted by a monster of no human birth; her front was the front of a lion, in the middle of her body she was a goat, she tapered away to a strong swift serpent, and she breathed flame from her nostrils. The King of Lycia, wishing to get rid of Bellerophon, had but to name this curse to his guest, who vowed that he would meet her if he might find her. So he was led to the cavern where she dwelt, and there he watched for her all night till the day dawned.

He was cunning as well as brave, and men asked him why he took with him no weapon but his sword, and two spears with heavy heads, not of bronze, but of soft lead. Bellerophon told his companions that he had his own way of fighting, and bade them go home, and leave him alone, while his charioteer stood by the horses and chariot in a hollow way, out of sight. Bellerophon himself watched, lying on his face, hidden behind a rock in the mouth of the cavern. The moment that the rising sun touched with a red ray the dark mouth of the cave, forth came the Chimaera, and, setting her forepaws on the rock, looked over the valley. The moment that she opened her mouth, breathing flame, Bellerophon plunged his leaden spears deep down her throat, and sprang aside. On came the Chimaera, her serpent tail lashing the stones, but Bellerophon ever kept on the further side of a great tall rock. The Chimaera ceased to pursue him, she rolled on the earth, uttering screams of pain, for the lead was melting in the fire that was within her, and at last the molten lead burned through her, and she died. Bellerophon hacked off her head, and several feet of her tail, stowed them in his chariot, and drove back to the palace of the King of Lycia, while the people followed him with songs of praise.

The King set him three other terrible tasks, but he achieved each of the adventures gloriously, and the King gave him his daughter to be his bride, and half of all the honours of his kingdom. This is the story of Bellerophon (there were other ways of telling it), and Perseus was determined to do as great deeds as he. But Perseus was still a boy, and he did not know, and no man could tell him, the way to the island of the Gorgons.

When Perseus was about sixteen years old, the King of Seriphos, Polydectes, saw Danae, fell in love with her, and wanted to take her into his palace, but he did not want Perseus. He was a bad and cruel man, but Perseus was so much beloved by the people that he dared not kill him openly. He therefore made friends with the lad, and watched him carefully to see how he could take advantage of him. The King saw that he was of a rash, daring and haughty spirit, though Dictys had taught him to keep himself well in hand, and that he was eager to win glory. The King fell on this plan: he gave a great feast on his birthday, and invited all the chief men and the richest on the island; Perseus, too, he asked to the banquet. As the custom was, all the guests brought gifts, the best that they had, cattle, women-slaves, golden cups, wedges of gold, great vessels of bronze, and other splendid things, and the King met the guests at the door of his hall, and thanked them graciously.

Last came Perseus: he had no gift to give, for he had nothing of his own. The others began to sneer at him, saying, 'Here is a birthday guest without a birthday gift!' 'How should No Man's son have a present fit for a King.' 'This lad is lazy, tied to his mother; he should long ago have taken service with the captain of a merchant ship.' 'He might at least watch the town's cows on the town's fields,' said another. Thus they insulted Perseus, and the King, watching him with a cruel smile, saw his face grow red, and his blue eyes blaze, as he turned from one to another of the mockers, who pointed their fingers at him and jeered.

At last Perseus spoke: 'Ye farmers and fishers, ye ship-captains and slave dealers of a little isle, I shall bring to your master such a present as none of you dare to seek. Farewell. Ye shall see me once again and no more. I go to slay the Gorgon, and bring such a gift as no King possesses – the Head of the Gorgon.'

They laughed and hooted, but Perseus turned away, his hand on his sword-hilt, and left them to their festival, while the King rejoiced in his heart. Perseus dared not see his mother again, but he spoke to Dictys, saying that he knew himself now to be of an age when he must seek his fortune in other lands; and he bade Dictys guard his mother from wrong, as well as he might. Dictys promised that he would find a way of protecting Danae, and he gave Perseus three weighed wedges of gold (which were called 'talents', and served as money), and lent him a ship, to take him to the mainland of Greece, there to seek his fortune.

In the dawn Perseus secretly sailed away, landed at Malea, and thence walked and wandered everywhere, seeking to learn the way to the island of the Gorgons. He was poorly clad, and he slept at night by the fires of smithies, where beggars and wanderers lay: listening to the stories they told, and asking old people, when he met them, if they knew anyone who knew the way to the island of the Gorgons. They all shook their heads. 'Yet I should be near knowing,' said one old man, 'if that isle be close to the Land of the Dead, for I am on its borders. Yet I know nothing. Perchance the dead may know; or the maid that prophesies at Pytho, or the Selloi, the priests with unwashen feet, who sleep on the ground below the sacred oaks of Zeus in the grove of Dodona far away.'

Perseus could learn no more than this, and he wandered on and on. He went to the cave that leads down to the Land of the Dead, where the ghosts answer questions in their thin voices, like the twittering of bats. But the ghosts could not tell him what he desired to know. He went to Pytho, where the maid, in her song, bade him seek the land of men who eat acorns instead of the yellow grain of Demeter, the Goddess of Harvest. Thence he wandered to Epirus, and to the Selloi who dwell in the oak forest of Zeus, and live on the flour ground from acorns. One of them lay on the ground in the wood, with his head covered up in his mantle, and listened to what the wind says, when it whispers to the forest leaves. The leaves said, 'We bid the young man be of good hope, for the Gods are with him.'

This answer did not tell Perseus where the isle of the Gorgons lay, but the words put hope in his heart, weary and footsore as he was. He ate of the bread made of the acorns, and of the flesh of the swine that the Selloi gave him, and he went alone, and, far in the forest, he laid his head down on the broad mossy root of an old oak tree. He did not sleep, but watched the stars through the boughs, and he heard the cries of the night-wandering beasts in the woodland.

'If the Gods be with me, I shall yet do well,' he said, and, as he spoke, he saw a white clear light moving through the darkness. That clear white light shone from a golden lamp in the hand of a tall and beautiful woman, clad in armour, and wearing, hung by a belt from her neck, a great shield of polished bronze. With her there came a young man, with winged shoon of gold on his feet, and belted with a strange short curved sword: in his hand was a golden wand, with wings on it, and with golden serpents twisted round it.

Perseus knew that these beautiful folk were the Goddess Athene, and Hermes, who brings all fortunate things. He fell upon his face before them, but Athene spoke in a sweet grave voice, saying, 'Arise, Perseus, and speak to us face to face, for we are of your kindred, we also are children of Zeus, the Father of Gods and men.'

Then Perseus arose and looked straight into their eyes.

'We have watched you long, Perseus, to learn whether you have the heart of a hero, that can achieve great adventures; or whether you are an idle dreaming boy. We have seen that your heart is steadfast, and that you have sought through hunger, and long travel, to know the way wherein you must find death or win glory. That way is not to be found without the help of the Gods. First you must seek the Three Grey Women, who dwell beyond the land that lies at the back of the North Wind. They will tell you the road to the three Nymphs of the West, who live in an island of the sea that never knew a sail; for it is beyond the pillars that Heracles set up when he wearied in his journey to the Well of the World's End, and turned again. You must go to these nymphs, where never foot of man has trod, and they will show you the measure of the way to the Isle of the Gorgons. If you see the faces of the Gorgons, you will be turned to stone. Yet you have vowed to bring the head of the youngest of the three, she who was not born a Gorgon but became one of them by reason of her own wickedness. If you slay her, you must not see even her dead head, but wrap it round in this goat-skin which hangs beside my shield; see not the head yourself, and let none see it but your enemies.'

'This is a great adventure,' said Perseus, 'to slay a woman whom I may not look upon, lest I be changed into stone.'

'I give you my polished shield,' said Athene. 'Let it never grow dim, if you would live and see the sunlight.' She took off her shield from her neck, with the goat-skin cover of the shield, and hung them round the neck of Perseus. He knelt and thanked her for her grace, and, looking up through a clear space between the forest boughs, he said, 'I see the Bear, the stars of the North that are the guide of sailors. I shall walk towards them even now, by your will, for my heart burns to find the Three Grey Women, and learn the way.'

Hermes smiled, and said, 'An old man and white-bearded would you be, ere you measured out that way on foot! Here, take my winged sandals, and bind them about your feet. They know all the paths of the air, and they will bring you to the Three Grey Women. Belt yourself, too, with my sword, for this sword needs no second stroke, but will cleave through that you set it to smite.'

So Perseus bound on the Shoes of Swiftness, and the Sword of Sharpness, the name of it was Herpe; and when he rose from binding on the shoon, he was alone. The Gods had departed. He drew the sword, and cut at an oak tree trunk, and the blade went clean through it, while the tree fell with a crash like thunder. Then Perseus rose through the clear space in the wood, and flew under the stars, towards the constellation of the Bear. North of Greece he flew, above the Thracian mountains, and the Danube (which was then called the Ister) lay beneath him like a long thread of silver. The air grew cold as he crossed lands then unknown to the Greeks, lands where wild men dwelt, clad in the skins of beasts, and using axe-heads and spear-heads made of sharpened stones. He passed to the land at the back of the North Wind, a sunny warm land, where the people sacrifice wild asses to the God Apollo. Beyond this he came to a burning desert of sand, but far away he saw trees that love the water, poplars and willows, and thither he flew.

He came to a lake among the trees, and round and round the lake were flying three huge grey swans, with the heads of women, and their long grey hair flowed down below their bodies, and floated on the wind. They sang to each other as they flew, in a voice like the cry of the swan. They had but one eye among them, and but one tooth, which they passed to each other in turn, for they had arms and hands under their wings. Perseus dropped down in his flight, and watched them. When one was passing the eye to the other, none of them could see him, so he waited for his chance and took it, and seized the eye.

'Where is our eye? Have *you* got it?' said the Grey Woman from whose hand Perseus took it. 'I have it not.'

'I have it not!' cried each of the others, and they all wailed like swans.

'I have it,' said Perseus, and hearing his voice they all flew to the sound of it but he easily kept out of their way. 'The eye will I keep,' said Perseus, 'till you tell me what none knows but you, the way to the Isle of the Gorgons.'

'We know it not,' cried the poor Grey Women. 'None knows it but the Nymphs of the Isle of the West: give us our eye!'

'Then tell me the way to the Nymphs of the Isle of the West,' said Perseus.

'Turn your back, and hold your course past the isle of Albion, with the white cliffs, and so keep with the land on your left hand, and the unsailed sea on your right hand, till you mark the Pillars of Heracles on your left, then take your course west by south, and a curse on you! Give us our eye!'

Perseus gave them their eye, and she who took it flew at him, but he laughed, and rose high above them and flew as he was told. Over many and many a league of sea and land he went, till he turned to his right from the Pillars of Heracles (at Gibraltar), and sailed along, west by south, through warm air, over the lonely endless Atlantic waters. At last he saw a great blue mountain, with snow feathering its crests, in a far-off island, and on that island he alighted. It was a country of beautiful flowers, and pine forests high on the hill, but below the pines all was like a garden, and in that garden was a tree bearing apples of gold, and round the tree were dancing three fair maidens, clothed in green, and white, and red.

'These must be the Nymphs of the Isle of the West,' said Perseus, and he floated down into the garden, and drew near them.

As soon as they saw him they left off dancing, and catching each other by the hands they ran to Perseus laughing, and crying, 'Hermes, our playfellow Hermes has come!' The arms of all of them went round Perseus at once, with much laughing and kissing. 'Why have you brought a great shield, Hermes?' they cried, 'here there is no unfriendly God or man to fight against you.'

Perseus saw that they had mistaken him for the God whose sword and winged shoon he wore, but he did not dislike the mistake of the merry maidens.

'I am not Hermes,' he said, 'but a mortal man, to whom the God has graciously lent his sword and shoon and the shield was lent to me by Pallas Athene. My name is Perseus.'

The girls leaped back from him, blushing and looking shy. The eldest girl answered, 'We are the daughters of Hesperus, the God of the Evening Star. I am Aegle, this is my sister Erytheia, and this is Hesperia. We are the keepers of this island, which is the garden of the Gods, and they often visit us; our cousins, Dionysus, the young God of Wine and Mirth, and Hermes of the Golden Wand come often; and bright Apollo, and his sister Artemis the huntress. But a mortal man we have never seen, and wherefore have the Gods sent you hither?'

'The two Gods sent me, maidens, to ask you the way to the Isle of the Gorgons, that I may slay Medusa of the snaky hair, whom Gods and men detest.'

'Alas!' answered the nymphs, 'how shall you slay her, even if we knew the way to that island, which we know not?'

Perseus sighed: he had gone so far, and endured so much, and had come to the Nymphs of the Isle of the West, and even they could not tell how to reach the Gorgons' island.

'Do not fear,' said the girl, 'for if we know not the way we know one that knows it: Atlas is his name – the Giant of the Mountain. He dwells on the highest peak of the snow-crested hill, and it is he who holds up the heavens, and keeps heaven and earth asunder. He looks over all the world, and over the wide western sea: him we must ask to answer your question. Take off your shield, which is so heavy, and sit down with us among the flowers, and let us think how you may slay the Gorgon.'

Perseus gladly unslung his heavy shield, and sat down among the white and purple wind flowers. Aegle, too, sat down; but young Erytheia held the shield upright, while beautiful Hesperia admired herself, laughing, in the polished surface.

Perseus smiled as he watched them, and a plan came into his mind. In all his wanderings he had been trying hard to think how, if he found the Gorgon, he might cut off her head, without seeing the face which turned men into stone. Now his puzzle was ended. He could hold up the shield above the Gorgon, and see the reflection of her face, as in a mirror, just as now he saw the fair reflected face of Hesperia. He turned to Aegle, who sat silently beside him: 'Maiden,' he said, 'I have found out the secret that has perplexed me long, how I may strike at the Gorgon without seeing her face that turns men to stone. I will hang above her in the air, and see her face reflected in the mirror of the shield, and so know where to strike.' The two other girls had left the shield on the grass, and they clapped their hands when Perseus said this, but Aegle still looked grave.

'It is much that you should have found this cunning plan; but the Gorgons will see you, and two of them are deathless and cannot be slain, even with the sword Herpe. These Gorgons have wings almost as swift as the winged shoon of Hermes, and they have claws of bronze that cannot be broken.'

Hesperia clapped her hands. 'Yet I know a way,' she said, 'so that this friend of ours may approach the Gorgons, yet not be seen by them. You must be told,' she said, turning to Perseus, 'that we three sisters were of the company of the Fairy Queen, Persephone, daughter of Demeter, the Goddess of Harvest. We were gathering flowers with her, in the plain of Enna, in a spring morning, when there sprang up a new flower, fragrant and beautiful, the white narcissus. No sooner had Persephone plucked that flower than the earth opened beside her, and up came the chariot and horses of Hades, the King of the Dead, who caught Persephone into his chariot, and bore her down with him to the House of Hades. We wept and were in great fear, but Zeus granted to Persephone to return to earth with the first snowdrop, and remain with her mother, Demeter, till the last rose had faded. Now I was the favourite of Persephone, and she carried me with her to see her husband, who is kind to me for her sake, and can refuse me nothing, and he has what will serve your turn. To him I will go, for often I go to see my playmate, when it is winter in your world: it is always summer in our isle. To him I will go, and return again, when I will so work that you may be seen of none, neither by God, or man, or monster. Meanwhile my sisters will take care of you, and tomorrow they will lead you to the mountain top, to speak with the Giant.'

'It is well spoken,' said tall, grave Aegle, and she led Perseus to their house, and gave him food and wine, and at night he slept full of hope, in a chamber in the courtyard.

Next morning, early, Perseus and Aegle and Erytheia floated up to the crest of the mountain, for Hesperia had departed in the night, to visit Queen Persephone. Perseus took a hand of each of the Nymphs, and they had no weary climbing; they all soared up together, so great was the power of the winged shoon of Hermes. They found the good giant Atlas, kneeling on a black rock above the snow, holding up the vault of heaven with either hand. When Aegle had spoken to him, he bade his girls go apart, and said to Perseus, 'Yonder, far away to the west, you see an island with a mountain that rises to a flat top, like a table. There dwell the Gorgons.'

Perseus thanked him eagerly, but Atlas sighed and said, 'Mine is a weary life. Here have I knelt and done my task, since the Giants fought against the Gods, and were defeated. Then, for my punishment, I was set here by Zeus to keep sky and earth asunder. But he told me that after hundreds of years I should have rest, and be changed to a stone. Now I see that the day of rest appointed is come, for you shall show me the head of the Gorgon when you have slain her, and my body shall be stone, but my spirit shall be with the ever living Gods.'

Perseus pitied Atlas; he bowed to the will of Zeus, and to the prayer of the Giant, and gave his promise. Then he floated to Aegle and Erytheia, and they all three floated down again to the garden of the golden apples. Here as they walked on the soft grass, and watched the wind toss the white and red and purple bells of the wind flowers, they heard a low laughter close to them, the laughter of Hesperia, but her they saw not. 'Where are you, Hesperia, where are you hiding?' cried Aegle, wondering, for the wide lawn was open, without bush or tree where the girl might be lurking.

'Find me if you can,' cried the voice of Hesperia, close beside them, and handfuls of flowers were lightly tossed to them, yet they saw none who threw them. 'This place is surely enchanted,' thought Perseus, and the voice of Hesperia answered: 'Come follow, follow me. I will run before you to the house, and show you my secret.'

Then they all saw the flowers bending, and the grass waving, as if a light-footed girl were running through it, and they followed to the house the path in the trodden grass. At the door, Hesperia met them: 'You could not see me,' she said, 'nor will the Gorgons see Perseus. Look, on that table lies the Helmet of Hades, which mortal men call the Cap of Darkness. While I wore it you could not see me, nay, a deathless God cannot see the wearer of that helmet.' She took up a dark cap of hard leather, that lay on a table in the hall, and raised it to her head, and when she had put it on, she was invisible. She took it off, and placed it on the brows of Perseus. 'We cannot see you, Perseus,' cried all the girls. 'Look at yourself in your shining shield: can you see yourself?'

Perseus turned to the shield, which he had hung on a golden nail in the wall. He saw only the polished bronze, and the faces of the girls who were looking over his shoulder. He took off the Helmet of Hades and gave a great sigh. 'Kind are the Gods,' he said. 'Methinks that I shall indeed keep my vow, and bring to Polydectes the Gorgon's head.'

They were merry that night, and Perseus told them his story, how he was the son of Zeus, and the girls called him 'cousin Perseus'. 'We love you very much, and we could make you immortal, without old age and death,' said Hesperia. 'You might live with us here for ever – it is lonely, sometimes, for three maidens in the garden of the Gods. But you must keep your vow, and punish your enemies, and cherish your mother, and do not forget your cousins three, when you have married the lady of your heart's desire, and are King of Argos.'

The tears stood in the eyes of Perseus. 'Cousins dear,' he said, 'never shall I forget you, not even in the House of Hades. You will come thither now and again, Hesperia? But I love no woman.'

'I think you will not long be without a lady and a love, Perseus,' said Erytheia; 'but the night is late, and tomorrow you have much to do.'

So they parted, and next morning they bade Perseus be of good hope. He burnished and polished the shield, and covered it with the goat's skin, he put on the Shoes of Swiftness, and belted himself with the Sword of Sharpness, and placed on his head the Cap of Darkness. Then he soared high in the air, till he saw the Gorgons' Isle, and the table-shaped mountain, a speck in the western sea.

The way was long, but the shoes were swift, and, far aloft, in the heat of the noonday, Perseus looked down on the top of the table-mountain. There he could dimly see three bulks of strange shapeless shape, with monstrous limbs that never stirred, and he knew that the Gorgons were sleeping their midday sleep. Then he held the shield so that the shapes were reflected in its polished face, and very slowly he floated down, and down, till he was within striking distance. There they lay, two of them uglier than sin, breathing loud in their sleep like drunken men. But the face of her who lay between the others was as quiet as the face of a sleeping child; and as beautiful as the face of the Goddess of Love, with long dark eyelashes veiling the eyes, and red lips half-open. Nothing stirred but the serpents in the hair of beautiful Medusa; they were never still, but coiled and twisted, and Perseus loathed them as he watched them in the mirror. They coiled and uncoiled, and left bare her ivory neck, and then Perseus drew the sword Herpe, and struck once.

In the mirror he saw the fallen head, and he seized it by the hair, and wrapped it in the goat-skin, and put the goat-skin in his wallet. Then he towered high in the air, and, looking down, he saw the two sister Gorgons turning in their sleep; they woke, and saw their sister dead. They seemed to speak to each other; they looked this way and that, into the bright empty air, for Perseus in the Cap of Darkness they could not see. They rose on their mighty wings, hunting low, and high, and with casts behind their island and in front of it, but Perseus was flying faster than ever he flew before, stooping and rising to hide his scent. He dived into the deep sea, and flew under water as long as he could hold his breath, and then rose and fled swiftly forward. The Gorgons were puzzled by each double he had made, and, at the place where he dived they lost the scent, and from far away Perseus heard their loud yelps, but soon these faded in the distance. He often looked over his shoulder as he flew straight towards the far-off blue hill of the giant Atlas, but the sky was empty behind him, and the Gorgons he never saw again. The mountain turned from blue to clear grey and red and gold, with pencilled rifts and glens, and soon Perseus stood beside the giant Atlas. 'You are welcome and blessed,' said the giant. 'Show me the head that I may be at rest.'

Then Perseus took the bundle from the wallet, and carefully unbound the goat-skin, and held up the head, looking away from it, and the Giant was a great grey stone. Down sailed Perseus, and stood in the garden of the Gods, and laid the Cap of Darkness on the grass. The three Nymphs who were sitting there, weaving garlands of flowers, leaped up, and came round him, and kissed him, and crowned him with the flowery chaplets. That night he rested with them, and in the morning they kissed and said farewell.

'Do not forget us,' said Aegle, 'nor be too sorry for our loneliness. Today Hermes has been with us, and tomorrow he comes again with Dionysus, the God of the Vine, and all his merry company. Hermes left a message for you, that you are to fly eastward, and south, to the place where your wings shall guide you, and there, he said, you shall find your happiness. When that is won, you shall turn north and west, to your own country. We say, all three of us, that our love is with you always, and we shall hear of your gladness, for Hermes will tell us; then we too shall be glad. Farewell!'

So the three maidens embraced him with kind faces and smiling eyes, and Perseus, too, smiled as well as he might, but in his eastward way he often looked back, and was sad when he could no longer see the kindly hill above the garden of the Gods.

- 3 -

PERSEUS AND ANDROMEDA

PERSEUS FLEW WHERE THE WINGS BORE him, over great mountains, and over a wilderness of sand. Below his feet the wind woke the sand storms, and beneath him he saw nothing but a soft floor of yellow grey, and when that cleared he saw islands of green trees round some well in the waste, and long trains of camels, and brown men riding swift horses, at which he wondered; for the Greeks in his time drove in chariots, and did not ride. The red sun behind him fell, and all the land was purple, but, in a moment, as it seemed, the stars rushed out, and he sped along in the starlight till the sky was grey again, and rosy, and full of fiery colours, green and gold and ruby and amethyst. Then the sun rose, and Perseus looked down on a green land, through which was flowing north a great river, and he guessed that it was the river Aegyptus, which we now call the Nile. Beneath him was a town, with many white houses in groves of palm trees, and with great temples of the Gods, built of red stone. The Shoes of Swiftness stopped above the wide market-place, and there Perseus hung poised, till he saw a multitude of men pour out of the door of a temple.

At their head walked the King, who was like a Greek, and he led a maiden as white as snow wreathed with flowers and circlets of wool, like the oxen in Greece, when men sacrifice them to the Gods. Behind the King and the maid came a throng of brown men, first priests and magicians and players on harps, and women shaking metal rattles that made a wild mournful noise, while the multitude lamented.

Slowly, while Perseus watched, they passed down to the shore of the great river, so wide a river as Perseus had never seen. They went to a steep red rock, like a wall, above the river; at its foot was a flat shelf of rock – the water just washed over it. Here they stopped, and the King kissed and embraced the white maiden. They bound her by chains of bronze to rings of bronze in the rock; they sang a strange hymn; and then marched back to the town, throwing their mantles over their heads. There the maiden stood, or rather hung forward supported by the chains. Perseus floated down, and, the nearer he came, the more beautiful seemed the white maid, with her soft dark hair falling to her white feet. Softly he floated down, till his feet were on the ledge of rock. She did not hear him coming, and when he gently touched her she gave a cry, and turned on him her large dark eyes, wild and dry, without a tear. 'Is it a God?' she said, clasping her hands.

'No God, but a mortal man am I, Perseus the slayer of the Gorgon. What do you here? What cruel men have bound you?'

'I am Andromeda, the daughter of Cepheus, King of a strange people. The lot fell on me, of all the maidens in the city, to be offered to the monster fish that walks on feet, who is their God. Once a year they give to him a maiden.'

Perseus thereon drew the sword Herpe, and cut the chains of bronze that bound the girl as if they had been ropes of flax, and she fell at his feet, covering her eyes with her hands. Then Perseus saw the long reeds on the further shore of the river waving and stirring and crashing, and from them came a monstrous fish walking on feet, and slid into the water. His long sharp black head showed above the stream as he swam, and the water behind him showed like the water in the wake of a ship.

'Be still and hide your eyes!' whispered Perseus to the maiden.

He took the goat-skin from his wallet, and held up the Gorgon's head, with the back of it turned towards him, and he waited till the long black head was lifted from the river's edge, and the forefeet of that fish were on the wet ledge of rock. Then he held the head before the eyes of the monster, and from the head downward it slowly stiffened. The head and forefeet and shoulders were of stone before the tail had ceased to lash the water. Then the tail stiffened into a long jagged sharp stone, and Perseus, wrapping up the head in the goat-skin, placed it in his wallet. He turned his back to Andromeda, while he did this lest by mischance her eyes should open and see the head of the Gorgon. But her eyes were closed, and Perseus found that she had fainted, from fear of the monster, and from the great heat of the sun. Perseus put the palms of his hands together like a cup, and stooping to the stream he brought water, and threw it over the face and neck of Andromeda, wondering at her beauty. Her eyes opened at last, and she tried to rise to her feet, but she dropped on her knees, and clung with her fingers to the rock. Seeing her so faint and weak Perseus raised her in his arms, with her beautiful head pillowed on his shoulder, where she fell asleep like a tired child. Then he rose in the air and floated over the sheer wall of red stone above the river, and flew slowly towards the town.

There were no sentinels at the gate; the long street was empty, for all the people were in their houses, praying and weeping. But a little girl stole out of a house near the gate. She was too young to understand why her father and mother and elder brothers were so sad, and would not take any notice of her. She thought she would go out and play in the street, and when she looked up from her play, she saw Perseus bearing the King's daughter in his arms. The child stared, and then ran into her house, crying aloud, for she could hardly speak, and pulled so hard at her mother's gown that her mother rose and followed her to the house door. The mother gave a joyful cry, her husband and her children ran forth, and they, too, shouted aloud for pleasure. Their cries reached the ears of people in other houses, and presently all the folk, as glad as they had been sorrowful, were following Perseus to the palace of the King. Perseus walked through the empty court, and stood at the door of the hall, where the servants came to him, both men and women, and with tears of joy the women bore Andromeda to the chamber of her mother, Queen Cassiopeia.

Who can tell how happy were the King and Queen, and how gladly they welcomed Perseus! They made a feast for him, and they sent oxen and sheep to all the people, and wine, that all might rejoice and make merry. Andromeda, too, came, pale but smiling, into the hall, and sat down beside her mother's high seat, listening while Perseus told the whole story of his adventures. Now Perseus could scarcely keep his eyes from Andromeda's face while he spoke, and she stole glances at him. When their eyes met, the colour came into her face again, which glowed like ivory that a Carian woman has lightly tinged with rose colour, making an ornament for some rich King. Perseus remembered the message of Hermes, which Aegle had given him, that if he flew to the east and south he would find his happiness. He knew that he had found it, if this maiden would be his wife, and he ended his tale by repeating the message of Hermes.

'The Gods speak only truth,' he said, 'and to have made you all happy is the greatest happiness to Perseus of Argos.' Yet he hoped in his heart to see a yet happier day, when the rites of marriage should be done between Andromeda and him, and the young men and maidens should sing the wedding song before their door.

Andromeda was of one mind with him, and, as Perseus must needs go home, her parents believed that she could not live without him who had saved her from such a cruel death. So with heavy hearts they made the marriage feast, and with many tears Andromeda and her father and mother said farewell.

Perseus and his bride sailed down the great river Aegyptus in the King's own boat; and at every town they were received with feasts, and songs, and dances. They saw all the wonderful things of Egypt, palaces and pyramids and temples and tombs of kings, and at last they found a ship of the Cretans in the mouth of the Nile. This they hired, for they carried with them great riches, gold, and myrrh, and ivory, gifts of the princes of Egypt.

– 4 –

HOW PERSEUS AVENGED DANAE

With a steady south wind behind them they sailed to Seriphos, and landed, and brought their wealth ashore, and went to the house of Dictys. They found him lonely and sorrowful, for his wife had died, and his brother, King Polydectes, had taken Danae, and set her to grind corn in his house, among his slave women. When Perseus heard that word, he asked, 'Where is King Polydectes?'

'It is his birthday, and he holds his feast among the Princes,' said Dictys.

'Then bring me,' said Perseus, 'the worst of old clothes that any servant of your house can borrow from a beggar man, if there be a beggar man in the town.' Such a man there was – he came limping through the door of the courtyard, and up to the threshold of the house, where he sat whining, and asking for alms. They gave him food and wine, and Perseus cried, 'New clothes for old, father, I will give you, and new shoes for old.' The beggar could not believe his ears, but he was taken to the baths, and washed, and new clothes were given to him, while Perseus clad himself in the beggar's rags, and Dictys took charge of the winged shoon of Hermes and the sword Herpe, and the burnished shield of Athene. Then Perseus cast dust and wood ashes on his hair, till it looked foul and grey, and placed the goat-skin covering and the Gorgon's head in his wallet, and with the beggar's staff in his hand he limped to the palace of Polydectes. On the threshold he sat down, like a beggar, and Polydectes saw him and cried to his servants, 'Bring in that man; is it not the day of my feast? Surely all are welcome.' Perseus was led in, looking humbly at the ground, and was brought before the King.

'What news, thou beggar man?' said the King.

'Such news as was to be looked for,' whined Perseus. 'Behold, I am he who brought no present to the King's feast, seven long years agone, and now I come back, tired and hungry, to ask his grace.'

'By the splendour of Zeus,' cried Polydectes, 'it is none but the beggar brat who bragged that he would fetch me such a treasure as lies in no King's chamber! The beggar brat is a beggar man; how time and travel have tamed him! Ho, one of you, run and fetch his mother who is grinding at the mill, that she may welcome her son.'

A servant ran from the hall, and the chiefs of Seriphos mocked at Perseus. 'This is he who called us farmers and dealers in slaves. Verily he would not fetch the price of an old cow in the slave market.' Then they threw at him crusts of bread, and bones of swine, but he stood silent.

Then Danae was led in, clad in vile raiment, but looking like a queen, and the King cried, 'Go forward, woman: look at that beggar man; dost thou know thy son?' She walked on, her head high, and Perseus whispered, 'Mother, stand thou beside me, and speak no word!'

'My mother knows me not, or despises me,' said Perseus, 'yet, poor as I am, I do not come empty-handed. In my wallet is a gift, brought from very far away, for my lord the King.'

He swung his wallet round in front of him; he took off the covering of goat-skin, and he held the Gorgon's head on high, by the hair, facing the King and the chiefs. In one moment they were all grey stones, all along the hall, and the chairs whereon they sat crashed under the weight of them, and they rolled on the hard clay floor. Perseus wrapped the head in the goat-skin, and shut it in the wallet carefully, and cried, 'Mother, look round, and see thy son and thine own revenge.'

Then Danae knew her son, by the sound of his voice, if not by her eyesight, and she wept for joy. So they two went to the house of Dictys, and Perseus was cleansed, and clad in rich raiment, and Danae, too, was apparelled like a free woman, and embraced Andromeda with great joy.

Perseus made the good Dictys King of Seriphos; and he placed the winged shoes in the temple of Hermes, with the sword Herpe, and the Gorgon's head, in its goat-skin cover; but the polished shield he laid on the altar in the temple of Athene. Then he bade all who served in the temples come forth, both young and old, and he locked the doors, and he and Dictys watched all night, with the armed Cretans, the crew of his ship, that none might enter. Next day Perseus alone went into the temple of Athene. It was as it had been, but the Gorgon's head and the polished shield were gone, and the winged shoon and the sword Herpe had vanished from the temple of Hermes.

With Danae and Andromeda Perseus sailed to Greece, where he learned that the sons of King Proetus had driven King Acrisius out of Argos, and that he had fled to Phthia in the north, where the ancestor of the great Achilles was king. Thither

Perseus went, to see his grandfather, and he found the young men holding games and sports in front of the palace. Perseus thought that his grandfather might love him better if he showed his strength in the games, which were open to strangers, so he entered and won the race, and the prize for leaping, and then came the throwing of the disc of bronze. Perseus threw a great cast, far beyond the rest, but the disc swerved, and fell among the crowd. Then Perseus was afraid, and ran like the wind to the place where the disc fell. There lay an old man, smitten sorely by the disc, and men said that he had killed King Acrisius.

Thus the word of the prophetess and the will of Fate were fulfilled. Perseus went weeping to the King of Phthia, and told him all the truth, and the King, who knew, as all Greece knew, how Acrisius had tried to drown his daughter and her child, believed the tale, and said that Perseus was guiltless. He and Danae and Andromeda dwelt for a year in Phthia, with the King, and then Perseus with an army of Pelasgians and Myrmidons, marched south to Argos, and took the city, and drove out his cousins, the sons of Proetus. There in Argos, Perseus, with his mother and beautiful Andromeda, dwelt long and happily, and he left the kingdom to his son when he died.

THE FABER CLASSICS LIBRARY